4-EVER

MM ROCKSTAR ROMANCE

WAYWARD LANE

AVA OLSEN

CHAPTER 1

FAISEL

AGE 10

It was my first day at my new school and I hated it.

Sitting on the bench opposite the playground, by myself, I stared at my classmates, who ran around, laughing and having fun.

I wanted to go back to New York. To Jackson Heights, the neighborhood in Queens that was the only home I'd ever known. Where my friends were. And my grandparents. Not here in Rhode Island, in this town where everyone stared at me. Here, the only people I knew were my parents and my brother.

"What kind of name is Faisel?"

I followed the voice, turning around. The boy standing behind me was familiar. He'd been in my math class, Nathaniel... something. He was popular and everyone in class talked to him.

Except me. I was too shy. When he glared at me, I didn't understand. And I didn't know what to say to him now.

What was wrong with my name? No one back home asked me about it.

"It's the name my grandparents gave me."

"It's weird," he sneered. "And so are you."

My face heated and I turned around again, not wanting to talk anymore. Wishing I could disappear. Or blink and open my eyes to find I was back in my old school.

Suddenly, I was pushed off the bench and I tumbled onto the grass. My knees hit the ground hard, and my hands after them.

Looking up, Nathaniel was staring down at me, his arms crossed.

"I don't like you and no one else does either. No one's gonna play with you. Go back inside."

Humiliation washed over me. I was frozen, unable to move. My eyes begin to fill up but I blinked fast and hard.

"You gonna cry now? What a big baby," Nathaniel muttered as he stepped closer to me. "I'm gonna tell everyone you're a scared loser."

Get up and run inside! Go find a teacher.

But I couldn't. I just sat there, protectively pulling my knees up to my chest. Nathaniel kicked my shins hard and I yelled out, but no one heard me. Or cared. Pain, humiliation, and fear welled up inside me. Tears rolled down my face and I tucked my head into my arms, trying to blockout everything.

Go away, please. Just leave me alone.

"Get away from him."

What?

Wiping my face, I glanced up to find another boy, one with dark brown hair and big blue eyes, standing in front of me. I couldn't remember his name, but he was also in my math class. He was bigger than Nathaniel.

This boy made silly faces and jokes, and the teacher told him to be quiet. A lot. Unlike other boys in the class, his hair was long. And even though the other kids kept asking him about it, he didn't seem to mind the questions or the stares.

Not like me.

"I didn't do anything," Nathaniel complained. "He's just a loser crybaby."

"And you're just annoying."

"Whatever. You've got a stupid name too, *Ronin*."

Ronin.

The boy towered over Nathaniel, and I hid my face again. I heard footsteps but I kept my head down until Ronin's voice echoed in my ear.

"He's gone now. Are you okay?"

I slowly looked up again and nodded. Even though I wasn't okay. I was still trembling. Today was turning out to be the worst day ever.

"Faisel, right?" Ronin asked, crouching down in front of me. "I'm Ro. Do you need help getting up?"

Shaking my head, I used my t-shirt to wipe my face and stood up on trembling legs. Ronin joined me, and when I stood up, I realized he was way taller than me. Bigger too. He looked like he was twelve or thirteen, not ten.

"Thanks," I whispered gratefully, a huge lump in my throat.

"No problem. I got a younger sister, Ciara, and I look out for her. I don't like bullies."

"I have an older brother but he's at another school."

The one for gifted students. Not average ones like me.

"Is this your first day here?" he asked.

I nodded. "I'm from New York City. I miss it already."

"I've never been there, but the city sounds cool. I wish I lived there and not here."

"Yeah."

"I moved here a week ago with my mom and sister," Ronin explained. "My parents just divorced."

"I'm sorry."

"I'm not. They argue *all* the time. Now at least I can sleep."

I didn't know what else to say.

"You want to go play on the jungle gym?" Ronin asked.

"Okay," I replied and looked back up at him. Ronin's eyes were so blue, like a summer sky. My stomach calmed and my anxiety started to fade away. "You can call me Faise."

He nodded. "You've got a cool name. I think being different is awesome. Who wants to be like everyone else?"

I did. I just wanted to fit in.

"People here don't seem to like different," I suggested.

"Then they're boring. And dumb."

And thinking about what he said, I began to wonder.

"Your hair's long," I blurted out.

Ronin laughed and I felt my face heat.

"Um, I mean, it's nice. Your hair. It's, um," I paused. "Yeah, different. But good."

Jeez, could I sound any more awkward? I began to walk away, flushed with embarrassment. I was never going to make friends here.

"I know what you meant," Ronin replied, and I stopped walking. "Thanks."

"What do you think of school so far?" I asked tentatively.

Ronin made a strange face, like he was going to be sick or something. Maybe I wasn't the only one who was feeling out of place.

"It's okay, but the teachers don't like me already 'cause I talk too much and joke around."

"I don't think they like me either. I'm only good at math. And music. It's my favorite. Everything else takes me forever to learn."

"Same. Music is the coolest thing ever. I want to play guitar. But I need lessons."

"My parents have me in piano class already. I can teach you to play. If you want."

"Really?"

"Sure."

"What else do you like?" Ronin asked me as we headed for the gym. "Do you play chess?"

I nodded.

"And video games," I added. "I have an Xbox. You want to come over and play sometime?"

Ronin smiled at me.

And just like that, I knew that everything was going to be okay.

Ronin

I glanced at Faisel and I was happy to see him smiling back at me.

His big brown eyes were no longer fearful or welled up with tears.

I hated seeing anyone get bullied. Ciara had been teased by her classmates at our last school. I'd been made fun of too, but it didn't bother me like it did her. And because I was bigger than most kids my age, no one picked a fight with me.

Faise was shy at first but once we got talking, he slowly came out of his shell. And he wasn't the only one who felt relief.

I'd finally made a friend. Me.

I joked around and because of that I got along anywhere, with pretty much anyone. But I didn't have any close friends. No play dates or sleepovers. Up until recently, I'd lived in a trailer park with my mom, dad, and sister but I never wanted to invite anyone home. Between my parents fighting and the state of the trailer itself, just… no.

I didn't tell Faise the reason why my hair was long. It was either leave it or let my mom give me her idea of a haircut, which was just shaving it off. Which I didn't like. We couldn't afford to go to the barber. We didn't have new clothes either. Or much of anything.

Being the poorest kid in the class, I didn't get invited to

parties because they knew I couldn't buy gifts. The only time we got nice stuff was at Christmas, when the local charity organized a donation drive. Last year, I got a video game console. I took extra care of it because I knew it would have to last years.

It was fine. We got by. At least me and my mom and my sister always had each other.

And I learned that if I could make people laugh, I'd get by, no matter what. Maybe now that my mom had two jobs, and we were in a new apartment, in a new town, things would be different.

Maybe.

But wishing for something and getting it were two different things. I gave up on wishes, along with believing in Santa Claus and the tooth fairy.

After Faise and I played for a while, it was time for lunch, so we headed back inside the school. We got our bags from our lockers and headed into the crowded lunchroom.

"What do you have to eat?" Faise asked me as we found two empty seats.

"PB & J," I replied. "My favorite."

It wasn't my favorite. It was what I ate every day because there was nothing else. Sometimes only the J.

"Do you want to try some of mine?" he asked as he opened his lunch bag.

He pulled out three metals containers packed with food.

"Wow, what's all that?"

It smelled amazing and there was so much of it.

"This is my mom's chickpea curry and veg, rice, and homemade naan bread. Orange and mango slices. And string cheese."

"String cheese?" I asked. "It doesn't sound like it goes with the other stuff."

"I love them," Faise giggled. "My dad too, but we hide them from Mom. She says they're processed foods."

"All I've ever eaten is that."

"Here," Faise said and passed me his fork.

"You have utensils too? What else is in there? A microwave?"

Faise laughed again and the sound made me smile. I tried a mouthful of the curry, and it was good but...

"That's kinda spicy," I replied and reached for a piece of the bread. "But really good."

Then I bit into the flatbread. "OMG, that's amazing."

Faise's face lit up.

We spent the rest of the lunch hour eating and talking, in our own world. We liked the same video games and TV shows. And music, too.

"Do you, I mean, would you like to come to my house on Friday after school?" he asked me. "We always have pizza night on Friday. But real pizza, from a restaurant, not the frozen kind."

Just the thought of fresh pizza had my stomach rumbling again.

"Yeah," I replied without thinking. "I'll check with my mom first, but it should be okay."

Then I felt guilty. I'd have loads of pizza and my sister and mom would be eating Kraft mac & cheese again.

"Um, I just remembered. I might need to babysit my sister Friday night."

"Bring her with you. We always have lots."

I nodded but I didn't reply.

"If you want," Faise added quietly. "You don't have to if you don't want. I mean—"

"I want to. I just, well—" I paused. I never told anyone about how we struggled, but suddenly, it just spilled out of me. "I won't be able to do the same. My family can't afford stuff like pizza nights."

Faise nudged me with his sharp little elbow. "I don't care. I still want you to come over."

Then he gave me a smile that had the dimples on his cheeks popping out.

Sitting there in the lunchroom, I knew right then that Faise wasn't going to be my friend.

He was going to be my best.

CHAPTER 2

RONIN

AGE 13

"Can I stay over at your place this weekend?"

My question was met with silence.

But that wasn't unusual. This was Faise I was talking to. He'd rather be playing on his drum kit than doing anything else. Including talking.

Not much had changed since we were ten.

Well, except for the surge of hormones running through our veins. Not to mention the pimples, underarm sweat that was so strong it would make you pass out, and longer hair.

Both of us hit a growth spurt this year. I was still towering over most people in my grade, including Faise. But where he was tall and lean, I was just big—big hands, big voice, big everything. And I was the first guy in our grade to have facial hair, too.

We'd just finished up our music class but we stayed on to get in extra practice. Like we did every Tuesday and Friday. Me on the guitar, and Faise on his drums. We already had it in our head that we wanted to form a band. Me and Faise had half-decent voices, but neither of us were great singers. Not that anyone would take our band idea seriously given our age. But still, when you know, you know.

Music was everything to me. It helped me forget about all the stuff I struggled with—at home and at school.

"You don't need to ask, Ro," Faise finally responded while he tapped out a familiar rhythm with his sticks. "Of course, you can stay over. Is your Dad visiting again?"

"Unfortunately," I shook my head and glanced at my friend.

Faise's brown eyes looked back at me with concern.

"The whole weekend will be nothing but my parents fighting and Dad on his phone with his new girlfriend. I don't know why he even bothers to visit. He never wants to spend time with us. All we do is sit and watch TV together, while he eats, drinks beer, and complains about his job at the factory. He arrives as late as possible Friday night and leaves first thing Sunday morning. And he doesn't even care to ask me about my music or anything that I'm interested in."

"I'm sorry, Ro. That sucks," Faise replied. "But you know my family thinks of you as one of our own. You're always welcome in our house."

It was true, I was. Faise's parents, Naleena and Aaron Reed, were like my own. Even though I wasn't sure that they were one hundred percent behind the friendship between me and Faise. Not that they'd ever said anything, but I wasn't a scholar like Faise's older brother Rae. Naleena was a chemical engineer and Aaron, a scientist who worked for the government. They had high hopes for their sons' academic and career futures. Hopes that didn't include friendships with below average classmates like me.

And I seriously doubted they'd want me around once they found out that Faise and I were starting a band. *Hey, we don't care about school. We want to become rockstars.* I'm sure that would go over well. Not.

But the bigger worry was them finding out about who I

really was. About the secret I'd been holding on to for a year. A truth I kept from everyone, including my best friend. Faise and I talked about everything, but not this. Not until I was sure. There was a weight inside me, a heaviness that secrets have, that I couldn't explain but needed to let out.

What if he doesn't want to be your friend anymore once he knows?

I was gay.

I knew it because girls in my class didn't interest me the way boys did. I wanted to tell my parents too, but I had no idea how they'd react.

I was dreading it. No, not that. I was terrified. But first, I had to tell Faise. Maybe it would be easier to start with him?

"I've got something important to tell you."

Faise stopped drumming and swiveled to face me, strands of his straight black hair falling into his eyes. He was growing it out. It wasn't shoulder length like mine, but it suited him.

"What is it?" he asked.

"It's something personal. I haven't told anyone. But I'm… I'm kinda afraid to tell you."

Faise placed his sticks aside and walked over to stand in front of me. The hurt in his eyes could not be mistaken.

"It's me, Ro, you know you can tell me anything."

"Yeah, but this is different—" I paused.

Shit, my pits were soaked now, sweat making my t-shirt stick to my body. And my heart was pounding like I'd just finished running several laps around the school track.

"Just tell me. Spit it out."

I wiped my face with clammy hands and took a deep breath.

"I'm gay. I don't want to date girls. Like, ever."

Faise stared at me for a split second and then nodded. "Okay."

Then he walked back over to his drum kit and began to play again.

What the hell?

"Did you hear what I just said?" I asked.

He nodded and kept playing. "Yeah, you're gay. I'm good."

"You're good? Just like that? I've known for almost a year, but I was too scared to say anything."

"You know no matter what, we're always gonna be best friends. Always. Nothing changes that."

I nodded, relieved. God, I was so freaking relieved. I picked up my guitar and began to play along with him.

"You really don't care?" I asked him.

Faise shook his head and grinned at me. "That you're gay? No, I don't. Whoever you like, you like. It's cool."

The weight I'd been carrying around finally lifted a little.

And then it got me thinking. I was curious about who Faise might be into. He was still kinda shy in school, and he kept his personal feelings close. He didn't seem interested in either guys or girls, but not everyone had that figured out yet. We were only thirteen.

It didn't matter anyway. I'd support him the same way he did me.

"So, pizza tonight?" Faise asked me, and I nodded in return.

I'd freaked out for nothing. Everything was fine, as it always was.

Until I got home and told my parents.

Faise

Ronin was always braver than me.

At school, when it came to music, when it came to anything.

Him telling me that he was gay sparked a panic inside me. Not that I had any issue with him being gay. Or that I let my anxiety show. But still, I was worried that he would somehow know that I felt the same way.

Like Ro, puberty hit me fast and hard this year and the changes in my body also gave me a realization.

I was queer. Gay.

But it was a truth that I didn't dare voice to anyone.

While my parents were accepting people, I couldn't recall anyone queer in my extended family. On either side. Mom was born in the U.S. to parents born and raised in Kashmir, India and my dad was from Northern Ireland. While my grandparents (on both sides) were what I would call conservative, my parents were not.

Still, I didn't know what to do.

Bad enough that I wasn't as book smart as my brother Rae. I'd let my parents down as soon as they found out I wanted to be a rockstar. Now this?

No. I wasn't ready to come out yet. Maybe Ronin was ready to tell people in his life who he was, but I wasn't. Which, for a moment, made me feel like a shitty person. But then I remembered that there was no timeline on this.

Right now, my focus was on supporting my best friend.

So, after we were done with music practice, I headed back with him to his apartment so he could change and grab his stuff for our weekend sleepover.

He wanted to tell his parents tonight. Not that I thought anything bad would happen. His dad and mom were kinda hands-off when it came to parenting Ronin and his sister, Ciara. To be fair, his mom was busy working two jobs to make ends meet so she had little time or energy left. His dad was another story. The guy didn't always pay child support—on time or at all. When his dad did show up to visit, it was usually not more than a day or two. Ronin was more of a father to Ciara than their dad was. Ro made dinner for him and his sister when their mom was working, and he helped

Ciara with her homework. He even took her to the doctor if his mom couldn't.

Surprisingly, when we got to his apartment, his mom, Callie, was already home and cooking dinner. She smiled and nodded when she saw me.

"You boys get washed up. Dinner's almost ready," she stated.

"I'm just here to grab my stuff," Ronin replied. "I'm going to Faise's for the weekend."

"Again? Okay, but—" she paused and turned back to the stove to stir the pot of what smelled like marinara sauce. "Your dad will be here in ten minutes. Don't you want to spend the weekend with him?"

"Why? He's always on his phone or asleep on the couch. We don't *do* anything," Ronin snapped and stomped off to his bedroom.

Leaving me alone with his mom.

"Is he keeping out of trouble?" she asked me.

I nodded. "He's good. We spend most of our time in the music room at school. He's a great guitar player."

"Ronin doesn't get that from me," she smiled at me. "Or his dad."

"Well, he's really good."

"I wish I could afford to send him for lessons," she sighed and turned back to the stove.

Ro came back into the kitchen, his gym bag in hand. He'd thrown on a clean white t-shirt and a denim jacket.

"Actually," Ronin started. "There is something I want to talk to you and Dad about. So, we'll wait until he shows up."

"Everything okay?" His mom turned off the stove and walked over to face us.

"Yeah. It's just something that I've been carrying around for a while. And I need to tell both of you."

His mom frowned. "You didn't get into a fight at school, did you?"

"What? No." Ronin shook his head. "Nothing like that."

"Then what is it?"

A knock at the door interrupted her question.

A few seconds later, Ronin's dad, Brad, appeared. He said hello to me and then reached over to hug Ronin. The hug was brief, almost awkward, and so unlike Ronin. When my best friend pulled away, he walked over to stand beside me.

"Like I was telling Mom earlier, I'm heading over to Faise's for the weekend, but first I wanted to tell you guys something."

I glanced at his face and noticed the beads of sweat and the paleness of his skin. His expression was suddenly so full of fear I nearly reached for his hand.

"Okay, so, the thing is, I'm gay," he blurted out.

Callie dropped the tea towel she'd been holding, and stood there with her mouth open, her blue eyes wide. Brad's expression, though, was shuttered. I couldn't tell what he was thinking.

Until Callie reached over and pulled Ronin in for a hug, holding him and rocking him in her arms even though he was four inches taller and twenty pounds heavier. She whispered to him that no matter what, she loved him and supported him.

"No," his dad snapped and shook his head. "Where did you get this idea? You're only thirteen for god's sake. You can't know if you're… if you're… that. No."

Callie pulled away to face Brad and I watched Ronin's face turn a sickly grey.

"I am," Ronin replied, his voice so low it was barely a whisper. "I've known for a while now. I'm gay. This is who I am."

"No!" his dad yelled.

"Brad, so help me God, if you don't support Ronin, you can get the hell out of my house right now!" Callie roared.

"This is your fault, Callie!" Brad shouted back at her. "Letting him grow his hair long, and encouraging him play that shitty music all the time. Filling up his head with your stupid, liberal ideas."

"Get out!" she screamed.

I glanced up at Ronin and his eyes welled up with tears. He was visibly trembling, so I grabbed hold of his arm and pulled him closer to me.

His dad and mom kept yelling at each other and then, suddenly, Brad pivoted and pointed his finger at Ronin. The hate in his eyes was unmistakable.

Without thinking, I stepped in front of my best friend.

Sure, I was shorter than Ronin *and* his father. But I wasn't going to let Brad hurt his son any more than he already had.

"Get out of my way," Brad threatened me, getting up in my face. "Did you do this to him? Did you touch him? Did you put that stupid idea in his head?"

I shook my head, astonished that any parent would react this way. But more than that, I was afraid for my friend.

"We're leaving," I announced with a shaky voice, my heart pounding out of control. "Right now."

His mom was crying, tears rolling down her face and she moved to step beside Ronin. Three against one.

Brad stared at us and shook his head. "I can't believe this. I won't."

And then he stomped out of the apartment, slamming the door behind him.

I turned to find Ronin still shaking, crying, and I hugged him as tight as I could. Me and his mom.

"What's going on?"

Ciara's sudden voice startled me.

"Why was Dad yelling?" she asked. "Ro, are you okay?"

My friend wouldn't answer his sister. Ro just stood there, shaking his head.

"Ronin?" I said his name and he finally wiped his face and took a deep breath.

"I told Dad I was gay. He didn't take it well. I don't think he's coming back."

His voice broke. Ciara rushed up to him and gave her brother a hug. All four of us stood in the kitchen in shock.

"Thanks," Ronin whispered as he stared at me. "For standing with me."

I reached for his hand and squeezed it tight. "There's no other place I'd be."

CHAPTER 3
FAISE

AGE 14

"My parents are sending me for testing tomorrow."

Ronin and I were in my bedroom, playing video games as we usually did after school. Well, when we weren't playing music. It was a Friday like every other. Except, I had news to share. News I'd been keeping to myself for a week now. But no longer.

"Testing for what?" he asked.

"A learning disorder. They think that's the reason I'm not doing well in English. Well, in most classes, except math. Despite having a tutor. And, depending on the results, they might send me to a new school."

Ronin placed the receiver on my bed.

"But they can't do that! So what if you're not great at writing boring essays? I'm not. It doesn't mean we're not smart. Just not book smart. You've learned to play the piano and drums in a couple of years. And you're not just good, you're amazing. How many of our classmates can do that?"

"I know that, you know that, but my parents don't care about the music thing. They want me to be like Rae and get straight A's. To go to college and shit. Become a scientist, or a mathematician or something. And I don't have a choice. I'm being tested whether I want to or not."

I should be grateful. I guess. Ronin's mom didn't have money to spend on tutors or testing. Not that I wanted to be tested. I already felt different from other students given my grades. I didn't need an exam to tell me that.

But I was really worried about the idea of being sent to a new school. About being separated from Ronin.

After Ronin's dad left a year ago, he never came back. Not a call or a visit, nothing. Ronin didn't talk about it, but he was hurting. Who wouldn't be after their father walked out like that? Just gone, forever? I couldn't even imagine. Ronin acted like his usual silly self at school, joking around, playing off like everything was okay.

But it wasn't. He wasn't.

Ronin liked to talk, a lot, but not about his dad. Instead, he dove into music and he didn't look back.

I'd finally started to come out of my shyness, and me and Ronin had made a few friends at school. Most of them were in the music program. And if Ronin or I got picked on by the popular students, we had each other's backs. So, thinking about leaving him, leaving my school behind, made me feel like I was gonna puke.

"Will you come with me?" I asked.

"What time?"

"Eleven. We could hang out after. Maybe check out that music store in Providence?"

"Sure. Maybe. I think," Ronin muttered and looked away from me. "Look, I don't feel so good. I'm gonna head home."

"Okay, but—"

Ronin grabbed his backpack and headed for the door.

"Ro."

He didn't reply. Instead, he left and slammed the door behind him.

I was too shocked to move at first. Then, I finally followed. But when I stepped outside my bedroom, and walked downstairs, Ronin was already gone.

"Everything okay?" My dad asked.

He worked from home now and had an office on the main floor of our house.

"I don't know. I told Ronin I was going to get tested and everything. And then he said he didn't feel good."

My dad walked over and gave me a reassuring pat on the shoulder.

"Probably all that junk food you guys eat when you're upstairs in your room."

I hid chips, candy, and soda in my bedroom, far away from my mom. Dad knew and had thankfully kept our secret. For now.

"I don't think that's it," I paused, feeling kinda sick myself, rubbing my stomach. "I'll go get tested but I'm not changing schools."

"What?"

"You can hire another tutor for me if you want. But I'm not leaving. I can't leave him there alone."

"But Faise—"

"No!" I shouted.

Which, for me, was unheard of. Least of all, to my parents.

My dad startled, then drew me in close and nodded. "I know Ronin's been through a lot. His father leaving. And you're a good friend to be concerned about him. But you also have to think about your future."

"I know what I want to do. And I don't like school. Writing and stuff is hard for me. Not like music. That's what I love. The only thing I want to do. Why don't you guys ever listen to me?"

My dad raised one eyebrow and I stopped talking.

I'd never been so vocal before.

Then, my dad surprised me and pulled me in for a hug. I

felt so bad that Ronin would never be able to do the same with his father. It made me want to cry and scream on his behalf.

"That's the first time you've ever talked back to me. And don't tell your mother, but I'm so damn proud," Dad whispered.

I hugged him tighter. I was worried about Ronin and I needed the feeling of home and safety.

"I'll talk to your mom," Dad murmured. "The testing is still a go, but if you really want to stay at your school, then maybe we should take that into consideration."

I was never going to graduate with honors like my brother Rae. And I was okay with that. But I hated the guilt of disappointing my parents.

My dad's cell rang. "I've got to take this. Once I'm done, we'll order pizza for dinner, okay?"

He walked back to his office.

I pulled out my phone and texted Ronin.

> Faise: You okay??

No response.

I waited for an hour and texted him again.

> Faise: I'm NOT changing schools.

I wouldn't. It wasn't respectful to push back against my parents, but I was fourteen now. Didn't that mean I had a say in where I wanted to go to school?

> Ronin: It's okay, boo.

I knew in my gut it wasn't.

———

A few days later, I had my answer. About my learning disorder. But still none from Ronin. He ghosted me over the weekend.

By the time Monday morning rolled around, I told my parents I was sick.

I wasn't, but I didn't want to go to school.

At least I finally had a name for my poor performance. Dysgraphia. Basically, I had difficulty turning my thoughts into written sentences. So, no wonder I sucked at writing reports and essays and basically everything except numbers.

And part of my therapy was journaling. It was physically painful for me to write most times, but especially now. But I managed to write a few lines. Better than nothing. And I'd have a special tutor for three hours a week, every week for the rest of the year. Great.

"Faise!" My dad called out, knocking on my bedroom door.

I glanced at my phone. It was already noon.

"Yeah, come in."

He opened it. "I have some soup for you. Do you think you can eat?"

I nodded, putting my phone aside. I'd been waiting all weekend for Ronin to respond and the longer the silence went on, the worse I felt.

"Also—" My dad's comment was interrupted by the sound of the doorbell ringing. "Take this. I'll be right back."

I took the offered tray, a steaming bowl of lentil soup and rice.

Too bad I didn't feel like eating at all.

Then I heard the heavy sound of footsteps, and suddenly, Ronin's voice.

When he entered my bedroom, I nearly jumped up and ran over to him. My dad nodded at us, then closed the door.

"Hey."

"Hey," Ronin replied as he stood there, hands in his

pockets, his toe tapping out a nervous rhythm. "I was wondering why you weren't in class this morning."

"I didn't feel good. And shouldn't you be there right now?" I asked.

Ronin shrugged. "I told the teacher I had stomach cramps. I'm not going back today."

"You wanna stay and play video games?"

He nodded, then finally dropped his backpack on the floor like usual and wandered over to sit beside me on my bed.

"How did the testing go?" he asked quietly.

"Okay. I have dysgraphia."

"Dis what now?"

I nearly laughed at his comment. "It means I have trouble getting what's in my head put into words on a page. Or a laptop screen."

He nodded.

"Does this mean another tutor? Or," he paused and licked his lips. "Another school?"

"Another tutor, three hours a week. I've already got homework."

Ronin's tight expression finally eased. He leaned over and bumped my shoulder. "Sorry I walked out on Friday. It's just—"

"I get it."

"No. I mean, you do get it, but I just… I didn't know how to talk about it. It felt like—" Ronin blew out a deep breath. "Like I was losing you. If you go to another school."

"Which I'm not. And you'd never lose me."

"I know that. But Friday, I thought maybe it was happening," Ronin looked down at his hands. "Ever since Dad left, I worry that people close to me will leave. And never come back."

Ronin's quiet admission made my stomach flip over. His dad cutting off contact like that was never going to stop hurting Ronin. I wished I could do something to help him.

All I could do was be his friend.

"Even if I had to go to another school, we'd stay besties," I replied and put my arm around his massive shoulders. "I'm not going anywhere. You're stuck with me. Forever."

Ronin laughed and turned to look at me. "That's a long time, boo."

"That's our friendship."

CHAPTER 4

FAISE

AGE 16

"See those guys standing at the end of the hallway?" Ronin asked. "They're gonna be in our music class this year."

I slammed my locker shut and glanced around.

You couldn't mistake the newcomers.

Both had long hair, like me and Ro. The first guy was tall and lean, with black wavy hair, and he wore makeup. Lots of eyeliner. Something that wasn't allowed in school. The guy turned and met my stare head on, but I looked away, turning my attention to the one standing next to him, the blond. Both guys were wearing ripped t-shirts, jeans, and converse. The blond one was talking and waving his arms around, while the other guy smirked and leaned back against his locker, like he didn't have a care in the world.

"Have you talked to them yet?"

"Nope." Ronin shook his head. "But I heard that the dark haired one has quite a mouth on him. It's his first day here and he already got threatened with detention from Mr. Stuart."

Mr. Stuart was our English teacher. If you could call him that. He didn't like helping the struggling students, aka me and Ronin. Instead, he red-lined our essays with nothing but a single mark, no feedback. I didn't give a shit. As long as I did well enough to pass, I was good. I didn't give a fuck about school anyway. My parents were disappointed in my grades but that was nothing new. And the older I got, the more I realized that I was never going to be like them. I'd have to forge my own path. Be bold.

Bold? Me? Yeah, I was working on that.

Speaking of bold, Ronin and I didn't have to walk down the hallway to talk to the new guys. They headed in our direction.

"Hey, I'm Brodie." The dark-haired one reached out with his fist. Ronin bumped it, then I followed. "This is Holloway. Cool shirts. I've been to concerts for both bands. They're fucking awesome."

I had on my favorite Foo Fighters t-shirt and Ronin, Green Day.

"Thanks," Ronin replied in his rumbling voice. He not only looked older, but he sounded it too. "I'm Ronin, this is Faisel. Where you guys from?"

"Just outside Providence. We used to go to a private school, but I got kicked out a month ago," Brodie smirked. "My parents shit their pants."

"I was next to go. Or rather, I told my dad I wanted out," Holloway shook his head. "Private school sucked. Too many rules."

"I like your makeup, but you better watch it," I warned. "The principal's gonna make you take it off."

"I'd like to see them try," Brodie scoffed. "It's a free country and I can do what I want."

This guy had fucking balls. I knew right then and there that the teachers would not be able to deal with his attitude.

"Public school is still a dictatorship," Ronin commented

with a grin. "Faise and I jam after music class. You guys play?"

"Fuck, yeah." Holloway smiled. "Brodie's got a kick ass voice and I play guitar. Just tell us when and where."

"Today?"

They nodded.

Brodie looked around. "Fuck, I hate school. Rules and more fucking rules. Me and Holls are gonna split town once we turn eighteen and gig across the country. Do our own thing."

I looked at Ronin and he smiled back at me. "So are we."

"No shit?" Brodie asked, a fire in his hazel eyes.

Ronin nodded. "I play bass, Faise, drums. We've been looking to form a band, but we haven't clicked with anyone yet."

"Are you kidding me? This is fucking perfect." Brodie leaned in close. "How about we jam and see if it works? If it does, we find a name, and start playing local gigs."

"But we don't even have our own instruments yet. Well, I don't," Ronin replied. "I'm working a job on the weekends to save up for a guitar."

"That's not a problem. I've got instruments you can borrow for now. We can practice in my basement, it's all set up," Brodie added. "I've already got a van, an old one that my parents don't need any more. We're gonna fix it up and then one more fucking year and we hit the road. Wait, how old are you guys?"

"Sixteen," I muttered. "Both of us turn seventeen in July."

Holloway cocked his head. "Me and Brodie are the same, but in April."

"Awesome," Ronin replied. "Well, we have math class and we better not be late. The last thing I need is extra homework."

"Mr. Lansing's class?" Holloway asked.

"Yup."

"We're in the same one."

The four of us walked to class together. Brodie got some long stares from the other kids, but all he did was give them the finger in return and kept strutting, cocky as fuck. I was awed by his confidence.

When we did make it to class, our foursome sat at the back and talked about our favorite musicians and albums. All four of us were obsessed with the idea of being in a band and making it big. And talking with Brodie and Holloway, I felt like I did when I first met Ronin. We became fast friends. Me and Ronin didn't have a wide circle of buddies in high school and that was okay. Not everyone did. We were video game geeks and music nerds. And a lot of the jocks in our class made fun of us.

One guy in particular, Ilya Vallen, the star quarterback and the most popular guy in our school, seemed to have a thing for stirring up trouble with Ronin.

Case in point…

"Ronin, why don't you shut up already? No one wants to hear about your stupid music," Ilya snapped, turning around and glaring at us. "Fucking queer freak."

"Fuck off, jockstrap," Ronin muttered back.

"Yeah. Turn your pretty boy face back around before I rearrange it," Brodie snarked. "And I'm queer too, so watch your mouth."

"Yeah," Holloway interjected. "Me, too. So shut the fuck up."

Holy shit! I couldn't believe how bold Brodie and Holloway were. They were brand new to this school and already, they took no shit. And they were both queer? And open about it? I was blown away.

"Just what we need, more weirdos. And wearing make-up?" Ilya sneered. "Disgusting."

"No, that's your face. Now turn around and mind your own fucking business," Ronin hissed.

Ilya made to get up, Ronin joining.

"Guys," I cautioned as the teacher entered the room and gave us a warning glance.

They both sat back down.

"Is there a problem?" Mr. Lansing called out, adjusting his glasses.

Brodie nodded and pointed at Ilya. "Just this dumb jock here being a complete asshat."

The classroom chatter turned to laughter.

"And you are?"

"Brodie James."

Mr. Lansing nodded. "Well, Mr. James, given that you're new to my class I will give you one reprieve. But I will ask that you please control your wayward tongue from here on out."

Wayward tongue? Brodie mouthed to us. I tried not to laugh but it was impossible.

"For you, and as a reminder to everyone in this class, that means being rebellious will not be tolerated and neither will cursing at other students. Do you understand?"

Brodie nodded but behind his desk, he was giving the teacher two middle fingers.

Shit, this was too entertaining. I glanced at Ronin, and he was trying to hold in a laugh too.

"Don't worry," Brodie whispered to us. "We've got your back."

I believed him. The guy was fierce, and he wasn't afraid of anyone.

After math class was over, Ronin and I headed to history and Brodie and Holloway went to English. Then all four of us met up again for music class, which was at the end of the day.

Once our final class was over and before we started jamming, I wandered out to use the washroom. The hallways were deserted now that school was done, no one in sight.

Once I was finished in the head, I washed up, and started back out.

Until I spotted Ronin and Ilya at the end of the hallway, in the alcove under the stairs.

But they weren't fighting like usual.

Ilya and Ronin were sucking face. And going at each other with the same intensity as their argument.

I flushed all over, embarrassed that the sight of them kissing turned me on and at the same time, made me angry. How could Ronin kiss an asshole like that? A guy who made fun of him all the time.

I didn't know what to do, so I crept back into the bathroom and waited a few more minutes. When I re-appeared and glanced again, they were gone.

I walked back to class, confused and shaken up. Brodie and Holloway were already playing. And singing. Fuck, Brodie could *sing*. A shiver passed through me. Somehow, just like I knew about Ronin, I knew that the four of us, right here, was the start of something special. I could feel it in my gut.

"You're so fucking good," I blurted out as I stood in the doorway, watching them.

Brodie's smirk made another appearance. "I know. But thanks."

"He's already got the rockstar ego," Holloway teased. "All we need now is a band name. Oh, and you know, a record deal."

"Where's Ronin?" Brodie asked.

I flushed, because, of course I did. "Um, I don't know. Probably the washroom?"

"He left ten minutes ago. Seems like a long time to take a piss," Holloway quipped. "Or a shit."

"Not for someone my size."

I turned at the sound of Ronin's voice. Of course, my eyes lasered in on his lips, which were swollen. Now that I'd seen him, with Ilya of all people, I couldn't unsee it.

"What about Wayward Tongue?" Brodie suggested.

I flushed again, my mind still thinking about that kiss, and shook my head. "What?"

"The name of our band. The teacher's comment got me thinking," Brodie explained. "Wayward means rebellious and that's what rock music means to us. Fuck the nine to five, yeah?"

"Wayward, I like. Tongue, I like." Holloway waggled his eyebrows. "Just not together. At least, not for a band name."

Brodie rolled his eyes. "Okay, fine. You suggest a name."

"Wayward Dick?" Holls snickered and Brodie gave him two middle fingers in response.

"Be serious for a moment," I added. "This name is one that all of us have to love. And it needs to be good. Something that has meaning. Something original."

Brodie nodded. "What about Wayward Stray?"

"Immediate veto," Holls snorted. "It sounds like we're lost. Or, you know, dogs."

"I like the Wayward part," I replied. "That sounds cool. Maybe just that?"

The guys shook their heads.

"We're not following along with everyone else, right? Taking our own path. So, how about something like Wayward Lane?" Ronin suggested.

"That sounds cool!" Brodie exclaimed.

Me and Holls nodded our approval. Holy shit, we had a fucking name.

We played a few songs from two of our favorite bands, Nirvana and Goo Goo Dolls, testing things out. We sounded great together, but I didn't want to jinx things by saying anything. Time would tell. We just met. And we were only sixteen, so who the hell knows what could happen in a year? Still, something about our coming together seemed like fate to me. All four of us wanted to be musicians and nothing else.

Most people would say we were crazy. Go to college, take

the safe job. Me? I couldn't sit at a desk for eight hours a day, day in and out. School was bad enough.

After an hour of playing, laughing, and listening to Brodie's smart-ass commentary about our playing, it was time to head home.

"See you guys tomorrow?" Brodie asked over his shoulder, as he and Holloway headed for the exit.

I nodded and waved at him, still unable to look at Ronin.

"What's wrong?" Ronin finally asked me as we walked out.

"Nothing."

"It's obviously something."

I paused on the steps of the school and finally looked up at him. "I saw you."

"Saw me what?"

"You and Ilya. After music class," I snapped. "Under the stairs."

Ronin

"Oh. That."

"It's none of my business," Faise bit out. "I'm just surprised that you want to kiss someone who talks shit about you all the time."

I shrugged. "Um, I don't know how to explain it."

That was a lie. I did, I just didn't want to have to. Not to Faise.

"I mean, it's hot," I confessed. "We hate each other, and we're arguing, and then suddenly—"

"And then he uses you," Faise snapped and took off down the stairs.

"Hey, that's not fair," I whispered as I followed him. "It's just a kiss. I'm using him too. It doesn't mean anything. It's just hormones. And lots of people are in the closet. They don't or can't come out."

Faise flinched.

I suspected that my best friend was queer, like me. But I never asked. I was ready to come out at thirteen, but everyone is different. And it wasn't easy. My dad walked out that day and I hadn't had contact with him since. Not that I had much contact before, but still. Being abandoned by one of your parents for just being you is the hardest thing ever.

"I don't like the fact that Ilya makes fun of you and then does that. Like you're a dirty secret. You deserve better."

That was Faise, always coming to my defense. I pulled him in for a side hug and ruffled his hair.

"Don't." He pulled back and swatted my hand away. "I'm still mad."

"There's nothing to be mad at. I'm fine. Like I said, it's just a kiss. And I was curious. And horny. It's not like I have feelings for the guy."

"Okay," he sighed. "As long as you're all right."

"I am. But thanks for your concern, boo," I teased.

I got his middle finger in response. Good, we were back to normal. We walked along the pathway that led to the bus stop.

"So, Brodie and Holloway, they're cool, eh?" Faise muttered, changing topics.

"Yeah, they are. I think we have a good sound together."

"Me too," Faise replied and bit his lower lip.

He always did that when he was working out a problem in his head.

"I think I'm ready to do this," he stated.

"Ready for the band? We can practice, and maybe play a gig here or there, but we still have another year of high school—"

"Not that."

We sat down on the bench at the bus stop. No one else was around.

"I'm ready to finally admit that I'm queer too," he whispered. "But I don't want to tell my family. Not yet."

"Okay," I acknowledged. "I mean, thanks for telling me. But yeah, you do you. You don't have to tell anyone."

Faise glanced up at me with those earnest brown eyes. He was worrying his lower lip again and rubbing his hand over his jaw. Unlike me, Faise didn't have pimples or facial hair. Just sharp cheekbones and wicked dimples.

"I was watching Brodie and Holloway in school, and they're so fucking confident. I want to be like that," he confessed.

I knew that Faise struggled with expressing himself and being social. But when he was in the music zone, he thrived. And I was sure that, given time, his confidence would follow.

"You'll get there," I replied. "It just takes some of us longer to grow out of our awkward teenage phase."

Faise sighed. "How long is that?"

"I have no idea. Ask me again in a few years."

CHAPTER 5

FAISE

AGE 18

A month ago, Ronin and I, along with Brodie, Holls, and the rest of our class, graduated from high school.

Now I was getting ready for my eighteenth birthday party. Well, two of them. The first, a formal dinner celebration with my family, and the second, a night out with my friends.

I threw on my blazer even though I hated formal wear. But my parents insisted. I wore jeans and a t-shirt underneath. The jacket would get tossed aside as soon as the family stuff was done.

But first, I had news to share.

I had to tell my parents tonight that A) I wasn't planning on taking a year off to figure out where I wanted to go to college because I was *never* going, B) I'm heading out with my friends to gig across the country because we wanted to be rockstars, and C) I'm gay.

Truthfully, the first two scared the shit out of me. More than the third. But I was eighteen. That meant I could do whatever the hell I wanted.

They would tell me the rockstar thing was immature and irrational, but I didn't care. This was what I wanted. Me and the guys had planned and practised. And we were good.

But instead of waiting until I got to the venue for our dinner, I wanted to tell my family now. Otherwise, I'd never be able to eat.

A knock at my bedroom door had me turning around.

"Hurry up, Faisel, we don't want to keep your grandparents waiting," my mom yelled out. "We're already fifteen minutes late."

I opened the door and she smiled at me. "Finally."

"Where's Dad?" I asked.

"He's waiting in the car."

Fuck.

"I'm ready."

I was so not ready. But, like my friends reminded me, it's now or never. If we wanted to make a real go at becoming professional musicians, we had to do it now.

My mom and I headed to the car, but my brother was absent.

"Rae is already at the restaurant with Hannah," Mom commented before I could ask.

Of course, my brother was. He was never late like me.

I slid into the backseat and slammed my door.

"I have something to tell you guys," I started.

Dad shifted into drive and pulled out onto the street. "Can't it wait until we're all together?"

"No," I blurted out. "I need to talk to you and Mom first. This year isn't going to be a gap year. I'm not going to college. Ever. Me, Ro, Holls, and Brodie are heading out on the road. As a band."

"Not this rock band nonsense again," my mother commented.

"It's not nonsense, it's what I want to do! It's all I want to do. And I'm going."

Dad was silent, glancing at me occasionally in the rearview mirror. I saw the worry in his green eyes. There was disappointment there too.

"I want to be a professional musician," I insisted. "And we have a great sound. We're gonna make it."

"Then apply to music schools. Go to Juilliard," Mom added.

"No. I hate school and I'm done with it," I spat out.

My mom looked at my dad and he shook his head.

"You're eighteen, Faise. We can't tell you what to do," Dad replied. "But that doesn't mean we aren't worried. Without a college degree—"

"I'll be fine. I know what I'm doing. And, one other thing—"

My mom sighed. "I don't know if I can take another surprise."

"I'm gay."

Dad braked so hard at the stop sign that all three of us pitched forward.

A cold sweat broke out all over my body. This was it. I was sure they were going to kick me out of the car.

Instead, he surprised me and kept on driving.

"Okay," Dad answered, glancing at my mom.

"Okay?"

"Fozzy," Mom replied, using my childhood nickname. "We love you no matter what, you know that. But thank you for telling us."

"You're not mad?"

"About you being gay? No. Of course not," Dad responded. "About you not going to college? That's another thing."

I sat back, nearly collapsing from the relief I felt.

Then I remembered my grandparents.

"I'll tell Rae, but not Nana and Dada. Not yet," I muttered. "Maybe not ever."

My grandparents' traditions and beliefs were different to mine. I knew they loved me, but I had no idea how they would take the news of my coming out. I respected them but I had to live my own life.

"That's your choice."

We finally arrived at the restaurant, and my brother and his girlfriend greeted us. I was relaxed for a change.

At the end of the meal, I pulled my brother aside and told him my news.

He wasn't surprised by any of it.

"Always gotta be the quiet rebel," he teased and gave me a hug. "You're gonna hit the big time, Faise, I know it. Just keep being you and do what you love. Play your music. Don't follow anyone else's path but your own. And be with whoever you want. No matter what, you'll always be my baby bro."

I'd never felt closer to Rae than in that moment. Hugging him back, all the stress and worry that had swirled in my mind finally settled. I was nearly in tears, but I managed to keep myself in check.

Once we had birthday cake and coffee, I said my good-byes to my family and grabbed a rideshare to meet up with the guys.

Brodie's parents were cool and allowed him to have massive parties at their home. And yeah, there was drinking. Let's face it, if I was old enough to vote, drive, and enter the military, I was old enough to drink. That was my reasoning.

At least this way, no one was drinking and driving. People crashed at Brodie's and went home the next day.

When I arrived at his house, the music was already blast-ing. I threw off my blazer and knocked on the door.

Ronin answered, dressed in his usual black jeans and a ripped t-shirt. He'd hit another growth spurt this year and was now towering over me, nearly six foot three to my five eleven.

The boom of the music was so loud that I felt the ground vibrating under my feet.

"My birthday boo is finally here!!"

My best friend leaned over and hugged me, crushing my ribs. He smelled like beer and spicy body spray. Then he kissed my cheek and kept his arm around my shoulder as he led me into the house.

"You get your birthday gift later, but for now, let's get you a drink."

"Beer please, stat."

Ronin nodded. "I take it you told your parents, and everything went fine."

"How did you know?"

"Because for the past few months you've looked like you were gonna puke. You're finally smiling."

He ushered me down the basement steps, hands on my shoulders, as the noise and laughter got louder.

"My parents and brother are fine. With me being queer, that is," I admitted. "The rockstar idea, not so much. Well, Rae believes in me."

"You're eighteen now, you can do whatever the fuck you want."

I wasn't religious, but I said Amen to that.

"Where're the guys?"

We stepped into the basement, which was hazy, filled with smoke from cigarettes and pot.

"Brodie's over there, sucking face with some guy," he pointed to the far corner. Sure enough, Brodie was kissing some big-ass dude with tattoos. Then Ronin pointed to the opposite end of the room. "Holloway's leading a drinking game."

Of course, he was. People crowded around Holls, chanting "chug, chug, chug," as he placed the end of the plastic funnel in his mouth and drank.

Ronin and I walked over to the makeshift bar—coolers

packed with beer and mixers—and Ronin passed me a can of my favorite IPA. I cracked it open and took a long sip, feeling my remaining tension ease. I downed the rest of the beer in three more gulps, threw the empty can in the nearby bin, and grabbed another one.

Meantime, classmates greeted me and wished me happy birthday. I didn't court attention, but it was nice. I'd come a long way from the shy boy I once was. Music was the biggest part of that. The more I played with the guys, not just for myself but for an audience, and seeing their positive reaction, the more my confidence grew.

And tonight was another turning point. Finally telling my folks who I was and what I wanted. And I wasn't backing down. I felt like a fucking adult for the first time in my life.

And speaking of being an adult, one of Brodie's friends, Jojo, sauntered up to me and gave me a flirty wink. Jojo's normally blond hair was now bright pink, and he had full lips that were slicked with gloss. "How about a kiss, birthday boy?"

"He needs that, and more," Ronin quipped and shoved me forward.

My cheeks heated but I wasn't going to let that stop me.

"How can I say no?" I replied.

Jojo grinned and took my hand and fuck, I was excited already. I'd yet to fool around with any guy. And while I knew that I was attracted to bigger dudes, a horny eighteen-year-old is a horny eighteen-year-old. Jojo was sexy AF in tight jeans and a cropped top. And it was time for me to do more than just fantasize about sex. I wanted to experience it.

Maybe it was the beer or maybe it was finally coming out on my birthday, but something needy inside of me roared to life. As soon as Jojo turned back to me, I pushed him against the nearest wall and kissed him. His lips were soft and eager, his hot tongue delving into my mouth, teasing me so good.

Holy fucking hell, kissing was even more amazing than I

imagined. My cock grew so hard, so fast. When Jojo reached down and cupped my dick, I was about ready to come.

"You know what you're doing," I blurted out when we finally came up for air.

Jojo smiled wickedly and dropped to his knees.

"Just wait," he licked his lips. "I think what you really need to celebrate tonight is a birthday blowjob."

I was too turned on to reply. Or to care that other people were nearby.

When he unzipped my jeans, I leaned back and caught Ronin staring at me.

Why the fuck was that even hotter?

Next thing I knew, my hard cock was in Jojo's hot, wet mouth, and the only sounds coming out of me were grateful grunts and moans. I gripped his hair, tight, and then wondered if I should. Until Jojo popped off my cock.

"Fuck my face," he demanded. "I love it."

I was so ready. It was like a switch inside of me, and when he swallowed my cock again, I did just that, punching my hips forward. His mouth was so much better than my hand.

All the while, people were watching us. Or, as much as they could in a dark basement. And it turned me on more than I'd ever imagined. I came embarrassingly fast, and watched as Jojo swallowed my cum.

Shit, was he okay with that?

"Sorry, I—"

"You haven't been with anyone, right?"

I nodded.

"So, there's nothing to worry about. I wanted to swallow your cum."

Fuck, just him saying those words to me had my cock jerking again. He tucked me in, zipped me up, and stood up. Then he gave me a kiss on the lips and tasting my cum on him was also hot.

Holy shit. Happy birthday to me...

Another guy came up to Jojo and the two of them headed off to dance. I finally managed to catch my breath and come down from my first-time sex high, heading back to find Ronin in a drinking contest with another student. I grabbed a can of beer and joined them.

A short while later, I looked around for Brodie and Holls.

Brodie pushed away from the guy he was kissing, and when he spotted us, he dropped his hot date and made his way through the crowd. Wearing jeans and nothing else, he strutted towards us, partygoers getting out of his way.

When Brodie drew closer, I realized he had what looked like cling wrap tied around his arm. There was a design on his skin underneath it, a clef surrounded by flames.

"Oh my God! You got tatted!" I blurted out.

"Fucking right I did. And I'm about to get lucky with the artist."

He pointed over his shoulder. Ah yeah, the guy he'd been kissing. He was hot.

"That's what I want to do. Tonight!" I exclaimed.

"Get lucky? I thought you already did that with Jojo." Ronin waggled his eyebrows and slapped my ass.

I elbowed him in response.

"I want to get a tatt. Oh, and some piercings."

"Your first one is on us. Happy fucking Birthday!" Brodie leaned over and hugged me.

Then someone jumped on my back, and I laughed, startled.

"Happy birthday Fozzy!" Holloway shouted in my ear, his beer breath so strong it was nearly toxic.

"Hey, hands off my boo!" Ronin warned him with a teasing grin and a playful shove.

When Holloway finally eased off me, he messed up my hair and then put his arm around Brodie's neck.

"Pack your bags, bitches, we head out in two days!" Holloway yelled.

Ronin passed us more beers. "I can't believe it's really happening."

"My parents think I'm crazy." I shook my head.

"Well, we *are* Wayward Lane," Brodie replied with a smirk. "And it's not crazy. Being a musician is all I've ever wanted. You guys are the same. We're following our gut. That can never steer us wrong."

Despite his sarcastic mouth, Brodie was right.

I had fears, but deep down, I was doing what felt right. Music was everything to me. To us.

We had drive, talent, and passion. But the reality of making a living off our music was a big unknown. We'd played a few gigs this past month in Providence to good crowds. But being popular in our hometown was one thing. Gigging every week in different cities and trying to get noticed by a record label was another.

Not only that, but all four of us were queer. And we weren't going to hide.

Would that impact our ability to make it?

"To Faise," Ronin called out, holding up his can of beer. "My best friend, and the best fucking drummer I've ever heard! Happy eighteenth birthday and many more!"

We raised ours in turn and I caught Ronin's stare. His belief in me had me choked up for the second time tonight. Instead of letting my feelings show, I took a sip of my beer.

When he blew me a playful kiss, I shook my head.

Tonight, we had no worries.

Teenage expectations, though, are a funny thing. Did we have what it takes to make our rock 'n' roll dream come true?

There was only one way to find out.

CHAPTER 6

FAISE

AGE 21

Another year, another city, another performance.

Me and the guys were finishing up our third year on the road, heading into our fourth, and while we'd had steady work, we were also dealing with frustration.

We had gigs lined up for the year ahead, two a week, almost every week, but always as the opening act, not the headliner. And we'd been invited to a few summer music festivals, but only as a backup if others cancelled.

The big break we were working for, well, it still hadn't happened.

Don't get me wrong, we were having a blast. No one to answer to but ourselves. The freedom and excitement of the road, new places, and people. Hanging out with other musicians, getting drunk, getting high, and having sex whenever and however we wanted. And never having to deal with a clingy hookup since we were usually out the door the same night and on to a different city.

And we were always working on improving our sound,

and our performance. Brodie wrote all our songs, with input from the rest of us, and he had a talent for catchy lyrics. Most of them raunchy as hell.

But performing live every week was physically grueling and so was traveling. Not to mention, trying to get our demo in front of *any* contact at *any* record label was no easy feat. The few so-called talent scouts that did approach us after our recent shows turned out to be nothing more than predatory assholes. *Sign here and give us all the rights to your songs and we'll take most of your money.* No fucking way.

Three years in and no record deal.

Personally, we were having the time of our lives, but professionally, frustrating was the least of it.

Plus, we lived together. Twenty-four seven. Either in our van, or in shitty motel rooms we had to share. And every month or two, there would be arguments. Not that we stayed mad for long. But still, living and breathing in the same tiny space was only possible when you loved what you did. And when you loved the people with you.

Holls, Brodie, and Ronin weren't just friends, they were my band brothers.

Well, Ronin was more than that. I didn't even have to speak to him half the time. He could just look at me and he knew exactly what I was thinking. Or feeling. The kinetic energy between us needed no explanation.

He was my ride or die. Platonically speaking.

Or so I kept telling myself. The older I got, the more complicated my feelings were for my best friend. Not that I would screw things up by making a move. All four of us made a pact not to fuck with group dynamics by, well, fucking each other. It was one rule we stuck to.

Curiosity was just that. Better left alone.

Besides, we were never short of male attention on the road.

And I wouldn't trade this life for a nine to five, no matter what. But earning just enough money to keep going meant we were barely getting by. It wasn't easy, but it was the life we'd chosen.

It's gonna happen. We're gonna make it. One day.

And it could be tonight. We were in Seattle, opening for Havenstone, one of the most popular local bands in the city. It was a sold out show so hopefully we would garner good press. At this point, any press at all was good.

Our dressing room wasn't much bigger than a closet. At least it had a lock on the door, and it was clean. Not like some of the dives we'd played in. Fucking hell, they were grunge. Like, literally, they hadn't been cleaned since the 90s.

When my phone buzzed, I glanced at the message. It was a notification from my socials. Most of our high school classmates were graduating from college and starting their first jobs. Or going to grad school. Including my brother. He was finishing his MBA and at twenty-four, he already had a job lined up at some fancy-ass marketing firm.

I glanced at the pictures, graduation photos with happy smiles and proud parents.

Not that I envied them. Well, maybe a bit.

My parents still thought I was going through a phase, refusing to grow up. I knew they loved me, but their approval was something I wanted. I believed in my dream, and I wanted them to believe in it too.

"Hey boo, we've gotta finish soundcheck. You coming?" Ronin called out from the other side of the door.

"I'll be right there!" I yelled back.

My pre-show ritual was important. I started off with stretches to warm up my shoulders and legs. Then I relaxed with a hit of coke, my drug of choice. I'd tried a lot of different ones, but I always came back to it. It helped me loosen up, and by the time the show was done, I was on top of the world and ready to party. For an introvert like me, it was a game changer.

I snorted the white power, wiped my nose, and took a shot of tequila. Then I put my phone in our lockbox, finished fixing my black eyeliner, and did my final stretches before heading out to join my bandmates.

The guys were busy setting up our equipment and already working up a sweat. Hauling our gear in and out of venues, including amps that weighed a fuckton, was no mean feat. We didn't need a gym because we worked out every fucking day. And often, we didn't have anyone, save the venue manager, to help us.

I sat down behind my kit and adjusted my stool and my kickstand, while Brodie tested his mic, and Holls and Ro, their guitars.

A half hour later, the manager told us the doors were opening and we could hear the crowd on the other side of the curtain as they filled the room. The venue could pack in a thousand easy and the stage was the nicest one we'd ever played on.

My adrenaline spiked as the minutes counted down to showtime.

Until Brodie's phone rang, and we all stopped talking so he could hear.

"Brodie James… yeah… uh huh… thanks," he said and tapped his phone. "Thanks for nothing! Fuck!"

"Another label said no?" Holls asked as he swiped a hand through his hair.

"Yeah, that was Ethan from Strattos. Apparently, we don't have the sound he's looking for," Brodie spat out as he paced.

"What does that mean?" Ronin asked.

"I don't fucking know! That's all he said!" Brodie snapped and stormed off to the wings.

I set my sticks aside and walked around my kit. "That's the second rejection this month."

"This is so goddamn frustrating!" Holls bit out. "And to think I fucked that guy."

"You what?" I asked.

"Ethan said he loved our music, and our deal was a sure thing," Holls explained with a shrug of his shoulders. "He was hot. We were celebrating."

"He was using you, for fuck's sake!" I snapped. "Think Holls, come on. No wonder he didn't take us seriously. What the hell?"

"Hey! I'm not the only one who fucks around with guys in this business. Don't make this my fault!"

Ronin stepped up and placed an arm around my shoulder. "Take it down a notch, Holls."

"Of course, you'd come to *his* defense," Holls bit out, pointing at me with his guitar pick.

"I'm not taking sides. Done is done. We just gotta stay cool and keep going," Ronin assured us. "So, they said no. Fuck 'em."

"Too late," Holls quipped, shaking his head.

"A bigger and better label will come along," Ronin insisted. "But Holls, maybe don't fuck someone at the label that's scouting us until we have a signed deal, yeah?"

"Ronin's right. About all of that," Brodie's voice piped up. "Fuck Strattos."

Brodie walked back on stage, hands on his hips. "I'm good. We're good. Fuck that asshole and his shitty label! He wouldn't know good music if it bit him on the balls."

"Small, hairy balls at that," Holls teased.

Our confidence had wavered, but it came back around like always.

Holls shook his head. "I just don't get it. Crowds love us, and so do other bands. I don't know what else we can do. Like, why other bands and not us?"

"I have an idea to switch things up," I offered. "I think we should change our scheduled plans for next year and go to Europe instead."

Ronin turned to me. "Europe? Why?"

"We've been touring the states for three years. Enough already," I tapped my sticks together. "Maybe a label over there will take notice? What do you guys think?"

Brodie nodded. "I like it. And a change of scene is what we need. I've got some savings that I can dip into to help fund our flights over there. Holls, Ro?"

"I call the window seat," Holls quipped.

"So, are we all in agreement?" I asked. "Ro?"

Ronin pulled me in for a hug. "Like you ever need to ask."

Nine Days Later

Ronin

Berlin was our cheapest flight option.

Germany was cool and kinda overwhelming, but in the best way. New people, different language. It was energizing.

Cancelling our US bookings however, made me nervous. At least back home, we *knew* we had gigs lined up. Here? Anything could happen.

And if we didn't get any bookings, if the fans didn't like us and we had to return home, we'd have lost out on money we desperately needed. Or that *I* desperately needed. Brodie and Holls didn't like to ask their respective parent(s) for money, but if they needed to, they could. And did. Faise too.

Everyone but me. And I didn't like the others funding my room or expenses. Brodie insisted that we were family, and it was no biggie, but I didn't like feeling the odd one out.

Someday, I was going to have enough money so that me, my mom, and my sister would never have to worry again.

For now, I put aside my fears and trusted in Faise's idea. It might be the change we needed.

It had already inspired Brodie to write a new song on the way over here. *Nine Gone Wrong* was going to be our debut when we hit the Berlin stage.

Our first night, we made fast friends with a bouncer at a

downtown club. Which led us to an invite to an underground party, queer friendly, and full of twentysomethings like us. We popped pills, snorted coke, and danced until we sweated it all away.

Most of the crowd spoke English as well as German, so we were gold. And we met a group of guys that were also struggling musicians. Bruno, Anton, and twins Elias and Carl were members of a rock group called Die Tier. Translation: The Beast. And fuck, they were all that and more. Talented, fierce, and sexy as hell.

After out-dancing and out-drinking us, they invited us to another after, after party. Instead, we invited them back to our hotel. I don't remember much except landing on one of the beds in the room, then it was lights out. I woke up the next day to a room that smelled like stale beer, cigs, and cum.

At least someone got lucky last night.

When I looked around, Holls was asleep beside me, and Anton beside him. Brodie was passed out on the sofa, with Bruno on the floor by his feet.

But where was my…

A loud groan had me rolling over to look for Faise.

He was lying on the second bed, his back against the headboard. But he wasn't asleep.

Carl and Elias, the blond twins, were keeping him company. Or rather, one of them (don't ask me which one) knelt between Faise's legs, sucking him off.

Without hesitation my hand reached for my cock, my morning semi turning to a raging hard on despite my hangover.

"Yeah, fuck, just like that," Faise moaned loudly. "Take it all. Suck harder."

For the quietest guy in the band, Faise sure was loud when it came to sex. I licked my lips as I watched him gripped Carl/Elias's spiky hair, taking control of his movements.

That was another thing I'd learned lately about my best friend. He wasn't the biggest or loudest guy around, but he could be a total power top.

God, they're so hot together.

The other twin sat up and leaned over, licking, and playing with Faise's pierced nipples. Goddamn it, the filthy echo of their grunts and moans had me working my dick faster. Spitting in my hand, I jacked off, needing to come so fucking bad.

"Yeah, just like that," Faise panted. "Are you gonna swallow my cum?"

The twin moaned; the sound muffled by the cock in his throat. But judging by the flush on the guy's body, and the way his hand frantically worked in tandem with his mouth, he looked eager as hell for Faise's cum.

Jesus.

Faise punched his hips forward and the twin gagged. Christ, my balls were drawing up so tight it was near painful. My climax was almost there.

"That's it, take my cock like the needy slut you are," Faise growled.

The bed creaked and groaned as Faise pumped his hips frantically. When his body tensed, the look of pure pleasure on his face was unmistakable.

"Yes!"

I didn't bother to contain my own shout as I came all over my hand and stomach, flooding the sheets with ropes of cum.

Welcome to Berlin, baby.

Faise's confidence—on stage and off—kept growing and it was something else. My dick was still half hard as I watched the twins masturbate, covering Faise's chest and abs in their cum.

Fucking hell, that was the hottest thing I'd witnessed in a while. Watching each other was always sexy. We didn't have hang ups about our bodies or sex. We were young and always primed to fuck. And to watch other people fuck. It was all good.

Until one of the twins crawled up Faise's body and leaned in to kiss him. My stomach flipped over and not in a good way.

It's just the hangover.

I looked away, rolling over. Holls and Anton were awake now and watching Faise and the twins too. Anton was sucking on Holls's neck and whispering that he wanted to fuck him.

My dick twitched but I was too exhausted after that monster orgasm to do anything about it.

The last thing I heard before I passed out was Faise's husky laughter. Which surprised me. But more than that, I was annoyed. Because *I* was the one who made him laugh. Me.

I didn't like this feeling at all.

CHAPTER 7
FAISE

AGE 24

The crowd was chanting "Wayward Lane! Wayward Lane!" as I sat behind my kit waiting for the curtain to rise.

I adjusted my earpiece and nodded at Ronin, who was warming up on his bass.

Then he sauntered towards me, and I swiveled on my stool. He crouched down in front of me, reaching out to place his hand around the back of my neck as I reached up and did the same to him, our foreheads touching.

It was our thing, before every performance. It started out the first time we did a show. Ronin was so nervous he thought he was having a literal heart attack. Until I placed a comforting hand on him and reassured the big guy that he was okay. We were gonna rock the shit outta that show. And we did. And we were still doing it.

I looked into Ronin's summer blues and nodded, feeling grounded, and at the same time, ready to kick ass.

He pulled his hand back and I watched him walk back to

take his mark on the stage. A few rolls of his shoulders and he was ready to go.

So was I. In more ways than one.

Touching my best friend was becoming a dangerous distraction. So, I did my own shoulder shrug, shaking off the intense ache that started in my chest and spread to the rest of my body.

This, I didn't need.

Not now. Not ever.

I could never lose Ronin, so I had to remind my body to get the fuck over it. These feelings were worse than playing with fire. And letting them loose would be setting my whole world ablaze.

Besides, I had plenty of male attention. Whenever we'd have a show, there were guys lined up to meet us. Before and after. Add to that, a hit of coke, a couple of drinks, and my feelings for my BFF faded away like my worries.

We were back in the States, at a sold-out stadium show in New York as we prepared to open for yet another headlining band. After a couple of years playing around Europe, we still had no record deal. Six years of working our asses off. No lie, sometimes it was difficult to keep positive. To not let our frustration get the better of us. Especially for a group of guys in our early twenties who're impatient for everything.

So, six months ago, we headed back to the US and started again. Not with our tail between our legs, but with an understanding that this was going to be our life. Only a small percentage of musicians got a record deal and made it big. It wasn't giving up. It was just accepting that being a working musician meant you had to keep going, no matter the size of the show or the crowd.

We didn't want to do anything else, and really? Life was still fucking good.

We had steady gigs lined up and made enough money to rent a studio and record a proper demo. We'd just sent it out to several labels and we were once again waiting for responses.

Tonight, we were playing our biggest audience to date. And judging by the screams and hollers already, there was electricity in the air.

I was pumped up, and like always, ready to play my heart out.

The stage manager waved from the sidelines and started the countdown.

I started our first set with the pulse-pounding drumbeat for *Never Look Back*. No matter how many times I played a song, the rush of making music with my friends never got old. Sometimes I'd close my eyes on stage and just marvel at the sound, my heartbeat times a thousand.

And performing, just like sex, was usually better with a partner. Or several. You can do it alone, sure, but the energy of a crowd amplifies the rush.

Music is, after all, one of the ultimate human experiences. That's pretty deep for a rockstar, right?

When the curtain finally dropped and the flash of lights exploded, so did the crowd. Brodie belted out the opening chorus and I could hear people screaming his name. That was new. And fucking awesome. It made all my senses ignite.

Since we'd returned to the States, with new songs and a strong backlist, our popularity slowly began to rise. We now had festivals and booking agents calling *us* for a change. I could feel the tide shifting in our favor. It was as real as the pedals at my feet and the sticks in my hands.

Brodie strutted across the stage, touching the hands of the lucky few in the front row and using his sex appeal to work them into a frenzy.

By the time we'd finished our fifth song, I was soaking wet. Jeans may look sexy, but for a drummer playing under the heat of the stage lights, my balls were now glued to my pants. I'd ripped off my t-shirt already and threw it in

Ronin's direction. He made a big show of sniffing it, then chucking it into the audience. The crowd screamed our names.

Fucking hell, that was a rush. People *knew* our goddamn names.

We closed out the set with *Nine Gone Wrong* and the roar of hollers and claps had all four of us shaking our heads in disbelief. After three bows, we took our leave, but the boom of the audience followed us, even backstage.

"What a fucking night!!" Brodie shouted and hugged us each in turn. "Did you feel that? Could you believe that?"

"They were yelling our names." Holloway grinned. "This is it, guys. We've arrived!"

"You were amazing, boo." Ronin hugged me, and kissed the top of my head, both of us slippery with sweat.

"Right back at ya," I replied. "That was incredible. Brodie, they were going nuts for you."

"For all of us," Brodie stated as he grabbed a towel and wiped his face.

"Excuse me, can I speak to your manager?"

A sudden, strange voice interrupted our celebration.

All four of us turned around to find ourselves face to face with a middle-aged guy in a pair of expensive looking jeans and a crewneck sweater. Not our typical fan. And judging by the severe expression on his face, not a happy one either.

"You're looking at him." Brodie pointed to his chest.

"It's about your set, I have to tell you—" the stranger started.

"Look, if you're here to run us down, or if you have a problem with our songs, you can go fuck yourself. You can still hear the fans out there screaming. That should tell you everything you need to know."

The guy shook his head and stepped forward.

"That's not why I'm here," the stranger insisted, and the boom of his voice had all of us, Brodie included, jolting. "I'm

Greg Haddley, the CEO of Bandit Music. I represent Chaotic Chains."

The headliners tonight were represented by Bandit Music, the biggest label in the country.

Holy fucking shit.

"I'd like to see your full demo. Email it to this address," he explained as he pulled out a business card. "ASAP, because I've got a very long list of bands who would kill for the same opportunity."

Was this guy for real or was this a prank? Or was I still high from the coke I'd had before showtime?

Brodie looked at us and we nodded like trained seals.

"We'll do that." Brodie cleared his throat, as he reached for the card. "But first, I want to check that this is legit."

What the hell? Was he crazy?

"Go ahead." Greg shook his head. "I'll give you twenty-four hours."

"And then what?" Holloway asked.

"If my exec team likes what we hear, we'll fly you to our head office in Nashville for a formal meeting."

"Cool," Brodie replied, cocky as fuck.

Greg nodded and stalked past us, heading for the dressing rooms.

"Did that just happen?" Ronin asked.

Brodie's hand shook as he held up the card. "Come on, I need my phone. Let's do some digging. If that really was Greg Haddley, then fuck me, we have more than just a concert to celebrate."

We all but ran to our dressing room and as soon as we had our phones in hand, we were googling everything we could about Greg and the label.

"Yup, that's him all right." Brodie nodded, his eyes widening. "Fucking Jesus, it's really happening."

We emailed Greg our demo not fifteen minutes after we met him. Still sweaty and dehydrated from our performance, we were too stunned to do anything but sit in our dressing room and stare at each other.

The next morning, we had a response. Along with tickets to Nashville.

Brodie hadn't lied when he said we didn't have a manager. We had a temporary one when we moved back to the US, but he turned out to be a skeevy perv, not to mention a thief. Stealing our hard-earned dollars to supply his gambling habit.

"They sent a fifth ticket for our rep," Brodie explained as we sat in our hotel room, eating breakfast. "Even though we don't have one. If you guys are okay, I'd like to invite my dad. Which sounds really lame, like I'm sixteen again or something. But at least he has experience with contracts."

"If they offer us one," Ronin added.

"They wouldn't be flying us down there unless it's a done deal," Holloway offered. "Right?"

"For sure," I replied. "I mean, I assume so. If we do get an offer, we should have a lawyer review the contract. To make sure we don't get screwed."

"We're getting ahead of ourselves." Holloway shook his head. "Meeting first. Brodie's dad can give us his initial impression and we go from there."

Three days later, we flew down to Nashville. First class.

We each had our own hotel room, but it was weird for me to sleep alone. So much so, that an hour after we'd gone our separate ways, I slipped out of my room and knocked on Ronin's next door.

"I can't sleep," I admitted. "I'm too amped up."

Instead of replying, Ronin gripped my arm and dragged me into his room.

This time, I was the big spoon. But I still couldn't sleep. And no wonder. Between the prospect of signing a record deal and having my best friend all to myself, I was floating.

"Things aren't going to change too much, are they?" Ronin whispered in the darkness.

"Between you and me? Never."

He sighed. "If we do get that deal, though, everything else will be different."

"Hopefully. That's a good thing. This is what we've worked the past six years for."

"I know, but it's weird. Now that it might happen, I'm really fucking scared."

"It's not weird at all. But we'll have each other's backs. No matter what."

Ronin gripped my hand tighter, holding it over his chest. His heart was racing as fast as mine.

There was no point in trying to sleep. I pulled my hand away, rolled over and turned on the lamp and then the TV.

"Movie?" I offered.

"Anything to distract me from the thought of this meeting tomorrow," Ronin agreed as he sat up.

"Anything?" I teased as I turned up the volume.

"Shut up, I can't hear the show."

CHAPTER 8

RONIN

AGE 25

Everything changed for us within a year. We signed that record deal, and ten months later, I was still in shock about the 180 in our lives.

We went from doing everything ourselves—booking our shows, hauling our gear, working on our demos—to having a full-time manager, a recording studio, and a road crew to set up our concerts. Which meant more time to play, rehearse, write songs (Brodie), and party.

And fuck, did we party.

Suddenly there were press events and invites hosted by the biggest names in music. And we were the ones that music journalists were clamouring to talk to. People stopped us for selfies and autographs everywhere we went. It was crazy, heady, and everything we'd ever dreamed of.

Our first album was set to release and we were finishing up a cross-country junket to promote it, ending up tonight in LA, at a party hosted by our record label. Or rather, at a mansion somewhere in the Hollywood hills. And we were accompanied by Ivan Cross—Van—our manager. After

Bandit Music signed us to a five-year deal, Van was assigned to look after us. Basically, to run things and deal with our rockstar antics. We lucked out. Our manager was a rarity in our business: he was trustworthy, and he knew his shit. Van played too, which was important. He understood not just the business, but the creative drive behind our music.

"Now remember, there's no formal press at this thing, and NDAs all around," Van started. "Still, watch what you say."

Van turned to look directly at Brodie and our lead singer rolled his eyes.

"Don't bother with the lecture, Van. You know that I say what I want, when I want, and nothing, not a record contract or a warning from Greg, is going to change that."

Van leaned forward and tapped Brodie's knee. "Just try not to piss anyone off this time, okay? Our PR team can only handle so many issues at once."

"I can't help it if people don't like to hear the truth. And you know that reporter in New York was being an asshole. He called us overhyped. You think I'm *not* gonna respond to that?" Brodie snapped and gripped Van's wrist in turn. "Stop worrying. I know what I'm doing."

He did. Brodie was snarky but that's what made him memorable. And quotable. He'd already gone viral for his sarcastic comments about the corporate side of the music biz, not to mention his biting responses to questions about our talent and criticism about his uninhibited performance style. He was also quick to fight when trolls hated on us for being openly queer. Brodie was never going to hold back and that's why he was loved. By us, and the fans.

Van nodded and pulled his hand back, running it through his thick brown hair. The guy was forty and had hardly any grey hair to speak of, but I had a feeling that was about to change thanks to managing Brodie. And his runaway mouth.

Unlike Faise, who was all but silent on the ride over here. Probably nerves. We'd landed in LA and driven straight from the airport, no time to decompress, AKA drink or get high. Okay, we had champagne, but we needed real liquor. And maybe a spliff to relax.

I looked over at Faise's profile, something I never got tired of studying. He was dressed in tight, bootcut jeans, and a white linen shirt that was open to his waist, all his golden skin on display, along with his nipple rings. Then I glanced up at his face, his black hair tousled, falling into his eyes. I didn't miss the clenched jaw, and the way he bit his lower lip. He was nervous for sure.

When Faise turned to me, I saw the worry in his amber eyes. They were always so expressive. The part of him he couldn't ever hide.

"Are those real?" I whispered.

"Are what real?" he asked.

"Your eyelashes."

Faise said nothing, but his eyes widened. He stared at me like I'd lost my mind.

"They're like, beautiful or something," I continued.

Beautiful? WTF? Shut up, Ronin. Stop talking.

I tended to blather when I was nervous. And holy fuck, since when did I care about shit like people's eyelashes? Obviously, Faise wasn't the only one who needed to relax. He shook his head and turned away. Thankfully, ignoring my inane chatter.

The limo came to a sudden stop a few minutes later.

When the back door opened, we stepped out, and were greeted by Greg. The CEO of our label owned houses in Nashville, LA, and New York, to name a few, and he was a big deal in entertainment circles. Still, he was a corporate suit, and we were definitely *not*.

"Come on in, guys, everyone's dying to meet you," Greg announced. "Including my wife."

"Which one?" Brodie quipped.

Greg's face flushed, but he shook his head and motioned

to the front door of his mega mansion. Van and Brodie headed up first, me, Holls, and Faise following.

Van gave Brodie an arm squeeze in warning. Brodie looked over his shoulder and gave us a wicked grin.

Faise stepped up ahead of me, and for some reason, my eyes were glued to his slim form, catching on his tight ass in those jeans.

Until Holloway nudged me and started talking. I was grateful for the distraction. My eyes had no business following my BFF like that. It was probably just frustration. I needed to get laid.

We entered the Spanish style house, and the boom of music and chatter filled the air. Greg guided us into the living space and introduced us to his wife (number three as it turned out), and several famous musicians and actors.

The booze was top notch and there was also plenty of drugs available. It was LA after all, and no party here would be without. Faise scored some coke, and we all took a hit. After a long-ass plane ride, the kick of energy was welcome.

"Thank fuck," Faise muttered and wiped his nose. "Now I'm good."

Faise had outgrown most of his shyness, but occasionally, in social situations, it still reared up. Not that I could blame him. It was weird to go from being anonymous to a face people recognized everywhere we went. Add to that, the barrage of media, which was something we were still getting used to.

I looked across the room and spotted a well-known TV actor headed our way.

"Fuck, is that—" I started.

"Yup, it's Reed Larkin," Holls whispered. "Wow, he's hotter in person. And fuck, he's coming over. To talk to us. Oh my God. Oh my God."

Faise snorted. "Way to be cool, Holls."

"I can't help it." Holls ran a hand through his hair. "I'm still not used to the celebrity thing."

Brodie shook his head. "You're one of them now. So, like Faise said, be cool."

Reed walked right up to us and held out his hand. "It's an honor to meet you guys. I'm a big fan of your music."

Brodie thanked him and did the intros. We all got to talking about our favorite bands and then the Hollywood scene.

"Can I get you a refill?" he asked Faise.

Faise stared at his empty glass and nodded. "I'll go with?"

Reed smiled at him, and yeah, the Hollywood actor was gorgeous. I watched my BFF wander off and a weird, unsettled feeling swirled in my gut.

"Looks like Faise is getting lucky tonight," Brodie commented. "I better be next."

"I think Van's gonna beat you to it," I replied and motioned to our manager with my drink. "That woman's all over him."

Brodie downed the rest of his drink in one go, slammed the glass on a nearby table, and took off into the crowd.

Holls and I were approached by a couple of guys, Sarin and Jayme. Both men were models and actors based in LA.

Jayme was all over me, but I was distracted, looking around for my BFF.

Faise was still talking to Reed, their heads close together. And I recognized the look on Faise's face, the dimples that only came out when he was smiling hard. When the two of them walked out of the room together, my heart pounded so fast I was afraid I was gonna faint.

Must be the coke.

I picked up my drink and downed it one go. Then I flagged down a server for another.

Jayme and I flirted, drank, and smoked pot for over an hour. I was finally relaxed.

"Come back to my place?" Jayme offered, his lush mouth curled in a seductive grin. "I want you to fuck me."

I was all for fucking but I wasn't in the mood to leave this party or my friends. "How about here and now?"

Jayme licked his lips. "You're on. Follow me."

I had no problem doing just that as he sauntered through the crowded room. We walked down a set of stairs, and along a wide hallway to another crowded room packed with partygoers.

Only, this room had no windows. And it made sense.

Because everyone in this room was having sex.

I spotted Holls and Sarin frotting on a nearby couch, several guys watching them, jerking off.

Brodie was leaning against a wall, getting sucked off by a couple of guys taking turns.

There were other groups of people fucking in the center of the room, being watched by others. The whole scene was sexy, heady, exhilarating. My dick pulsed hard and hot in my jeans.

Then I looked over and spotted Faise having sex with a big ass dude. Not Reed Larkin. I was relieved, and yet, still unsettled. Whoever the stranger was, he was bent over a chair and Faise was railing his ass. And I couldn't look away.

Faise had his shirt off, his head thrown back, his arms and neck rigid as he fucked into the man at a frantic pace. The scene turned me on more than any of the other filthy sights and sounds in the room. But watching the look of bliss on the other guy's face made me furiously angry for some reason.

Fuck, that coke must've been laced with some weird shit.

I turned to Jayme, determined to screw this odd feeling out of me. "Get naked. Show me that hot ass of yours."

Jayme stripped off his clothes and turned around, bending over the nearest couch, his pale cheeks on display. I reached into my pocket for the packet of lube and a condom. Once my fingers were slick, I slid them over his crease, teasing his asshole. Jayme spread his legs wider, and took his dick in hand, jerking off.

I pushed one finger inside him.

"You prepped," I grunted as I added another finger and shoved them deep, the glide smooth.

"For a party with rockstars? Fucking right I did," Jayme hissed. "Now shut up and get your cock inside me."

I quickly unzipped, suited up, and added more lube to my covered dick. As I pushed my cock inside the model's ass, my attention snagged on a loud groan from across the room. I looked up, my eyes locking with Faise as he came long and hard. And yeah, I knew he was coming. Fuck, I knew his orgasm sounds as well as my own.

An angry pressure swelled up inside my chest that needed to be let out. I fucked into Jayme with fast, hard strokes, the model making dirty sounds that should've had all my attention.

I could've been fucking my fist for all it mattered.

And I didn't want to think about why.

CHAPTER 9
FAISE

AGE 27

No one partied like rockstars in Vegas.

We were celebrating the recording of our second album and our number one hit single, *Filthy Pain*. Bandit organized a massive event at the gaudiest hotel on the strip, complete with top-notch booze, hot as fuck celebrities and models, and the best damn coke I'd ever sniffed in my life. And I'd sniffed a lot of it.

With our growing fame came more fans, and press, and money than I'd ever had in my life. Luxury houses, fast cars, and a troupe of bodyguards. A whole team of them, including Dawson and Lennie, who were standing watch over us as usual. Not that we let our detail stop us from doing what we wanted.

Which was more parties, more men, more drugs of every kind.

Coke was my comfort zone and one that I could readily afford now. It gave me the energy to keep going, to wake up and rock out, on stage and off, one late night after another. It made me forget that I was sometimes hesitant in social situations. And it had the added benefit of obliterating—temporarily—the stupid urges I had rattling around for Ronin.

Which was fucked up. Ronin saw me as his BFF, not a man he wanted to get down and dirty with. I told myself to let it go. But this year, it had only gotten worse. He was all I wanted.

Too bad my heart—and my dick—never listened to my brain.

I glanced across the crowded party and watched Ronin making out with one of the stunning models. In the past, the sight would've turned me on and gotten me off. And that would be that. But recently? I didn't want to look at him touching someone else. It made me want to punch a hole through the nearest wall. And the thought of so many strangers touching Ronin, the one person who was always mine, was fucking with my head. Both of them.

I pulled out a baggie and dumped the white powder on the table in front of me. Checking my pockets, I realized I'd forgotten to grab my snake, my metal straw. Whatever. I used my driver's license to divide up the coke into several lines, plucked out one of the straws from my drink, leaned over, and inhaled.

It was my third pull tonight and fuck, it was good. Some of the best shit I'd ever had.

I snorted the rest of the powder and wiped my nose. Euphoria cascaded through my body, one lightning wave after another. I didn't notice Ronin or my feelings. I was too stoned to worry about anything.

"Take it easy, Faise. We have all night to party," Brodie warned me as he surveyed the room. "Hey, do you know that guy talking to Van?"

I looked across the room and squinted. "No fucking clue. And shouldn't you be more concerned with finding some rando to suck your dick rather than mooning over our manager?"

"Fuck off," Brodie sneered.

"Ooh, testy," I quipped. "Too bad Van's straight."

At least, I thought so. I didn't know. Van kept his private life, private. Never saw him hook up with anyone since we'd started working together, man or woman. He was always working.

"Don't start," Brodie warned.

"Take a hit, you'll feel better," I suggested. "You'll forget about you-know-who."

Brodie shook his head. "Been there, tried that."

I looked over at Van again. He was kinda handsome. If you liked older guys. Which Brodie did. And our frontman was shit at hiding how he felt. He had the same pained expression that I was probably, inadvertently, wearing earlier. Like he was about to walk over and tear into the person making a play for the man he so obviously had the hots for.

Holloway suddenly appeared and jumped on top of me and Brodie, crushing us into the sofa. "What's up bitches?"

"Get off me, weirdo," I pushed at him until he rolled onto the floor.

I glanced up, mid-laughter, and spotted Ronin headed our way with his latest fuck buddy in tow. *Great.* Reaching into my pocket, I pulled out another baggie and emptied it on the table in front of me. I felt everyone's stare and noticed Brodie and Holls looking at me with concern.

I shook them off. It was no big deal. The guys did their share of drugs too. Brodie was popping sleeping pills lately like rock candy. Who the fuck was he to judge?

"I know what I'm doing," I snapped at them.

Unfortunately, the cocaine didn't mix well with the bourbon I'd drank. And the orange pills I'd slid under my tongue before we got here. That last snort pushed me right over the edge, my head pounding, my stomach throbbing painfully. I started puking before I could even sit up.

"Faise, what the hell, are you—oh shit." Brodie's voice was muffled, like he was yelling from far away.

"Let's get him to the head."

Ronin.

The room was spinning, but Ronin was here, so I knew I'd be safe. My mouth filled with bitter bile, and I wanted to ask for water, but I couldn't form the words. Someone was holding me up, both arms, and then I puked again and fuck, it was coming out of my nose and everything.

I came to in a low-lit bathroom, the smell of vomit and air freshener making my stomach roil again. But this time, there was a toilet within reach. One of my arms was still pinned, though, and I started to panic, pulling away.

"Calm down, boo. I'm trying to help hold you up."

It was Ro. Thank fuck.

"I'm d-done. I'm… good. S'all gone," I muttered as I made to stand up. "M' fine."

When Ronin led me out of the stall, Holls and Brodie startled.

"We need to get him out of here. Now," Ronin demanded. "Get Van and Dawson."

"On it," Brodie replied and turned away.

"I said m'fine. K," I mumbled. "S-stop t-talking like I'm not here. I'm right here, Ro. Why c-can't you s-see me?"

Then I looked up and caught my reflection in the mirror above the sink. My face wasn't just covered in vomit. There were streaks of crimson paint running down my nose, around my lips and chin.

But the overwhelming smell, the copper. No, it wasn't paint. It was blood. So much blood. But nothing hurt. Not even my stomach. I was floating too high. Beyond pain.

"So f-funny," I pointed to my reflection. "B-bloody beard."

No one else was laughing.

"S' funny, right? I l-look like D-Dawson with the r-red beard. Red face," I snickered. "But only with Holls."

"We need to get him to a hospital," Ronin snapped, his voice cracking.

God, I'd never heard him so angry before. Or scared. Maybe both? I was too high to figure out which. Then the room spun faster and faster, so out of control that I couldn't see clearly anymore. Or catch my breath.

"I'm gonna… l-lie… d-down."

Ronin

I sat by Faise's bedside in the hospital as he lay sleeping. He was hooked up to monitors and machines.

He looked like death and death stared back at me. It was scary as fuck.

Chills wracked my body. The incessant trembling started three hours ago in that club bathroom and hadn't settled since. Glancing at his face, I noticed a streak of blood on his jaw that the hospital staff had missed. With a gentle hand, I reached for a tissue and wet it, wiping it off, being careful not to wake him.

He was stable now and breathing normally. But doctors had warned me and the guys that it was a close call. A near fatal overdose. His septum was damaged. Which accounted for all the blood.

But it wasn't just his nose. Doctors suspected he might have a stomach ulcer, since there was more blood mixed in with his vomit.

Jesus Christ, how did we end up here?

Thank fuck Dawson and Van got us out of that club without pause. Vegas had plenty of private hospitals and they'd seen to Faise right away.

But I didn't know what I was going to say to Faise when he woke up. Partying was all good and fun, but he'd taken it to the extreme this year. His moods were the same way, going from uncontrollable laughter one moment to aggressive anger the next. There was something going on with him. I could see it in his eyes every time he looked at me.

A struggle, a secret. One he didn't share.

For the first time in seventeen years, I didn't know what to say to my best friend. How to help heal whatever was going on inside him.

"How's he doing?"

I turned at Brodie's voice to find him, Holls, Van, Dawson, and Lennie standing behind me. What had started out as a night to celebrate one of our career milestones had ended up here. I still couldn't believe it.

"He's stable," I replied, swallowing past the lump in my throat. "But he'll probably be out of it for another few hours."

Holls stepped up and placed a comforting hand on my shoulder. "Why don't you take a break and go get something to eat. We'll be here."

I didn't know what time it was, and I couldn't remember the last time I had anything to eat or drink. But I didn't want to leave Faise.

"I'm staying. Could one of you get me a sandwich and coffee?"

"I'll get it," Lennie offered. "Anyone else?"

"Just coffee. Thanks, Len," Brodie replied as he walked to stand around the other side of the bed, Van by his side.

Brodie looked over at me, his hazel eyes welling up. He blinked and wiped his eyes, shaking his head. It wasn't often that our frontman got teared up. And when Van placed his arm around Brodie, our lead singer didn't hesitate to turn and bury his face in our manager's shoulder.

Van's worried blue gaze hit mine and I let out a shaky breath.

"He needs rehab," Van whispered. "This has been going on for a while now, but it's gotten out of control."

I didn't like the idea of being separated from Faise, but Van was right.

Faise needed help. Help that I couldn't give.

———

Two days after his overdose, Faise admitted himself to a rehab center in California. For three long months, with no visitation. It was the first time he and I had been separated from each other in almost two decades. And the distance between us was so damn painful I was afraid *I* was going to head down the same path as him. I'd been hitting the alcohol hard to counter my state of depression, but it only made my sadness worse.

We should've been out on tour at this point, but we'd delayed it until Faise was ready. So, it was weird for me to have so much time on my hands. I hung out with Brodie and Holls. But with Faise gone, Wayward Lane was incomplete. Truthfully, I was incomplete. I still played and practiced but it was habit more than anything.

The need to keep busy, to keep my mind from swirling out of control about all the what ifs about my bestie. But the passion, the energy that I took for granted in my music, was missing.

I didn't realize until Faise left that he was more than my BFF. He was my muse.

And something else I didn't know how to define.

New questions and unexplained feelings about my relationship with my best friend were now staring at me in the face.

But, in typical rockstar fashion, I shoved that shit away and threw myself back into the party scene. I fucked my way

through town, clubbing, drinking, trying anything and everything to forget the reality of the past few months.

The reality of life without Faise.

I was never alone, but I sure as fuck was lonely.

CHAPTER 10

FAISE

AGE 28

"Are you ready to talk about him?"

I ignored the question, or rather, I was mulling it over.

Sitting across from my therapist, Kenzie, I stared out the window at the dark clouds that hung over Nashville.

They suited my mood perfectly.

My inclination was to answer her question with a 'no'. But after two stints in rehab and coming out a clearer, stronger version of myself, I knew that it was time for me deal with one of the issues that had brought me to the brink. The feelings that made me want to numb myself, to forget that I felt anything at all.

But I didn't know if I could do it. I was brave in other ways, much more than when I was younger, but not in this.

"It's just the strangest thing," I replied, finally looking at her.

"What is?"

"It makes me uncomfortable to talk about him. With you.

When he's not here," I explained. "I mean, he's been my best friend for two decades. What do you want me to say?"

"Whatever it is that you're holding on to."

I shook my head, reactive as always to the thought of revealing myself.

"We've tackled everything else in your life—your family, friends, your work," she paused. "But not Ronin. Even at rehab, according to the notes I received, you refused to talk about him."

"We'll be here forever if you want to open that box."

She nodded. "You've mentioned before that you find it difficult to express your deepest feelings out loud."

"I do."

"And what comes to mind when you think of Ronin?"

Everything.

"If it helps, use music as an analogy to describe him."

"Booming," I laughed and some of the tension in my stomach eased. "He's a big guy, with a big voice, and his bass playing is the same. Loud. But he's such a teddy bear inside. Always protective of me, his family, and the guys."

The more I talked, the bigger the lump in my throat.

"He makes me laugh like no one else and he kicks my ass at video games. Says he doesn't know how to write a song, but I've seen his poetry. It's beautiful. He keeps a journal... shit, I shouldn't be repeating that. No one else but me knows."

"It's safe with me," Kenzie reassured me.

I nodded.

"I've never doubted that he cares about me. There's always words of encouragement, rib-crushing hugs, and sometimes, slaps on the ass," I quipped, shrugging my shoulders. "He's very touchy-feely with people he's close to. And he's a major flirt."

"Does that bother you?"

"The touching?"

"The flirting."

I shook my head. "No. He does it with everyone."

"Does he have a partner or partners?"

"Like me, Ro doesn't do relationships. Just casual sex. Not that I keep tabs or anything. Or that we watch each other. Not anymore."

"And by 'watch', you mean?"

"Voyeurism," I blurted out.

"And how did you feel when you watched him having sex with someone else?"

At first, turned on. Then, later, irritated. Frustrated. Angry. Jealous as fuck.

"It was hot. At first."

"If you went to see him now and he was with one of his lovers, how would that make you feel?"

I shook my head.

"Faisel?"

I leaned forward and gripped my hands together tightly, the calluses scratching my knuckles.

"I just can't jeopardize twenty years of friendship because my dick wants his attention."

I was incredibly relieved and anxious about voicing how I felt.

Kenzie gave me a small smile. "It sounds like it's more complicated than that."

"Is it? Because if it's not about sex, then I don't have a clue."

"Are you sure?" she asked.

No. But I didn't want to go there.

"I think it's about more than sex and that's why you're struggling. No doubt sexual desire on its own can be powerful and lead to intense feelings. But you and Ronin have been friends for a long time. There's a lot more involved than just pheromones."

My chest was suddenly tight.

"I didn't always feel this way. Before, watching him was like watching Holls or Brodie. It was sexy but that's all. Nothing more."

"When did you notice him differently?"

I let out a big sigh. "Before we became famous. A few years ago."

"And you never told him?"

"Hell no. There was no point. Like I said, I'm not risking our friendship for a fuck."

"Have you ever been in love?"

I jolted. Love was not a word I used, or thought about, or said, lightly.

"Nope. Never had more than a two-night stand. I have no need for a boyfriend or a relationship. Not with my schedule. And now my addiction. I don't think I could handle it."

"And Ronin?"

"He's the same."

Kenzie stared at me intently. "Other than concerns about your addiction, why are you so certain that you'll never have a need for an intimate relationship?"

"No lover will ever be more important to me than him."

And there it was. As soon as the words left my mouth, I realized what that meant.

Had I ever been in love?

I think I'd already been there. But I refused to admit it.

"No. No fucking way. I can't…. No." I stood up and paced the room. "He doesn't see me that way and telling him how I feel will ruin everything."

"You don't know that."

"But I know *him*. He's not shy about letting people know how he feels. If he did want me, he'd have told me by now," I reasoned. "No. I can't. And I'm not losing him. I'm just going to have to find a way to get over these feelings. I can work on that, right?"

Kenzie glanced at her watch and then back at me. "Unfortunately, we're out of time for today. See you next week?"

I'd be there.

Six Months Later
Ronin

Faise was ignoring my calls and texts. Again.

A few weeks ago, he claimed he was sick and wanted to be alone. But after three more weeks of barely any communication, outside of our recording sessions, it was obvious to me that he was lying. He was avoiding me.

And it hurt.

Fed up with his silent routine, I grabbed my keys and headed for my car. We lived a short drive from each other but lately, even that felt like a huge distance between us.

He wouldn't be using again, would he? *No. Don't go there.*

I paid attention in the recording studio when we were working, and he'd been his usual self. Quiet but giving it his all.

When I pulled up to his property, I entered the code, and the gates opened. But there was a car there I didn't recognize. Maybe Van? Or one of our security team? I parked my car and stepped out, stalking up to the front door and banging on it with my fist.

No answer. Again.

Then I texted him.

> Ronin: I'm here. You don't answer in five and I'm using my key.

> Faise: I'm busy. Come back in a few days.

A few days?

> Ronin: Busy? With what?

That was bullshit. He was *never* too busy to see me.

> Faise: I've got company and I don't want to be disturbed.

I was worried sick about him, and he was getting off? And what the fuck did he mean by a few days? Was he seeing someone?

> Ronin: Sorry to interrupt your afternoon blowjob, but I thought something was wrong. You keep avoiding my calls and texts.

> Faise: We're cool. But maybe it's time we start doing our own thing, yeah? We don't always have to be in other's back pocket. I'm seeing someone. He's a great guy. But we need our privacy. Try to understand.

Understand? Faise had a boyfriend? Since when? How? And he needed space? From me?

For a moment, my stomach heaved, and I swore I was going to throw up. Right there on Faise's front steps.

> Ronin: I don't know what's going on with you, but we're not done with this.

> Faise: Later

"Fuck!" I yelled out.

I had to a mind to use the key anyway, but I didn't. Instead, I got back in my car. Tapping on speakerphone, I dialled Brodie.

"Hey Ro, what's up?"

"Can I come over?"

"Sure, everything okay?"

"No," I paused, my throat closing over. "It's not okay. It's Faise."

"Shit, what happened?"

"I don't know. I'll be there shortly."

I pulled out of Faise's driveway, hitting the accelerator hard.

When I arrived ten minutes later at Brodie's, he welcomed me inside.

"I hope I'm not interrupting—" I started.

"No way." Brodie replied as he started walking towards his living room. "I always have time for you. Is Faise all right?"

I shook my head and leaned against the doorjamb.

"He wouldn't let me in the house. Said he's seeing someone. And he won't take my calls or texts. This past month has been—" I paused, completely out of breath. "He told me we shouldn't spend so much time together."

"What?" Brodie stopped short and turned around to face me.

He looked as shocked as I felt.

"Do you think he's using and trying to hide it?" he asked.

I walked over and sat down on the sofa, staring out the window. "No, I don't think so. He looked fine the last time we were in the studio. Why? Have you noticed anything?"

"No. He seems quieter, maybe, but there's been no mood swings, not like before." Brodie joined me and sat down. "And he claims he's seeing someone? Since when?"

I nodded, feeling like I might throw up again.

"A few weeks. Why wouldn't he tell me before today? We don't keep shit like that from each other. He's never—" I started, my hands shaking. "What if he meant what he said? I can't lose him, Dee."

"Hey, you're not gonna lose him. It's Faise. He'd never do that to you."

"He's doing it now."

I couldn't even believe it.

Brodie sighed and ran a hand through his dark curls. "I'll go over and see him tomorrow. Maybe he'll talk to me. Or Holls. It's worth a shot."

"Thanks."

"You want a drink?" Brodie asked. "I *know* I could use one."

"You? What's up with you?"

"Nothing. Just another disagreement with Van."

"Anything the rest of us should be concerned about?"

"Nope." He looked away and bit his lower lip. "I'll figure it out."

"Do you mind if I stay here for a bit? Crash? I don't want to go home," I confessed.

"'Course. Let's have a drink and watch mindless reality TV shows."

His phone buzzed and he glanced at it. "It's Holls. He's on his way over."

———

Ten minutes later, the doorbell rang.

"That was fast."

Brodie got up and glanced at the security monitor. "It's not Holls. It's Faise. And he's not alone."

My body locked up tight, tense as fuck. I stayed in the living room, listening to Brodie greet Faise and whoever it was. I didn't recognize the third voice and I started to sweat. I wished to hell I'd already had a second drink.

"Come on in. Me and Ro were just having a few drinks, chilling. Holls is on his way."

"We'll stay for a bit, but not long. Is that okay, Dean?"

We? Dean?

Brodie stepped into the room and gave me a warning glare. I stood up, wiping my clammy hands on my jeans.

"Hey, Ro," Faise greeted me like everything was normal. "Sorry about earlier. Dean and I were—"

"I get it," I snapped, glancing at the man beside him.

Dean was pretty. If you liked hot guys with big muscles, dark hair, and blue eyes. Instead of telling the guy to get the fuck gone, I put on a good act.

"Ronin Stadler, nice to meet you."

I offered my hand. Against my better judgement. He took it and I squeezed tight, until he winced, and I dropped his hand like I'd been poisoned.

"Dean Ralston. I've heard a lot about you."

"Really?" I bit out. "I've heard nothing about you."

Dean flushed and glanced at Faise, who slid his arm around Dean's waist. I bit down on my inner cheek so hard I tasted blood.

"Well, you can get to know him now," Faise offered.

"How about a drink?" Brodie asked. "Bourbon? Tequila? Beer?"

"Yes," I replied at the same time as Faise.

"Just water for me, thanks," Dean commented with a grimace. "I don't drink at all. It fucks with your sleep and your stomach. You really should limit yourself. Given the hours you work and all your travel, your sleep is already compromised. Alcohol won't help."

"Dean's a holistic nutritionist." Faise smiled at him.

"Naturopath," Dean corrected.

"Sorry," Faise laughed but it sounded forced. "I keep getting that wrong."

Wrong was an understatement. I glanced at my best friend, and something was way off. He didn't date. And he wasn't gaga over some guy. Any guy. His fake laugh alone had all the warning sounds in my head thrumming louder than my bass line.

I turned to Faise. "Can I talk to you for a sec? In private?"

"Sure."

He turned to Dean and kissed him.

All the air left my lungs. I wanted to ram my fist into the nearest wall. Or into Dean's smug fucking face.

"How's that drink coming?" I reminded Brodie, who was staring at Faise like he'd never seen him before.

You and me both, Dee.

"Uh, yeah." Brodie shook his head. "Dean, come join me. You can look through my fridge and tell me what I'm eating wrong."

"If you want a consultation, you'll need to book a—"

The rest of Dean's annoying words faded away as he made his way down the hallway with Brodie.

"What the fuck is going on?" I growled.

"I'm dating. Just like I told you. He's great."

I scoffed. "You don't date."

"I guess I do now."

"Why? A few months ago, you didn't even want to leave the house. Now you're playing it with *that* guy?"

Faise shrugged. "When I'm not working, I go stir crazy all alone. And I need more than jamming and playing video games. It's time to grow up. I want more than a hook up. And being your eternal wingman."

I stepped back like I'd been slapped.

"Where is all this coming from? Talk to me," I implored him.

Faise looked away, shaking his head.

"Nothing changes. We can still hang," he whispered. "But maybe, with other people too, yeah?"

I was about to argue when he looked up at me, and I saw the determined look in his eyes. I didn't want to lose Faise, so I accepted what he was telling me. His stubborn nature meant arguing with him was futile. I was gonna go along, to get along. But that didn't mean I was going to accept this total about face.

Then, I didn't have to worry at all. Or, so I thought.

Two weeks later, Faise and Dean were done. I never asked. He never said.

My boo was back.

Only, things were never quite the same.

CHAPTER 11

FAISE

AGE 29

My experience dating Dean—if you could call it that since it only lasted five weeks—left me convinced that I was not cut out for a relationship.

He was charming and the sex was great, but my heart wasn't in it. How could it be when it already belonged to someone else? I put that experience behind me, acting like it never even happened. Frustration turned to acceptance. Of a sort.

Then I had no time to worry about my feelings. Not about my unsuccessful attempt at a relationship and not about Ro. There was my family to consider. Even though my brother and I had walked different paths, we always stayed in touch by text and via calls. But lately, he stopped replying, and a gnawing ache in my gut told me that something wasn't right.

I had a week off before me and the guys were headed to NOLA for a charity concert on Halloween. While I was getting my shit ready for our trip, my mom called.

I hesitated to answer it.

Things were tense between us since I'd come out of rehab. Not that my family didn't love me, but they worried, and they wanted me to get out of the rock n roll business and into something more stable. It didn't matter where I worked. The temptation would always be there. An addict will find a way to get what they want, no matter where they live or work. I explained this to my mom, but I don't think she or my dad fully understood the nature of my illness.

Finally, on the fifth ring, I answered. "Hey Mom, what's up?"

"Rae's in the hospital."

"What? What happened?"

"The doctor said he," she paused, sobbing. "He overdosed."

I sat down on my bed, my legs numb, my heart beating wildly. No way. Not Rae. He'd never.

"But how—"

"I went over to visit him last night because he wouldn't return my phone calls. When he didn't answer, I used the spare key and found him lying in his bathroom," she choked out. "Hannah left him months ago. All her stuff is gone. There was hardly anything left in the condo. Everything is a mess."

"I'm heading home."

I didn't think twice. I didn't even text the guys. No point saying anything until I knew for sure what was going on.

The only person I told was our security lead, Regan, because if I didn't, she'd have reamed me out. That evening, with her in tow as my bodyguard, and after jumping on the quickest available flight, I found myself back in Rhode Island. I went to the hospital first and met my parents there.

"How is he?" I asked as I walked up and gave them each a hug.

"He's awake. Can you talk to him? He doesn't want to see us," my mom cried, and Dad pulled her into his arms.

I understood. The shame and the guilt of being an addict

can weigh as heavy as the addiction itself. I gave my parents a reassuring squeeze and let go. Without pause, I entered Rae's room, Regan waiting at a distance. My brother's pallor was grey, and he had lost so much weight I hardly recognized him.

It was scary, because looking at him now was like looking at myself.

As I stepped closer, I spotted the track marks on his arms. And the angry red scabs, old and new, that littered his body, his face.

Jesus fucking Christ.

He blinked and finally opened his eyes. They were blood-shot, weary, so unlike my brother that it knocked the remaining breath right out of me.

"Hey big brother. It's been a while," I stated, sitting down in a chair by his bedside.

His eyes welled up, but he shook his head. "Go away."

"No."

"Faise—" he warned.

"Me of all people? Come on, Rae. Talk to me. What the fuck happened?"

He barked out a laugh. "Don't make me laugh."

"What?"

"Talk to me? You?"

"Okay, so I'm not the best at communicating—"

Rae scoffed.

"—but I've been here myself, remember? How the hell did this happen?"

He let out a shaky sigh.

"Hannah left. I lost my job at the firm thanks to downsiz-ing, and I couldn't find another one. Well, one that paid as much. Money was tight. We were spending more than we were taking in. And when I finally confronted her and said we'd need to cut back, that's when she told me she was having an affair. She's taken up with some other guy. Rich as fuck. Just like that, she left me. So much for sticking it out for better or worse."

"Fuck, Rae, I'm so sorry."

"After she left five months ago, I started going out a lot. Dive bars, strip clubs. Anything to forget," he whispered, his voice raw. "I started partying with people I met there. At first, it was just booze and pot, and a few pills to get high. Then I needed more. Everything was getting worse. My depression. My money problems. I got another job, at half the pay, but I was staying out all hours and I couldn't get up in the mornings. Lost that job too."

He coughed and cleared his throat. There was a glass of water on the table beside him, so I grabbed it and held it up to his lips.

"Thanks," he whispered. "Fuck, my life is a total mess."

Guilt hit me hard and fast. "I wish I'd have reached out more often, maybe I could've—"

"I didn't want to say anything. To let you down. I'm the one who's supposed to have it together, to look after you," he let out a sigh. "Not that I did a great job of that either."

"What are you talking about?"

"Nothing."

I touched his arm. The one that didn't have an IV attached.

"Rae?"

"When we were growing up, you were bullied. And because we went to different schools, I couldn't help you," he bit his lower lip. "Thank fuck for Ronin. How is he, by the way?"

"He's fine," I bit out.

I didn't want to talk about Ronin at all.

Rae's eyes narrowed. "Something happen between you two?"

I shook my head quickly. "Nope."

My love life—or lack thereof—was the least of my worries.

"Are Mom and Dad still here?"

I nodded. "They want to see you."

"No. I can't face them. Not after what I've done. I just can't."

"They love you."

"They love the successful version of me," he spat out. "My MBA, my job, my perfect wife. Not this. A heroin junkie."

"They just want you to be okay. And speaking of that, remember that rehab centre in California I went to? I'll make a call."

Rae reached out and grabbed my wrist, holding tight. "I don't know if I can do it, Faise."

"I'll fly out there with you and everything. Trust me?"

Rae's wan smile had tears welling up in my eyes.

"My little brother is all grown up. And taking care of me. Fuck, how did that happen?"

"Life happens. And we take care of each other," I replied and squeezed his hand tight. "I swear I'm going to do better. To reach out more. And you have a chance to get sober and rebuild your life. It's not easy, but I know you. You can do it."

Rae let out a shaky breath and wiped his eyes.

"Okay."

"And let Mom and Dad see you. They're scared out of their minds."

Rae nodded and I slowly let go of his hand.

"Will you stay with me today?"

"As long as you need. Let me go get Mom and Dad first."

I got up and headed for the door. By the time I spotted my parents, I was shaking all over.

"He's ready to see you. Just—" I paused, unsure if I should say anything.

I respected my parents, but I also wanted to protect Rae.

"Just don't start asking him a lot of questions, okay? He's

sick. If he wants to talk, let him. But you can't push. Not at this stage. He's fragile. Answers will come when he's got the strength to give them."

My mom nodded while my dad pulled me in and hugged me so tight, I couldn't breathe. I'd never heard him cry before but he started sobbing into my shoulder. For the first time in my life, I was the one comforting him. Mom grabbed onto me too.

Once they'd calmed, they headed in to see Rae. I got on the phone and arranged his rehab.

———

Two days later, me, Rae, and Regan were booked on a private jet to California.

Ronin had been texting me, but I just said I was visiting my folks last minute.

I would tell the guys everything about Rae, in person, in private, when I was ready.

But of course, I felt guilty about not telling Ro. It was physically painful for me to keep shit from him. Just like my experiment with Dean, I kept pulling away, protecting myself, but in the end, I was still hurting.

But I kept reminding myself that there were other, more important things than my stupid heartache.

After I got Rae settled into rehab, I flew back to Nashville to get my shit ready for our next show. Dealing with Rae's financial mess would have to wait for another week. His condo mortgage was in arrears and Hannah's lawyer had sent a follow up email regarding the splitting of their assets. Not that there was much to split anymore. I contacted my lawyer and we decided to offer Hannah a settlement, in Rae's name, but it would have conditions. No more contact with Rae, no further requests for spousal support, and she would have to sign an NDA.

By the time I packed up to head out on the road again, to the charity concert in NOLA, I was exhausted, physically, and mentally. And a right pain in the ass to everyone who tried to come near me.

The night we headed out of town, on our tour bus, I got in my usual bunk, and the guys were in theirs. Ro was underneath me, with Brodie and Holls across the aisle.

Tired but wired, my mind was running in ten different directions. I couldn't sleep. I could hear Van and Brodie arguing—yet again—but I was too tired to get up and say anything.

"You awake, boo?" Ronin asked me, like he could read my mind.

I pushed the curtain aside and leaned over my bunk to look down at him.

"Yeah. What's up?"

"Come here," he murmured as he crooked his finger at me.

Oh God, Ronin wanted to cuddle. He was always like this, especially on the road for some reason, but we hadn't done that in a while. I wanted to say no. But if I refused, he'd know for sure that something was up. The questions would start.

So, against my brain's better judgement, I slid off my bunk and into his.

Ro wasted no time wrapping me up tight against his bigger body. I finally felt the stress of the past week ease out of me, one shaky breath at a time.

Fuck, I'd missed this. Missed him.

I was surrounded by his heady scent, and those incredible arms of his that were the stuff of my secret fantasies. Big biceps, veiny forearms covered in dark hair and tattoos, a strong, callused grip... and fuck I needed to think about something, anything else, to calm my excited dick.

He gently kissed the top of my head, and to my complete horror, my eyes started welling up.

That was new. Not the kiss, but my reaction.

Words I wanted to say were trapped in my throat. So, I did what guys always do when they don't want to deal with something. I made a joke.

"You smell like funky cheese."

His boisterous laughter vibrated through my body.

"Well, I found an old cheeseburger wrapper in my bunk from our last trip. I guess the air freshener wasn't strong enough to get rid of the odor."

"Gross. That was months ago."

"Tell me about it. How could our cleaning crew miss it?"

"Was it hiding under your mattress? That's where you stash all your garbage. And sex toys," I snorted. "Maybe that's the source of the smell. You gotta clean the dildo occasionally. You don't want to get an infection."

"So funny," he chuckled and reached down to pinch my ass.

I jolted, my semi turning to a raging hard on. Shit. I tilted my hips back and tried to shuffle away from him. Without falling out of the bunk, of course. But there was no room to move, so I flipped over, my back was to his front.

"This is nice. Feels like old times," he whispered.

"Old times? What are we? Ninety?" I laughed. "And it hasn't been that long."

"Yes, it has. I've missed you, boo."

My heart was in my throat again.

"I've missed you, too."

"Are you—" he started, and his body tensed. "Have you been, you know, seeing anyone, like, lately?"

I glanced over my shoulder, his face barely visible in the darkness. "No. I told you, I'm not doing that again. I'm not cut out for that shit."

"Okay. Cause you've been almost silent the past week. I thought maybe—"

"Nope. It was something else. Family stuff," I rested my

head against his bicep. "We'll talk about it tomorrow. Right now, we need sleep."

"Yes, sir," Ronin replied.

His arms tightened around me. If this was the only way I was going to get Ro, I was gonna shut up and take it.

"Hug me tighter."

CHAPTER 12

RONIN

The past seven months had been one major change after another.

The first came when Brodie, the loudest and snarkiest fuckboy of us all, finally got his man. Unfortunately, Van quit being our manager after Greg Haddley outed him, and his relationship with Dee, to the press.

But everything worked out eventually. Van and Brodie eloped to Vegas. And it turned out that Van was moonlighting as a songwriter with a pseudonym, and now he was writing full time, for us. With Brodie. And other artists. So, we lost a manager but gained a permanent songwriter. And an honorary fifth member of the band. A family member.

Then came the second major shock of the year.

Holloway fell. For Dawson no less—our lead bodyguard, and a single dad. Turns out, Holls' desire to escape Dawson and Dawson chasing after Holls, well, it was just their weird kind of foreplay. It worked for them. Those two were so in love, they were almost as nauseating as Brodie and Van.

The third major change? We cut ties with Bandit Music.

Again, thanks to Greg's stupid ass behavior. And to top it all off, we were turning thirty this year. A new decade and more changes were coming with it.

Faise and I grew closer. Now that Brodie and Holls had partners, all four of us didn't hang like we used to. And us single guys gotta stick together.

But ever since Faise's relationship with Dean, I didn't look at my best friend in the same way. The rift between us had made me pause and question my feelings. I'd always been comfortable in his personal space but now it was more like a need than a want. We were shifting, and I just hoped that whatever was going on, it would bring us closer together, not push us apart.

Today was another big step. We had a full day with our new label, Hardwick, and their VP of Marketing, Averell Jones. The CEO couldn't make it, so they sent the next best thing to officially welcome us to their team.

Me and the guys gathered around their boardroom table, our security team patiently standing guard outside.

We'd been waiting for over half an hour when suddenly, a tall, lanky guy in a red plaid suit stalked into the room. With an angular face, a messy mop of auburn hair, and a wicked grin, he nodded at us, phone in one hand and a stack of papers in the other.

"Averell Jones, at your service," he announced in a crisp British accent. "Apologies for the delay but I just got a new phone and it's my first day here in Nashville, so, of course, I have no idea where to find anything, including my schedule. I swear, I feel like Mr. fucking Bean today."

The image of that character had me biting back a laugh. Then I reminded myself to pay attention. *Ignore the smile and the charming accent.* After our experience with Greg, I was wary of music executives and their motives.

"So, welcome," Averell added as he looked around the table.

When he spotted Faise, he paused. The once over was subtle. But I noticed.

My protective hackles activated.

"It's my great honor and pleasure to bring a talented group as yours into our team. I've got some ideas I'd like to share but first, I'd like to hear from you about your expectations moving forward."

"To start, we're not working with homophobic dickbags," Brodie announced.

I bit back a laugh at our frontman's blunt words.

Averell nodded, seemingly unfazed by Brodie's direct manner. "As a proud gay man myself and one of the leaders of our management team, I can assure you that will never be a problem."

One fear laid to rest.

"Our main issue is trust," I added, and Averell turned to me. "Off the record, things happened with our former label. Shitty things. They pretended to protect us but, in the end, sold us out. And I don't mean ticket sales."

Averell leaned forward. "Our job is to market you to the fans, not throw your personal life to the media wolves. If there are any concerns, you bring it to your manager. And of course, my door is always open."

That sounded right, but only time would tell.

"And our contract has a three-month trial when it comes to our new manager, right?" Holls asked. "If we don't like whoever it is, we can request someone else?"

Faise tapped the table. "Our last manager was Greg's spy. And given that we're here, with you, no guesses as to how that went down."

Averell nodded. "I'm familiar with Mr. Haddley and Mr. Hines's reputations. Be assured, that won't happen with us."

"We want someone like Van," I suggested.

"No one will be as good as my husband," Brodie interrupted with a cocky grin. "But yeah, as Ro said, someone like him. In fact, if my husband doesn't know our new manager, it's a no go."

Averell leaned back and nodded.

"All that's fair. We've assigned Jesse Aimes to your group. He's been working in the UK as a manager for almost a decade. We sent his resume to your agent this morning so you can review it. His reputation is stellar. First things first, though, we're going to get new promo materials done. We've got you scheduled with our studio photographer after this. Then we're back here for lunch. Jesse will join us for a meet and greet and then it's on to the PR team. And of course, tonight we have a party to launch our kickoff. Everyone and anyone who's in the music business will be there."

"What about dates?" Faise asked.

Averell smiled at him. "Love them. You?"

The fuck? Was he flirting with Faise? So much for being professional.

"I meant the upcoming schedule," Faise replied with a cheeky grin as he leaned forward. "Not mine, but the tour dates."

And Faise was flirting back? Not that I hadn't witnessed that before. But why this guy? And why did I fucking care?

A sudden tightness in my chest left me uncomfortable and edgy.

"Ah, yes. We're working on that now. We'll have an update by EOD. It looks like a local concert the first week of June and then down to Florida, and nearby states. We'll start close to home given the timing. Then you fly out to LA for a show on July 1 to kick off the west coast leg." Averell's phone buzzed. "Excuse me, I need to take this. Head on down to the studio on the tenth floor. I'll meet you there in a bit."

With a nod, he stood up and headed for the door.

When he stepped outside of the boardroom, I turned to the guys. "What the hell was that?"

"What?" Brodie asked. "I like him."

"Me too," Holls nodded.

"He seems great," Faise replied. "A cool guy."

I crossed my arms. "Really? Was I the only one who saw what happened?"

The guys looked at me like I'd lost my mind.

I stared at Faise. "This is our first-time meeting with him and he's flirting with you? The fuck is that?"

"You mean, that whole thing about dates?" Faise scoffed. "It was a joke. He was just teasing."

"Uh, no boo," I insisted, my heart pounding out of control. "Open your fucking eyes."

"Right back at you."

"What does that mean?" I asked and reached across the table for him.

He shrugged my hand off. "Nothing. And so, what if he did? This is the biz, yeah? Happens all the time. We've fucked plenty of people we worked with. It is what it is. If there's consent, there's no problem."

"I *don't* like him."

"You don't have to sleep with him," Faise countered. "What's it to you anyway? If I wanna flirt or fuck, it's my business. He's hot."

Brodie and Holls murmured their agreement, and I gave them my best fingers as my mood nosedived.

"So, you're gonna fuck with someone at our new label? Jesus Christ, are you nuts? We just signed our contract."

"I can separate work and play," Faise insisted. "And we work with our manager, not directly with Averell."

"I can't believe I'm gonna say this," Holls interrupted. "But Ro does have a point."

"Said the man who slept with his bodyguard. And don't start either, Dee, given Van was our manager," Faise snapped and held his hands up. "Look, I never said I was gonna have sex with the guy, all right? It's harmless flirting. We all do it. Or, we used to, before everyone started pairing up. It's no big deal, just chill. It's time to head off to the studio to get our shots done anyway."

"Maybe you can fuck the photographer too while you're at it," I bit out and stormed out of the room.

"Ro!" Faise shouted but I didn't want to look at him right now.

A firestorm burned in my gut.

I stalked over to the elevator and slammed the button for the tenth floor. Suddenly Faise was there, and our bodyguards too.

"What's going on with you?" Faise asked.

"I just don't want you to make a mistake. Like Dean."

A visceral jealousy burned through my veins, turning my rational thoughts to ash.

Even though Faise was right, he could fuck whoever he wanted, it ate away at me. Which was so fucked up since he and I weren't... we were just... shit, I didn't even know anymore.

Brodie and Holls walked over to join us, and our lead singer gave me *the* look.

No way was I going to spill my guts. Not here. Not now. Maybe not ever.

"Don't Dee. I'm fine," I insisted. "I'm just worried about optics, is all."

Yeah, right. Because that was me. Always worried about what other people thought.

Not.

Faise wasn't in the wrong. I'd fucked plenty of people at our old label—music execs, PR staff, hair and makeup, the list goes on. So, who was I to judge? But the thought of him with Averell, or, fuck, any guy, was making me feel shit I shouldn't be feeling.

The elevator ride down was awkward, with no one uttering a word. Faise stood farthest away from me, biting his lower lip, his toe tapping out a nervous rhythm. I wanted to reach out but when Faise looked over his shoulder, the pissed look on his face stopped me short.

When we stepped out of the elevator, we were greeted by Averell's EA, Caley, who introduced us to the photographer, a thirty-something guy named Evert Jackson, and his assistant, Bailey. There were the usual lights, backdrop, and camera equipment being set up.

Evert's face was familiar to me, but I couldn't pinpoint exactly where and when I'd met him.

"Evert? Didn't you do the cover shoot for our second album?" Brodie asked.

"That's right, about four years ago," Evert replied with a smile.

"You're from down east, right? Boston?" Holls mentioned.

"Maryland, but I split my time between Nashville and LA. And please, call me Ev. It's an honor to work with you guys again. New label, new look, eh?"

"Only if we can convince Ro to shave his head," Holloway joked.

"Never gonna happen," I replied, and placed a protective hand over my hair.

No one touched my hair. Except my boo. If he still *was* my boo. I glanced at Faise but he refused to look at me.

"I'm with you there." Ev pointed to his head.

Like me, Evert had long hair. But while mine was loose and messy, he wore his dirty blond hair worn in a tight braid down his back.

Wearing a pinstriped vest—no shirt—and baggy jeans with chains that hung from his belt loop, he had that effort-less style that celebrities paid big money for. Colorful tattoos snaked up both his arms, and beaded bracelets rattled as he moved his hands. His green eyes were framed by wire-rimmed glasses. When he smiled, the crinkles at the corners of his mouth deepened, the glint of his gold lip ring catching the light. As an artist who captured the essence of rockstars on film, he could have easily been one himself.

"I'm just finishing my setup. Head on back to wardrobe, hair, and makeup."

We were ushered into a change room and given our first outfit for the shoot. A denim kilt for Brodie and skin-tight jeans for the rest of us. Nothing else. Nothing odd about that.

An hour later, our hair styled, make up done, and our bodies oiled up, we headed back to the set. Evert was standing on a ladder, adjusting one of the lights.

"You guys look great," he offered with a smile. "Hold on one sec."

I spotted Averell entering the room, moving to stand on the periphery, watching us. I could feel his stare. Not aimed at me, but at Faise.

Not in the mood to share, I turned and gave Averell my back, blocking Faise from his view.

Fat chance, fucker.

CHAPTER 13

RONIN

"Okay, guys, we're good to go," Evert called out as he hopped off the ladder and walked around to grab his camera. "First pose, Faise and Ronin, I want you on your knees, and spread them wide."

"I thought the sex party was happening later on," I quipped.

Evert sighed and shook his head. "As I was saying, on your knees. Ronin, your right leg should be touching Faise's left. Brodie and Holloway, stand behind them."

Forcing back an eyeroll, I kneeled down as instructed, and thankfully, on a thick rug that covered the floor.

For the most part, I hated posing for pictures. Being on stage was one thing. Being under this kind of spotlight was another. Because I wasn't a model and I sure as fuck wasn't as pretty as the rest of the guys. I looked more like a bearded mountain man than a rockstar. Plus, posing for any length of time made me restless.

"Ronin, put your arm around Faise's shoulder," Evert instructed. "Lean into each other."

I did as he directed, but when my palm touched Faise's slick skin, he jolted. And he wasn't the only one.

That's weird. I touch him all the time.

"Ronin, relax your arm and Faise, turn your head towards him. Look at each other."

Clicks and flashes echoed around me but all I could hear was the rapid pounding of my heartbeat. Even though I wasn't moving, my pulse raced out of control. Like I'd just finished a long-ass set.

When Faise turned his head, and our eyes met, I struggled to look anywhere else. As I stared down at the long, dark lashes that framed familiar amber eyes, I was suddenly out of breath.

"That's it, perfect. Now move in closer."

Closer? Any closer and our mouths would be touching.

Fuck, don't think about that.

Then Faise licked his lips and my cock jerked hard in my jeans. No, this could *not* be happening.

A lock of my hair slid over my heated face and Faise reached up and tucked it behind my ear before I could blink. Fuck, his hand barely brushed my skin and I wanted more. My best friend was looking at me so intensely, I shivered.

Out of my peripheral vision, I spotted Evert walking towards us.

"Amazing, beautiful," Evert whispered. "Brodie, wrap your arm around Holloway's waist and lean against him. Give me that trademark smirk."

More clicks and flashes.

"Great," Evert added. "Let's try a new pose. Ronin, I want you to sit down with your legs splayed wide. Faise, sit between Ronin's legs."

"Um, excuse me?" I blurted out, my face flushing hotter.

I swear I heard Brodie and Holls laughing but I didn't dare look behind me.

"Let's go Ronin," Evert directed with an easy grin. So I did as instructed and sat down, opening up my legs. "Come on Faise, slide between Ronin's legs, nice and tight."

Nice and tight…fucking Christ, my dirty mind was like a runaway train at this point, and it could not be stopped. And there was nothing I could do about the fact that my dick was rock hard and straining against my jeans. Reluctantly, I lowered my knees and opened my legs.

Thank fuck no one seemed to notice the bulge in my crotch.

Until Faise did as Evert asked and slid in between my legs. When that taut ass snuggled against my dick, shit, I liked that a whole fuckton. The heat in my face spread down my neck and chest. Faise's heartbeat was racing, thrumming against me as his smooth back made contact with my hairy chest. He sure as hell could feel mine pounding out of control.

"Faise, lean back and rest your head on Ronin's left shoulder. Give me a seductive smile. Ronin, wrap your arms around Faise's waist and then look up at me."

I did as Evert directed, my hands shaking.

Come on, you hug Faise all the time. It's the same thing.

It was *not* the same thing.

Because my body wanted more than a friendly hug. If my wayward cock was any indication, I wanted Faise without the layers of denim between us. The picture was so clear in my mind. Me and Faise doing dirty, dirty things together. Sure, I'd noticed that my best friend was beautiful, hot, sexy as hell. I'd admired his body many times. But I'd never wanted to rub myself all over him like I did now.

I bit back a groan, desperate to think of something, anything, to get rid of those filthy images in my head. But a sexy vision of Faise riding me bareback was suddenly all I could see.

"Holloway, move in closer. Tilt your head and lick your lower lip. That's it," Evert whispered as the click of his camera continued. "You guys look great. One more shot before we change, but—"

Evert paused and stopped.

"Okay, I want to try something more provocative. Faise, I need you to straddle Ronin's hips, and Ronin, reach up and splay your hands on Faise's chest."

Spontaneous combustion turned out to be a real thing.

Faise

I hope to fuck Evert didn't notice my raging hard on. If he did, he was gonna have to edit these photos before they went public.

Not that I was paying attention to what Evert was saying, or what Brodie or Holls were doing behind us. How could I with Ronin's huge, hard cock snug against my ass? How many times over the years had we hugged, cuddled, wrestled? Too many times to count. But suddenly, it was like I was sitting in the arms of a stranger. A hot, sexy stranger who knew me better than anyone.

A man I wanted to fuck.

And judging by his erection, I wasn't the only one. Holy hell, a filthy image of me ripping these jeans off and riding Ro flashed in my mind. And then I had to do just that, sit on Ronin's lap. This was the sexiest photo shoot we'd ever done, and that was saying a lot.

As I got into position, Ronin's arms trembled, surprising me. I straddled his hips as instructed, and then his hands snuck up and over my chest. It wasn't the most intimate touch I'd ever experienced but it sure as fuck felt like it, his rough fingertips sparking ripples of hot need along my skin.

Even though we weren't alone. And touching each other was nothing new to us.

I didn't think it was possible to faint while sitting down but I was about to prove otherwise. My nipples were hard, begging to be teased, the silver piercings rubbing against my sensitive skin. Ro's fingers were just shy of them, and fuck, I wanted to move his hands north.

I was sweating hard, and between his callused grip and the slick oil, my skin was on fire. Every time Ronin so much as breathed against my neck, or shifted his hips in the slightest, I was fighting back the urge to moan out loud. As soon as we were done here, I was going to find the nearest bathroom to rub one out. Or risk coming in these damn jeans like a teenager.

I had no idea what kind of expression was on my face, but Evert seemed pleased as he moved closer to us and snapped away.

"That's it. Right there," Evert muttered as he worked. "Jesus, that's beautiful."

Yeah, I couldn't argue with that. I'd never felt more aware of my body or Ronin's. I could only imagine the intense expression on my face.

Evert paused and finally lowered his camera. "Okay, this set is done. Time for an outfit change. Next up, we'll have you pose individually, and then another group photo."

His clipped words hit me like a bucket of ice water.

Ronin's hands slipped away, and I swallowed hard at the loss.

Evert's assistant handed us towels and I gratefully wiped my face and held it over my lap as I slid away from Ronin's body and stood up. But I moved too fast, unsteady, keeling forward when a strong hand gripped me and held me upright.

"You okay, boo?"

Was I okay? *No, Ronin, I'm so fucking far from okay.*

"Fine. I must've slipped on the carpet."

On my tongue, more like it.

"Are *you* all right?" I asked him.

What the hell had just happened? Was he turned on just because, or because of *me*? Not that this was the time or place for that. If there ever was. Fuck.

As soon as I felt steady, I pulled my arm away. Glancing

up at Ronin, he was looking anywhere but at me. Had he seen my hard on? Did I embarrass him? Nah, we'd seen each other naked so many times that neither one of us batted an eye. Same thing with sex. We'd seen it all. It couldn't be that.

But what if… did he have any clue as to I felt about him? Suddenly the fear of losing my best friend was all too real and my stomach clenched painfully.

"That was incredible," Averell announced as he stepped up to us, giving me a long once over. "The fans are going to go wild when they see those pictures."

He gave me another flirty grin and I was tempted to take him up on his offer, if only to prove that my feelings for Ronin could be overcome.

This had potential disaster written all over it. But what the hell? I needed to let off my frustration and why not with a sexy, powerful guy like Averell? Nothing like starting off a new contract with a bang. A literal one.

I smiled back and wiped my chest with the towel, watching the way Averell ran his eyes down my body. While I didn't have huge biceps and a broad chest like Ro, I was toned, and worked out regularly. More so since my time in rehab when working out was my only means of stress relief. When we were on tour, I sweated off the pounds every week, so it was necessary to take care of my body.

Weird thing was, I wasn't feeling much of anything from Averell's attention. My cock was still half-hard, but it wasn't for him. Still, if I didn't fuck someone, anyone, I'd be wallowing again. And that's the last place I needed to be. Nothing good came of it.

"I have to get back to my office, but I'll see you guys for lunch," Averell stated and glanced at me again.

"Looking forward to it," I replied and licked my lips, walking closer to him so only he could hear. "In fact, how about a drink later?"

"At the party?" he asked.

I nodded my head. "And maybe one after. My place?"

"You're on."

Averell quickly nodded and turned around, walking off the set.

"I can't believe you're going to fuck that guy."

I turned at Ronin's comment. What right did he have to cockblock me like this? Between his pissy attitude and my unrelenting hard-on, I'd had enough. I gave him my response via my middle finger and stalked off, heading for the dressing room.

"Faise!"

"Don't, Ronin. This is not up for discussion."

Ronin wasn't one to give up, though. He followed me into the dressing room. I tried to close the door, but his arm held it open. He slid inside the room with me and slammed the door shut.

Fuck this.

Instead of letting that stop me, I began to unzip my jeans.

Ronin could stand there all he wanted. I wasn't going to change my mind about Averell. In fact, given how stressed I was about today, I needed a fuck more than ever. Something quick and dirty. And that sexy Brit was just the kind of distraction I needed.

"Why are you doing this?" Ronin asked me.

"Again, I'm not sure what your problem is. Why are you so ticked off that I might hook up with Averell? Explain it to me."

Was it possible that Ro was jealous? That thought made my heart take off running again. Ronin stared at me with his mouth open, but no words came out. I guess I had my answer.

I pushed the jeans off my hips and the jockstrap along with it.

His eyes slid down my body like a heated touch and the

longer he looked, the harder my cock grew. Jesus Christ, so much for convincing myself to remain unaffected.

"This is why I need to hook up," I pointed at my dick and shrugged it off. "It's been a while."

"He… I—" Ronin ran a hand over his face and finally met my eyes. "He's not good enough for you."

"For a fuck? Gimme a break! Since when do you give a crap about who I have sex with?"

Ronin stepped towards me, but a knock on the door startled us.

"Hurry the fuck up, Evert's waiting!" Brodie called out from the other side of the door.

Ignoring my erection, I took a deep breath and willed my dick to calm. Then I reached for the next set of clothes on the hanger and threw Ro's at him.

"I swear, this is not going to affect our record deal, all right? I'll make it clear that it's a one-time thing," I explained. "Now let it go and let's finish up our job here."

Ronin said nothing in response. He yanked his jeans off, threw them across the room, and stepped into another pair. Then he plucked a white tank top from the hanger and pulled it on.

Turning my back, I got changed and finally, my cock cooperated.

Nothing more was said. There was only the heavy fall of Ro's footsteps, then the slam of the door. I finally breathed a sigh of relief.

One of these days, I was gonna fuck Ronin out of my system.

One of these days.

CHAPTER 14
RONIN

The rest of the photo shoot was, thankfully, boner-free. Never thought I'd be happy about saying that…

I didn't have to pose with Faise again. Of course, he stood as far away from me as possible. Which made me both insanely relieved and curiously annoyed. Why did things have to be so awkward between us now? And my irritation at his flirtation with Averell was like a cut that wouldn't heal.

I was frightened of this shift between us. I didn't want to think about the intensity of my feelings. And what that meant for our friendship.

On our way back up to meet our new manager, my phone rang.

Ciara calling.

Shit, I was so distracted that I almost forgot that my sister and her boyfriend were flying into town for the launch party.

I tapped the screen. "Hey Ci, where are you?"

"On our way to the hotel."

"You should've stayed at my place—"

"It's fine," she interrupted. "I'll text you when we arrive at the venue, okay? Bye."

Before I could reply, the call dropped, and I was staring at my phone.

Faise wasn't the only one acting weird lately.

My sister had been all but silent for the past few months. I chalked it up to the fact that she'd moved from Rhode Island to New York City to start a new job. One in social media for a fashion brand. She was excited about the move, and I was excited for her. Ciara and I remained close despite my schedule and the travel distance between us. Or so I thought.

Two months ago, my calls started going unanswered and she was only texting once every couple of weeks. The sudden drop off made me wonder and worry.

Apparently, she'd met her boyfriend, Dallas, a few weeks after she landed in the big apple. I still hadn't met the guy so all I knew was that that he was ten years older than her, and he worked in law enforcement. Ciara hadn't volunteered any more details, but it didn't stop me from asking.

Usually when she visited me in Nashville, she'd stay at my house. This time, though, she insisted on staying at a hotel and paying for it herself. I admired her independence, but I liked treating my family. After all the years of struggle, it felt right to spoil them. All this to say, I was hurt. Why the sudden change? I had a five-bedroom house, so there was plenty of room and privacy. And we always had a good time when she stayed. Faise, Holls, and Brodie, hell, everyone we worked with, loved her and loved to hang out with her.

I glanced at my phone, tempted to call her back. There was no point. I'd rather talk to her face to face later.

"How's your sister?" Brodie asked.

"She's good. I think. She's on her way to the hotel."

"But she always stays at your place," Holls commented.

"Right?" I said to him. "She brought her boyfriend this time, so—"

"Ooh, now it's getting interesting," Brodie rubbed his hands together. "Have you met him yet?"

"Nope. It's not just that, she—" I paused, looking over at Faise.

He was staring at me like he wanted to say something. But what?

That was another first. In the past, I always had a sense of where his mind was at, like we shared a psychic connection. But now? My sixth sense was jamming and I wasn't talking about music.

"She's barely contacted me since she moved to New York," I confessed as I looked at him.

His eyes softened for a fraction.

"It's a big move. Maybe she's just overwhelmed by it all?"

I shrugged.

"We hardly talk anymore. It's left me worried. And hurt," I admitted.

And I wasn't just talking about my sister.

Faise bit his lip and looked away.

"I'm sure you guys will work it out. You'll get to chat with her tonight," Brodie replied, gripping my shoulder. "And we can help you interrogate the boyfriend."

"Oh, fuck."

Everyone laughed at that.

We entered the boardroom, and Averell was already sitting at the head of the table, waiting. But not alone. A man in his thirties wearing dark-framed glasses, a button-down shirt, and suspenders, sat beside him. The guy was so corporate looking.

Please tell me this is not our new manager.

Until he moved to stand up and then I noticed the rolled-up sleeves and the black-lined tattoos that covered his forearms.

"Jesse Aimes, meet Wayward Lane," Averell announced. "This is Brodie—"

"Come on, Av, I know all their names and songs," Jesse

interrupted with a shake of his head and walked around the table to greet us. "It's an honor and an absolute pleasure."

Averell told us that our new manager had been working in the UK, so I wasn't expecting the American accent. Or how blunt Jesse was, even with his boss. This was going to be interesting.

Averell's EA entered the room and brought us all water and coffee.

"Grab a seat, let's get to work," Jesse demanded. "And yes, I am always this bossy."

Judging by the smiles around the table, that eased a bit of the tension in the room but not all of it.

"You guys got fucked over by Bandit, but as I'm sure Av's told you, Hardwick is the antithesis of Greg Haddley's music label. We don't play by old, archaic rules where the CEO says 'jump' and you say 'how high'. We are a band-first company. What does that mean? It means most of us who work on the corporate side have played professionally and we know what musician life is like. It means you have more creative control over your songs and brand. It means we're fiercely protective of your space. No one, and by that I mean the tabloid press, fucks with our people," Jesse insisted. "I'll be your sounding board as we create the new album, the marketing, and tour schedule. And whatever you need, any time, day or night, I'm here. Any questions?"

Brodie leaned forward.

Jesse raised his hand. "And yes, I know all about Van and how he managed you. I did my research. Whatever you want to ask me, go ahead. I'm always upfront about everything. Even the tough shit."

"Good, 'cause I always get right to the point," Brodie smirked. "But what I was going to say was, we had a lot of creative differences with Greg when it came to our songs. He kept pushing in one direction, but I always fought back. And that will never change. So, be prepared."

Jesse nodded. "I tracked every song from every album you've produced and it's clear that Van's songs and then your co-writes with him are the best-sellers. You know what you're doing. I'll give my input if I feel it's warranted but otherwise, you have control over your song choices."

Brodie nodded but said nothing else.

"Going back to the media," Faise added. "On our last European junket, that interview with the French press went too far and our manager played a key role in letting it happen. We're not putting up with that crap again. My brother's been followed around ever since he got out of rehab."

Averell placed a hand on Faise's arm, and I nearly shot up out of my chair. Fucking around was one thing. But touching Faise like that? That was personal.

"You have my guarantee that it will never happen again," Averell replied.

"I think he was asking Jesse," I snapped.

Faise pulled his arm back, turning to stare at me.

"Not to mention the story about my mom," Holloway added.

Jesse ran a hand through his short hair. "Like I said, we protect our own. That kind of stupid PR stunt isn't happening on my watch. It creates mistrust, and that's not a recipe for success. I know you did your due diligence. There's a reason bands are signing with Hardwick. And when I'm managing a band, I'm your shield. I stand between you and all that crazy shit."

I liked what I was hearing but everyone put on a good face on opening night.

"Can you give us the names of some of the musicians you've managed?" I asked. "I mean, all this sounds great, but we don't know you."

Jesse nodded and tapped on his phone. "I'll send the list now. Feel free contact anyone you want."

I nodded. Before, I automatically trusted in our label and their staff. But not anymore.

Averell leaned forward. "Any other pressing questions before we move on to meet with the PR team?"

"I have another one for Jesse." Brodie crossed his arms. "What song of ours is your favorite, and can you sing it, right fucking now?"

Jesse scoffed, then cleared his throat and belted out Filthy Pain like *he* was the rockstar and *we* were the audience.

When he finished, we were all too shocked to do anything.

"Why the fuck aren't you on stage?" Brodie asked with wide eyes.

It took a lot to impress our lead singer.

Jesse shrugged. "I was, fifteen years ago. I played lead guitar and backup vocals in a band called Ruthless Kane. I had longer hair back then. And no glasses."

"Holy shit, why didn't I make the connection!" Holloway exclaimed. "Your lead singer was Landry Soames. Didn't you guys have a song called *Take Me Under?*"

"That's right, it was our biggest—and last—hit single. Unfortunately, after three years together, we broke up. My desire to be on stage after that wasn't the same. But music is still my passion, so I started to work behind the scenes."

"What caused the breakup?" Brodie asked point blank, cocky as ever. "I'm a nosy fucker so get used to that, too."

Jesse let out a sigh. "I fell in love with my bandmate. He didn't feel the same. I couldn't move past it, and neither could he. That was that."

Suddenly, Faise's arm jerked and he knocked a glass of water off the table. The accident broke the awkward tension in the room as Faise made his apologies.

I hadn't been expecting that revelation.

That was that, all right.

———

The broken glass was a premonition. The day would only get worse from there.

I couldn't focus on what anyone was saying. Every time Faise and Averell made eyes at each other, or traded flirty jokes, I wanted to puke. All my appetite vanished as I watched my best friend act like a horny teenager with a crush.

Someone was going to get crushed, I thought as I glared at Averell. The guy was too fucking smooth for his own good.

My head was so messed up. Ever since Jesse told us about his band breakup, I couldn't focus on anything but that. Couldn't make conversation or anything. Jesse probably thought I was being a dick, but it wasn't that I didn't want to talk. I was too much in my head. There were lots of conversations going on around me but I had no idea what anyone said.

When me and the guys finally had a moment alone, they asked me what I thought of our new manager.

"We asked questions and he answered, no hesitation," I replied. "That's gotta count for something. I say we give him a chance."

Brodie, Faise, and Holls liked Jesse, too. I guess we'd see how the next three months rolled out.

We'd finished up our day with PR, had dinner out, then changed and headed over to the launch party at a club on Brooklyn Street.

I glanced around the packed venue and spotted Jesse chatting up Van, Holls, and Dawson.

Things with me and Faise were still tense, though. And my sister hadn't arrived yet.

Faise spent the whole time glued to Averell's side, hanging on his every word. And I spent the whole time following them around. So much that an hour into it, Brodie and Holls intervened.

"You've been like this all day, Ro. Don't you think it's time you get that stick out of your ass?" Brodie quipped.

I scoffed. "If our record deal gets thrown out next week, don't come running to me."

"It's already signed and sealed. A done deal. No backing out. Now, it's time to celebrate," Holls reminded me as he passed me a glass of bourbon. "Remember? That's when you talk and joke around with your friends and have fun?"

Across the room, Averell let out a loud laugh and Faise soon followed. I shot up off the lounger.

"I have to get out of here."

Brodie placed a hand on my forearm which I shrugged off. I didn't want anyone to touch me right now.

"Maybe think about why you're so upset with Faise," Brodie suggested. "No one else has an issue with who he fucks, even if it's Averell."

"Yeah, bud. It's time you shit or get off the pot," Holls added.

"Nicely put," Brodie snarked, then gave me a stare that meant serious business. "We can't have this tension in the band. Deal with your feelings for your best friend."

How could I when I was still confused myself? So what if my dick got excited today visualizing me and Faise fucking? That's normal. He's hot, I'm horny. It's not like I hadn't noticed how sexy he was before. But whenever that inconvenient urge popped up, I always managed to shove it away. Acting on that would cause a mess I wasn't prepared to deal with.

Right?

"What about our promise to each other? No fucking around, nothing that screws with the band dynamic? Look at what happened to Jesse," I argued.

Holls and Brodie exchanged a long look.

"When we started out, yeah, that was a valid concern,"

Brodie explained. "But you're not eighteen anymore. And this is you and Faise, not Jesse and whoever. Figure it out."

"I think it's too late."

I motioned to Faise and Averell, standing way too close, in each other's personal space.

"Yo, Faise!" Holloway called out and waved his arms in the air.

"What the fuck are you doing?" I bit out.

"Giving you a much-needed kick in the ass," Holls chuckled.

What the fuck did he mean by that?

My best friend ambled over in a graceful strut, a lock of black hair falling down over his eyes, a curious look on his face. My heart beat double time, triple. The closer Faise got, the higher the beat, until it was all I could hear.

I looked over and caught Averell's gaze across the room. The challenge in them was unmistakable.

He's not yours, asshole.

"What's with the glare?" a familiar voice called out. "I thought you'd be happy to see me."

CHAPTER 15

RONIN

jumped at the sound of my sister's voice, turning to find her standing behind me.

"Baby sister!"

Ciara was beautiful as always, in a fuchsia pantsuit with her long, dark hair in a high ponytail.

But she looked different somehow, slimmer than the last time I saw her. Her face was pale and her eyes red-rimmed, and puffy. Maybe from travel?

"Took you long enough to get here," I teased and pulled her in for a hug.

She jolted in my arms and that was fucking new. Ciara was used to my bear hugs.

Something was wrong.

"Ci, what's going—"

"You have to meet my boyfriend," she interrupted with a tight smile and turned her head. "Dallas Bledsoe, my brother, Ronin."

A bulky guy with a shaved head and a stern expression stepped forward, offering his hand. His other one gripped my sister's arm tightly.

"I thought for sure Ciara was lying when she said her brother was famous, but I guess the joke's on me."

Strange intro, but okay.

"Nice to meet you," I replied politely and shook his hand. "Welcome to Nashville. Meet my bandmates, Brodie and Holloway."

Dallas shook their hands. Then the guys gave Ciara a hug in turn.

"Don't wait so long between visits," Holloway teased her.

"I'll try. But New York life is crazy busy," she replied.

Jesse was waving at us from across the room and called out Brodie and Holloway's names. They left me to my sister and her boyfriend.

"This is quite the party," Dallas muttered as he looked around. "I can see the appeal."

Two stunning models walked by, and Dallas stared at them far too long for my liking.

"They go all out when you sign with a new label," I replied, trying to ignore my irritation. "So, how was your flight? How's life in the big apple?"

"Good, even though Ciara made us late to the airport. You sister is never punctual. I'm surprised she can make it to work," Dallas sneered and shook his head. "We only had time to check in and drop off our luggage. I'm thirsty as hell. Is there any booze at this party?"

Dallas' tone pissed me off and my big brother defense system was about to unleash. Until I saw the pleading in Ci's eyes.

Be nice.

I kept my mouth shut and motioned for a server. Bourbon on the rocks for me and Dallas, and nothing for my sister. Which was odd. She always enjoyed a drink or two.

"How did you two meet?" I finally asked as I motioned to a couple of chairs so we could sit and relax.

"I—" Ciara started.

"I'm a patrol officer," Dallas talked over her. "I ticketed her."

"Parking in a restricted zone?" I quipped as I glanced at Ciara, but she had her eyes downcast.

"Speeding," Dallas replied and rolled his eyes. "She can't remember the rules of the road. I have no idea how she survived before she met me."

My protective hackles engaged. I didn't appreciate the way he spoke about Ciara. And it wasn't like my sister to let an insult, even one disguised as a joke, go by without a response.

My gut instinct was pinging loud as fuck.

Just when I was about to confront Dallas about his comments, Faise sat down next to Ciara. "Ci, long time no speak!"

"Faise! It's so good to see you," she replied as she hugged him with one arm.

Dallas still hadn't let go of her other one. As soon as Faise leaned back, Dallas yanked Ciara back to his side, and glared at my best friend.

Now, I didn't know shit about romantic relationships, but I knew that Dallas' hold on my sister felt off. It wasn't possessive, like Van and Brodie, or Holls and Dawson. Because Dallas looked downright angry, and Ciara looked downright scared.

"I'm Dallas, Ciara's boyfriend," he announced as he continued to glare at Faise. "You seem to know her well."

"Naturally," Faise addressed him. "I'm Faisel Reed, Ronin's bestie. I've known Ciara since we were kids."

Dallas nodded at him, his gaze slightly less menacing. Thankfully, our server returned to ask if we wanted another round.

"Double whiskey, neat this time. And make it a real double," Dallas demanded. "And a glass of sparkling water."

"Gotta keep hydrated," I muttered.

"It's for Ciara," Dallas explained. "She doesn't drink."

"Since when?" I scoffed and looked at my sister.

"Oh, just recently," she whispered, rubbing her hands together. "It's fine. Better for my health."

"I reminded her that she's almost thirty." Dallas raised one eyebrow. "Gotta cut that shit out if you want to stay prime, right babe?"

Prime? Who the fuck was this douchebag?

"As long as it's her decision," I bit out.

It had no effect on Dallas, he just grunted and glanced around the room.

I needed that second drink. Right fucking now.

When I glanced at Faise, the look he gave me said he was just as worried as I was about this dickhead Ciara was dating. And her sudden change in behavior. Since when did she let someone else tell her what to do?

"I need to hit the head," Dallas announced and stood up.

"Back of the room to the left," I offered.

"I'll be back in a few, stay here." Dallas commanded and squeezed Ciara's shoulder, then walked away.

"What the hell's going on, Ci?" I asked her as soon as Dallas was out of earshot.

"What do you mean?"

"Why are you letting that guy talk down to you like that? And why've you stopped calling me? That's what I mean."

"I told you, I've been busy," Ciara replied but refused to meet my eyes.

"Too busy for family?"

She gripped her hands together tightly. "Dallas keeps telling me I need to be more independent. I'm too reliant on you and Mom."

"That's ridiculous. We're not just siblings, we're friends. That's only normal. And you're plenty independent. You live in a different city, and you have your own life."

Ciara bit her lower lip and let out a shaky sigh.

"You're acting nervous, and it's not like you. And he's talking out of his ass. So, tell me the truth. What's going on?" I asked again.

"I can't." Ciara shook her head. "Please, Ro. Not now."

"What about Mom? She hasn't heard from you in weeks either."

Ciara still wouldn't look me in the eye. I was so frustrated I wanted to scream.

Until Faise leaned forward. "Ciara's here for a couple of days, right? You have plenty of time to catch up."

I reluctantly nodded, despite my gut telling me to push my sister for answers. Then I spotted Brodie stalking towards us.

"Hey, Ro, Evert wants you for a photo op with Averell and Jesse."

Great.

I reached for my sister's hand, which was ice cold, and she startled. I gave it a reassuring squeeze. "I'll be right back."

She nodded but didn't say anything, pulling at her jacket sleeves.

When I got up to leave, Faise leaned in close to Ciara and started talking to her in that calm tone of his. Some of my tension eased. Maybe she'd at least tell *him* what was going on.

I made my way through the room and found Evert standing near the entrance, on a platform with a podium and a mic. Like with any of these official events, we always had photographs taken for the press and our PR team to use. Averell was nearby, schmoozing with a journalist, eagerly courting the media attention.

Jesse was deep in conversation with Evert, until the photographer suddenly raised his camera and took an impromptu snap. Jesse laughed it off, pretending to cover his face.

"Where do you want me?" I asked Evert as I stepped up to meet them.

"Hold on, where's Av?" Evert looked around and then motioned for the marketing VP to join us. "Okay, Ro, lean against the backdrop wall. I want Jesse and Averell on either side."

"Do I really have to be part of—" Jesse started.

Evert shook his head and stepped forward. "Yes, you really have to be in the picture. Stop procrastinating and get your ass up there."

Jesse's face reddened and it was the first time all day I'd seen him lost for words.

"I thought I was the bossy one," Jesse replied.

"You haven't seen anything yet," Evert quipped.

When Averell joined us, it was all I could do not to say, fuck it, and just walk away. I did *not* want to stand beside the guy standing between me and Faise. But I bit back my desire to leave and did as I was told. Sort of.

I turned my head towards Averell, muttering under my breath. "Hurt him and I don't care about our fucking contract, I will not hesitate to end you."

Averell bit out a laugh. "So dramatic. Why don't you just relax and mind your own business?"

Evert lowered his camera and motioned for us to lean in closer. "Shake hands and stop talking, please."

I gripped Averell's hand so hard I was in danger of hurting my own fingers. Not smart for a bass player.

"I mean it," I hissed. "Leave him alone."

"Uh, guys—" Jesse interrupted.

I forced myself to smile. Another flash.

Evert stopped and sighed. "Once again, please look in my direction and no talking, thanks. Just a few more shots and we're done."

"You're done, all right," I whispered.

Then I shut up, smiled, and let Evert get his shot.

One last flash, and then Averell turned to me. "What do you think you're doing?"

"I could ask you the same thing," I spat out. "The last thing Faise needs is to get mixed up with someone he works with."

Averell stared at me with a knowing grin.

"What?" I snapped.

"Are you and Faise involved?"

I coughed into my fist, nearly choking on my spit. "No. Of course not. We're just—"

"Best friends who share everything? Everything but—"

"Stop," I interrupted. "He's had a rough time with his brother lately, okay? I don't want to see him get hurt. I'm just looking out for him."

"Well, as far as I can tell, Faise is all grown up and he looks after himself. And I can assure you that a relationship is the last thing I'm looking for. Like I said before, relax. You have nothing to worry about."

That didn't calm the storm in my gut. Not at all. I hated the idea of him and Faise together. Even if it was just a casual screw.

"Now, if you'll excuse me, I have to do the rounds. Enjoy the rest of the party."

Averell dismissed me and walked away.

"So, you got it bad for your BFF bandmate?"

Jesse's question startled me since I all but forgot he was standing on my other side.

"Not you too," I groaned.

Jesse rubbed a hand over his face. "I told you, I've been there. It happens a lot. Band members share a bond that's like nothing else. It makes for heady chemistry. But you better be sure you want to go there. Cause once you let them know, there's no going back."

Jesse patted my shoulder and gave me a sympathetic look, then headed out into the crowd to join Averell.

I shook off his warning and headed back to find my sister. I expected to find her and Faise sitting together, talking.

But she was nowhere in sight. And neither was Faise.

CHAPTER 16

FAISE

I couldn't wait to call an end to this day.

Ronin and I could hardly talk without it turning into an argument. It had me fighting the urge to run right the hell out of the venue. To get high. To do anything to take away my frustration. Add to that, Averell's attention, though flattering, was making my anxiety spike. It should be exactly what I wanted. Averell should be who I wanted. Easy, no strings sex.

Why couldn't I just cut off these feelings for Ronin and focus on someone else?

But the longer I talked to Ciara, the more I realized that my problems had to take a backseat. I knew her almost as well as I knew Ro, and something was painfully wrong. She was way too quiet, and along with the boyfriend making disturbing comments, warning signs flashed in front of me like pyrotechnics on stage.

"Ro's just being a typical big brother," I reassured Ciara. "He misses you. And he worries."

Her phone vibrated and she pulled it out of her pocket. "I have to take this. I'll be right back."

I watched her get up and head to the exit. I flagged down

a server for another drink.

Booze in hand, I looked around for Ronin, but he was nowhere in sight. So, drink in hand, I did my bit and made the rounds of the room while I continued to search him out. I'd become more comfortable in the PR area with each passing year. It helped that I was a familiar face to music fans, so they often came up to talk to me. In a room with other musicians, or with fans, no worries, I could talk shop all day. But with suits and sponsors? Not my thing. Not for any of the guys, but me least of all.

Halfway through my drink, I headed back to where I started from.

I found Ronin sitting by himself, head down, checking his phone. While we had a moment alone, I considered opening pandora's box by asking Ro about what happened at the photoshoot.

Was I really ready for his answer?

"Hey."

"Where'd my sister and her boyfriend go?" he asked me.

"Uh, her phone rang when I was talking to her. I assumed it was work or something, I think she went outside to take the call. I have no idea where Dallas is."

"I'm going to find her. I need to know why she's dating that douchebag."

"No shit. That guy gives me the creeps."

Ronin nodded. Before I could say anything else, he stood up and took off. Instead of sitting around feeling unsettled, I went in search of Brodie and Holls. They were with their men and chatting up Evert and Jesse.

"Where's Ronin?" Holls asked.

"He went to find Ciara."

"Is she all right?" Van asked. "I saw her walking by and she looked upset."

That anxious feeling wouldn't leave my gut and I couldn't let it go this time. "I don't know. She's been acting odd lately, not contacting Ro for weeks at a time. And her boyfriend said some pretty shitty things to her. Disturbing things. I'm gonna go look for them."

Before anyone could say otherwise, before I could even tell my protective detail I was leaving, I headed for the door. Whatever, the place was crawling with security and I was just going to pop outside for a moment.

Averell stopped me on the way out. "You ready for that drink now?"

An hour ago, I would've said sure. And fuck knows, I needed to get my mind off Ronin. But there were more important things than my dick.

"Sorry, but I've changed my mind." I shook my head.

Averell gave me a knowing look and nodded, pursing his pouty lips.

"What about tomorrow?"

My silence to Averell's question said everything. He knew, I knew, fuck, everyone probably knew that all I wanted was Ronin. Well, everyone except the man himself.

"If you change your mind, give me a call," Averell offered with a flirty smile, then he walked away.

I kept walking out of the venue and into the spring night and looked around. No sign of Ro or Ciara. No one, in fact. I turned around to head back inside but then I heard a shout.

"Let her go!"

I'd recognize that voice anywhere. I followed the sound around the corner of the building to the alleyway and peered around to find Dallas with his hand around Ciara's neck, Ronin standing across from them, his arms raised.

What the fuck was happening?

Dallas shifted and it was only then that I noticed the broken beer bottle in his free hand. It was aimed at Ronin. I could've sworn my heart stopped beating, but thankfully, the rest of my body was working.

Pulling out my phone with shaky hands, I texted Lennie

our emergency code and then cautiously slipped around the corner, trying not to startle Dallas.

"Hey," I whispered as quiet as I could, walking up to stand beside Ronin.

Dallas startled and aimed the bottle at me. I held my hands up in surrender. "Put that down, man, there's no need for that. Come on. Please. Put it down. Let's talk it out."

Ciara's face was wet with tears, her hands frantically pulling at Dallas's tight grip on her neck.

Dallas shook his head, then shoved the bottle closer to Ronin again. "Coming here was a mistake. I heard what you said to her. You told her to dump me! But that won't happen. She belongs to me. To me! She does what I say! You get that?"

"Okay, all right," Ronin whispered, his voice cracking. "I get it. I was in the wrong. Just calm down and let her breathe, please."

"I'm always calm, that's what makes me a great cop!" Dallas snapped and shook his head. "I shouldn't have let her out of my sight. She didn't listen to me and now look what's happened!"

This guy was fucking crazy.

I glanced at Ronin, and I'd never seen him so fearful. My stomach pitched and I willed myself to hold on.

"You can walk away," Ronin pleaded. "Just don't hurt her, please."

"Hurt her? What are you talking about? I love her!" Dallas shouted. "But she needs to do as I tell her! I know what's best."

"Yes, okay, you do," Ronin repeated, his voice wavering. "Faise and I are going to step away, all right? You can put the bottle down now. We're going to back away."

Footsteps echoed in the distance, getting louder, and I prayed, closer. It had to be our bodyguards.

Dallas suddenly shoved Ciara away, against the brick wall, and then lunged at Ronin.

"No!" I shouted and reached for Dallas' arm, pushing him against the wall as hard as I could, until I saw the bottle drop out of his hand.

He swung his other arm around and hit me in the face, the pain searing my jaw.

The next moment was a haze of shouting and screams, and the arrival, thank fuck, of Lennie and Petyr and Regan.

When they pulled Dallas away, I noticed Ronin collapsing, holding his hand to his chest.

The last thing I remember was him calling out my name.

"Faise, wake up."

Brodie?

I blinked and opened my eyes to find him and Holls standing beside me. I was lying in a bed, but definitely not my own. It was the smell. Disinfectant and plastic. Oh God, not a hospital.

My face was aching, like I had a sore tooth. Then I remembered the party, and searching for Ronin. Ciara's boyfriend holding her against the wall. Dallas lunging at Ronin.

Ronin…

"Ro!" I shouted and made to get up off the bed.

"He's getting stitches, he's okay," Holls reassured me. But his red-rimmed eyes told me just how upset he was. He and Brodie both had wet streaks down their faces, and bloodshot eyes. "You guys scared the crap out of us."

Van and Dawson were standing in the corner of the room, talking quietly, along with Petyr, Valen, and Regan.

"Ciara?"

"She's fine, they gave her a sedative. Police are on their way to take your statements if you're up to it."

"Fuck." I rubbed my eyes as the tears flowed. "I need to see him. Now!"

"I'll see if he's ready," Brodie nodded and stalked out of the room, Van following him.

"Thank fuck you texted Lennie when you did," Holloway's voice shook. "God knows what would have happened. Shit, it's like my fucking stalker all over again."

He bit his lower lip, and his eyes were as watery as mine.

"I shouldn't have left the party without telling Len. It was stupid. I just ran out the door 'cause I wanted to find Ro."

Brodie re-entered the room and Ciara was with him. Her makeup was streaked, mixed with tears, as she walked up to the bed and leaned down to hug me.

When she cupped my face in her hand, I spotted the dark bruise just above her wrist.

And the red marks around her neck. Dallas' handprint. Jesus Christ.

"I'm so, so sorry," she cried as she sat down beside me.

"This is not your fault."

"But it is." She sniffled. "I should've known better. He's been getting worse. And tonight, when Dallas saw me talking to you—"

"How long has he been abusing you?"

She choked on a sob and swiped at her face.

"About a month after we started dating." She paused and rolled up her jacket sleeves.

Holloway gasped. Or maybe that was me. Both of Ciara's arms were littered with violet bruises.

"This one on my wrist is from three nights ago. I was late getting home. He doesn't hit as hard when he knows I have to report to work. Not as long as I do as he says."

It shouldn't happen at all. No wonder Ronin had confronted Dallas.

"Ci, no one should hurt you like that," I implored. "No matter what."

Ciara's eyes welled up.

"I know. I know. I just... I just don't know how all this

happened. How it got so bad. When I moved to New York, I didn't know anyone. I felt so alone. Suddenly, Dallas was there, and he was relentless in pursuing me. I just couldn't help falling, at first. But then," she paused and wiped her eyes. "After we were dating a few weeks, things were different. He started in on me, telling me I'd forgotten things, like when to meet up for our dates. I started to wonder if maybe he was right. Maybe I was stupid and forgetful. Then he told me to stop texting Ro. Said I was too dependent on my family, I needed to toughen up. I knew something wasn't right, but I kept thinking it was just my imagination. I thought it was just me."

She leaned forward and let out a shaky sigh. "Then Dallas started losing his temper at the slightest thing. When he hit me the first time, I was too shocked to believe it. We'd been at a bar that night, and he thought I was flirting with someone else. He slapped my face so hard my jaw ached for a week. But he was apologetic afterwards, said it would never happen again. Until a week later, only, this time he made sure to hit me where no one would see. And what could I do? He's a police officer. Who would believe *me*?"

She wrung her hands together, pausing to wipe her face.

"Dallas didn't want to come down to Nashville, but I insisted. Something was telling me I needed to see Ro. I thought maybe, I could finally admit what was going on. But I was still scared. And now Ro's hurt, and you're hurt, and it's all my fault."

Her words were muffled by her sobs as she shook her head.

"Hey, no, it's okay. Ro's fine," Holloway reassured her. "So's Faise."

I nodded. "I am. And you're gonna be too."

"I'm scared to go back home."

I reached for her hand, and she tentatively took it. "You can stay with Ro for now."

"But my life in New York, my job, the lease—"

"You can find another job. And apartment leases can be broken."

"Yeah, what Faise said."

The sudden interruption of Ronin's voice had fresh tears welling up in my eyes.

A nurse wheeled him into the room. Ronin was pale, with dark circles under his eyes, and a large bandage on his chest.

When his eyes met mine, I knew right then that tomorrow couldn't wait.

"I'm so sorry about all this," Ciara whispered. "I'm so embarrassed."

"Nothing to be embarrassed about. We've all dated dickheads," I remarked, trying to ease the tension.

"You have," Ronin quipped from the other side of my bed. "Not me."

I gave him my favorite finger, and he blew me a kiss. We were back to status quo.

Ciara shook her head and looked at me and then Ronin. "You guys never change."

"I don't think that's entirely true," I replied as I stared into Ronin's unforgettable blues.

The intense look he gave me told me that maybe, just maybe, he was thinking the same.

A lot had changed. For the better or worse, I still didn't know yet. But I knew I had to find out.

"Everything is so fucked up," she sighed.

She slowly peeled off her suit jacket to reveal a roadmap of bruises up and down both arms.

"Jesus Christ!" Ronin hissed. "Ci—"

"It's been happening a while now," she whispered as she put her jacket back on. "That's why I came down here. I didn't want to tell you over the phone. Then I got scared."

"Anything you need, anything, I'm here."

"That goes for me too," I added.

"I haven't told Mom," she confessed. "I couldn't. I was so ashamed. That's part of the reason I stopped calling. I just knew that as soon as you heard my voice, you'd know."

"Hey, it's all right," Ronin whispered as he reached across the bed for her hand. "You know you can always come to me. And thank fuck you did."

Van and Brodie, accompanied by Jesse, Averell, and Dawson, entered the room, concern all over their faces.

"How's everyone doing?" Van asked. "Do you need anything?"

Brodie's husband wasn't just our former manager. He was part of our family.

"Everything I need is right here," Ronin declared.

I couldn't have said it better myself.

CHAPTER 17

RONIN

put on a good face in front of my sister, but I didn't lie to myself.

Dallas was an abusive asshole and people like him didn't take no for an answer. His arrest tonight would probably only fuel his anger towards her. Not to mention, news of the incident was going to be plastered all over the tabloids sooner rather than later.

Jesse had assured me the label was doing their best to keep the incident low profile. But a cop, arrested for assault on his girlfriend and her famous brother, and bandmate, was hard to keep silent. Someone would inevitably talk. And I had a bad feeling it might be Dallas himself. Jesse agreed and, in conjunction with our PR lead, Zoe, issued a statement on my behalf.

Right now, all I cared about was Ciara's security and that of our band family. We needed to get my sister's things from the hotel and have her speak to a therapist. Then, I was going to bury Dallas Bledsoe in so many lawsuits, *he'd* be the one fleeing New York.

I watched my best friend as he talked to my sister. Faise's

gentle manner with her had my heart squeezing tight in my chest.

Tears threatened again as I realized how lucky I was to have him in my life. For his calm way with Ci, for sticking up for her and for me, for coming after me, for protecting me. For always being there when I needed him.

"My phone is blowing up," Ciara admitted as she passed it to me.

"We'll get you a new number," Jesse replied. "We'll take care of it now."

"Can I be discharged?" I asked. "I want to go home."

"What about our statements for the police?" Faise asked.

Lennie stepped forward. "I'll have a word. They can meet us at your house."

While Van and Jesse arranged for our discharge, Len and the security team, including Regan, had us recall the events of the night, taking detailed notes.

By the time we got out of the hospital and made it back to my house, I was wiped. And the wound on my chest was itching. Thirteen stitches was gonna take a bit of time to heal. The doctors warned me it might scar, and referred me to a plastic surgeon, but I didn't care. I was okay, and honestly, a scar was the least of my worries.

Sore, exhausted, and in dire need of peace and quiet, I just wanted my bed.

Unfortunately, sleep would have to wait. An unmarked black sedan was waiting just outside the gates to my place.

"It's the detective assigned to your case," Regan announced.

Once we drove past the gates and parked, Lennie and Petyr helped us inside and Regan met with the driver of the car.

A blonde woman in a black pantsuit walked up to us and held out her hand. "Sergeant Ailey Collins, I work in the major crimes division."

"Ronin Stadler, this is my sister Ciara, and my band mate Faisel Reed."

After the initial introductions, we walked inside and gathered in the living room.

"So, tell me what happened tonight," Ailey asked. "Ciara, why don't you go first?"

Ciara held a shaky hand to her head. "Dallas left to go to the bathroom and Faise and I were talking for a while. Then my boyfriend texted me and told me to meet him outside. I told Faise I had to make a call and left the venue."

"Why outside?"

"Dallas said he was smoking."

"The hospital took photos of your injuries. Am I correct in assuming that all the bruises on your body are from him?"

Ciara nodded.

"How long has the abuse gone on?" Ailey asked softly.

"Two months," Ciara admitted. "At first it was things he would say. Telling me I'd forget stuff and making me question my memory."

"Gaslighting."

Ciara sighed. "Yes. Then, he'd grab me and shake me when he'd get angry. Once, he slapped my face. Most of the time he left marks where no one could see."

The longer Ciara spoke, the worse my trembling. Hearing it all over again made me angry and afraid for her.

"And what happened when you left the venue to find him?"

"Dallas was standing right outside and he… he grabbed me and started yelling. He accused me of flirting with Faise. He wanted to leave but I insisted on going back in to say goodbye to Ronin. That's when he put his hand around my throat and—"

Ciara paused, shaking her head.

"Take your time," Ailey encouraged.

"And then," Ciara started with a shaky breath. "Dallas

dragged me into the alley around the corner of the building. I n-nearly tripped because the ground was littered with bottles. Then he hit me so hard I fell down, we struggled, and next t-thing I knew, he had one h-hand around my neck again and a broken bottle in the other. Dallas dragged me up to my feet. He's s-so strong that I couldn't fight him off. Suddenly, Ronin was there, and Faise. They tried to get Dallas to calm down but he wouldn't let go of me. I heard footsteps, someone else was coming near us. That's when Dallas attacked Ronin and Faise intervened."

Ailey nodded and passed her tablet to Ciara. "Thank you. I know that wasn't easy. If you could please e-sign your statement and add your contact details."

Regan's phone rang and she answered it in clipped tones. "Petyr, what do you have? … yes… good, send me the link."

She nodded at Ailey. "The venue has CCTV footage of the street. It corroborates Ciara's statement about Dallas dragging her away. And it shows Ronin walking in the same direction shortly thereafter, Faise doing the same, and lastly, our security team. No footage on the actual assault though. It doesn't cover the alley."

"This guy is supposed to serve and protect, not assault," I muttered.

"Oh God, I just remembered that he brought his gun with him, he left it in the room safe," Ciara admitted, her face pale. "What am I going to do? What if he comes after me again? I can't go back to New York. He's got friends there, and most of them are in law enforcement."

"Hey," I reached over and pulled her in tight. "You don't have to do anything right now. And there's no way you're going back there by yourself. We'll figure something out."

"Can we continue this tomorrow?" Ciara asked. "I need to lie down."

"Of course, I have enough for now," Ailey replied. "I'll get working on the footage and go from there."

"I have my purse and all my ID with me, but my clothes and other things are at the hotel."

"We'll have a police escort so you can collect your items."

"And bodyguards. Two of my security," I added.

"Sounds like a plan." Ailey nodded and pulled out a business card, offering it to Ciara. "Here's my contact details if you need to reach me."

"Thank you," Ciara whispered.

Then Ailey glanced at Regan. "Walk me out?"

Regan headed out with the detective.

"I'm going to head up," Ciara said.

"Your usual room?" I asked her and she nodded, wiping her eyes.

"I can stay in one of the spares on this floor," Faise offered.

"No," I replied, my face flushed. "Can you… I mean—" Fuck, I was never this awkward with him before. But I knew one thing for sure. I didn't want to be alone. "Stay with me."

We shared beds all the time—first in our van, then crappy motels, and now five-star hotels and tour bunks. It was no big deal. Only, it felt like it now.

"All right."

Faise smiled at me, and my body calmed. I couldn't put into words how grateful I was that he was here.

I'd had my share of hookups spend the night, but I never *needed* them to stay. Not like I needed him.

That realization hit me with greater force than all the other shocks tonight.

CHAPTER 18
FAISE

The rest of that night was a blur. I didn't remember walking upstairs, I didn't remember anything. Just the sound of Ronin walking beside me and the heavy fall of our footsteps.

And it wasn't light streaming through the windows that woke me up the next day.

It was Ronin's body heat. And the ache in my jaw.

Usually I was the little spoon, but with his stitches, it was my turn to hold him. My face was smashed against his bare back, and my cock was taking way too much interest in our early morning cuddle. His breathing was soft and even, and with my arm wrapped around his waist, I didn't want to be anywhere else.

Of course, my mind started on that dangerous path again, imagining myself waking up next to him like this every day. Being his lover, his partner, living together.

Fuck.

"Morning," he muttered.

He pulled away from me at first and rolled over, until we were eye to eye.

Ronin smiled, leaned over, and kissed me.

On the mouth.

What the everloving fuck? Was I still dreaming?

Then he winked at me, a wicked grin on his face.

"What's up?" he asked, as if nothing had happened.

I couldn't move. Ronin had kissed me. On the lips. Like we did this every day.

"Fuck, these stitches are itchy," he grumbled as he slid to his back. He turned his head and gave me a slow perusal. "How's your face feeling? Did you sleep?"

I opened my mouth, but the words were stuck in my head.

"Faise, you okay?"

No, no I was not fucking okay.

"Uh, yeah. I mean, sure. My jaw aches a bit but I passed out right away. You?"

"Same. All the stress from last night. Holy shit, I can't believe we were attacked like that. It doesn't seem real."

Ronin stretched and sat up, the sheet falling down around his waist. Then he chucked the sheet aside, and stood up, his naked ass right there in front of me. When he turned around, I was greeted by his morning wood.

My own hardened in response. Hell, just that one single touch of our lips meeting had my body lighting up like most incredible fireworks. I glanced up at him, confused, shocked, and fucking horny. Until I zeroed in on the bandage on his chest.

"Last night," I croaked, a sudden lump in my throat making it difficult to speak. "If it had been worse. If anything had happened to you, I don't... I don't think I can—"

I held my face in my hands, too choked up to breathe, everything hitting me all at once.

The bed depressed but I didn't look up. My eyes were a blurry mess, the tears coming out of nowhere, sliding down my face. Ronin gently took my hands and placed them over his pecs. I reached higher, my fingers clutching his shoulders, so solid, warm, and real.

He was right here with me. I couldn't ever lose him.

"I'm okay," he reassured me. "You can see I'm fine. It's over."

He pulled me into his arms and wrapped me up tight.

"But your wound, doesn't it hurt?" I protested and made to move away, but Ronin wouldn't let go.

"It's fine. I've got my medicine right here," he replied as he squeezed me tighter.

I snorted at his corny joke.

Like always, I notched my face under his bearded chin and breathed him in. Neither of us had showered last night, so we smelled like stale sweat and booze. But it didn't matter. He clutched me so tightly I couldn't take in air. Didn't need to. If I didn't have him, I'd have no reason for oxygen.

"Ro," I whispered against the heated skin of his neck. "I've got to tell you—"

The knock on his bedroom door had us jolting. He slowly pulled away from me and I shivered at the loss.

"Don't move," he demanded and reached for his jeans.

He slipped them on and padded over to the door while I lay back down, dizzy, my heart pounding hard, my vision spinning.

My lips tingled, and I rang my fingertips over them, still in awe. Had that really happened? Had Ronin kissed me? Was it just him being more affectionate than usual or...

"Faise?"

I didn't even hear Ronin's return to bed.

"Yeah?"

"The police are back. They got Ciara's stuff from the hotel, but they still have questions for her."

"Of course. I'll get dressed and out of your way."

"No, that's not what I meant." He shook his head, the dark waves of his hair falling around his face. "Please stay. She needs you. I need you."

I nodded, pulling the sheet around me. "I'll just take a quick shower and meet you downstairs."

Ronin smiled and headed for the bathroom. Maybe he wanted to use it first? There were plenty of bathrooms in the house, I could just use another.

I slid out of bed, my head still reeling, and dropped the sheet.

Then I heard the shower running. Instead of waiting for my turn, I reached for my pants.

"Where do you think you're going?" Ronin asked me.

I turned to find him still in his jeans.

"I'm gonna go wash up downstairs."

Ronin shook his head and offered his hand. I was so fucking confused.

"You want me to go first?"

He chuckled and bit his lower lip. "No, boo."

"Then I don't understand."

"Do you trust me?"

I stared at him like I'd never seen him before. "What kind of a question is that? Of course, I trust you!"

"Then take my hand."

I watched the expression in his eyes change from amused to smoldering hot and I swallowed hard. There was no way for me to mistake that look. I'd seen him give it to plenty of men over the years.

But now? Aimed at me? Fucking hell, those molten blues had me unable to move an inch. I didn't know whether to move towards him or run away.

I worried for a second that I might be hallucinating. Until Ronin stepped towards me and took my hand. Mine was shaking, and so was his. This was no high. It was the most real thing I'd ever felt in my life, and it was fucking amazing.

He said nothing, tugging me forward. I let my pants fall to the floor and followed my best friend into the bathroom. He opened the shower door and ushered me inside, the hot water sluicing over my skin. I watched from the other side of the glass as Ronin slowly peeled off his jeans. It was my own private strip show from my favorite dancer. He looked up and gave me a wicked grin as he kicked the jeans aside and reached for the door.

Suddenly, reality intruded my sexy thoughts.

"Your bandage! Don't get it wet."

"It's waterproof," he assured me as he stepped up close.

I looked up at him, unsure of what else to say.

Ronin cupped my face in his massive palms, rubbing his callused thumbs over my lips. I couldn't help the needy moan that erupted from my throat. My cock jerked hard against my stomach, my balls aching and full. He pulled me in closer, our wet skin making contact head to toe, his hard dick sliding against mine.

It almost distracted me from the fact that my best friend was looking at me the way I'd been longing for.

So long. Years.

The trembling started again, my arms and legs shaking like I was just finishing up a show.

"Why are you suddenly looking at me like this?" I asked him. There was no more time to be evasive. "Why now? Is it just a reaction to what happened last night?"

Ronin leaned his forehead against mine, closing his eyes and taking a deep breath. He blinked and opened his eyes again. There was no denying the truth in those bottomless blues.

"I've been looking at you like this for a while. I was just too scared to show you. To accept what it meant. First Dean, and then yesterday with Averell, it just pushed me over the edge. I can't take it anymore. I don't want you to be with them," Ronin growled, the possessive sound making goosebumps pop out all over my skin. "You belong with me."

"You're jealous?"

"Fuck, yes," he bit out.

"You're not the only one," I whispered my confession. "You have no idea how long I've been wanting you. And wanting to tell you. Why do you think I was dating Dean in the first place? I was trying to stop thinking about *you*."

"Don't mention his name ever again," Ronin hissed, and I smiled at his reaction.

"Done."

Then he leaned down and we shared one breath, our lips barely brushing. I wanted his kiss more than anything, but I was scared as hell about how he would react afterwards. If Ronin walked away from me… I didn't want to think about it.

"But you have to be sure, Ro. This isn't something we can take back," I admitted, reaching up and grabbing hold of his forearms. His pulse beat steady and strong under my fingertips.

"I am," he nodded, his eyes darkening. "Are you?"

The fear lingered but I shoved it aside.

I finally had the courage to speak the words that echoed in my heart for years.

"You don't need to ask. There's only ever been you."

Ronin reached down and I reached up, and twenty years of our life together flashed before my eyes like a movie reel. The highs, the lows, and every damn moment in between. No matter what, it all led back to him.

But everything I'd imagined about kissing my best friend was blown to pieces when it finally happened. I slid my tongue between his lips, tasting him for the first time. It was heady, decadent, and I needed more. Just like our music, the kiss was passionate, explosive—a collision of sound, taste, and touch that could only be experienced, not explained.

He groaned, and I followed, nipping his lips, licking to soothe the sting, then sucking on his tongue. Fuck, I was starved for him.

Ronin pushed me up against the shower wall, and I pushed back, my lips as aggressive as his. Pulling on my hair, he angled my head and I kissed him deeply, fucking his mouth the way I wanted to fuck him. I clawed at his shoulders, then up higher, gripping his neck, holding on tight.

"What the fuck?" Ronin moaned against my mouth. "Jesus, boo, your lips are dangerous."

"Just wait until I wrap them around your cock."

He grunted and kissed me again, and I reached for his dick, feeling the slick, heavy weight of it in my hand, tugging fast and hard. Then I took both our cocks in hand, jerking frantically, too overwhelmed and excited to slow down and make it last. Every touch was more desperate than the last.

"Don't have time," I panted as my hand worked frantically, my blood racing hotter, faster. "You... Ro... fuck."

I was so far gone, I wasn't making sense. My brain was shutting down as pleasure took over.

"Make me come," Ronin whimpered. "Yes. Just like that."

I stroked harder and faster as Ronin's body tensed. He was so fucking gorgeous like this. With me.

"Next time, I'm gonna suck this monster dick down my throat until you scream my name."

"Faise, oh God," Ronin moaned and punched his hips forward, fucking my fist.

"That's it, baby, let go. Come all over me. Cover me in your cum."

"Fuck!" Ronin roared as his body jerked hard, hot cum lashing my hand.

I followed, coming all over him in a hot rush, so fast, so hard, I couldn't breathe. I was lightheaded, dizzy with desire.

"Goddamn it," I panted. "I haven't come that fast since I was eighteen."

"You and me both."

Ronin turned me away from the water, placed his hand over mine, rubbing our combined cum on my skin, over my abs and up my chest. Then he held his fingers up to my mouth and I slid my tongue around them, sucking on them, letting out a filthy groan as I tasted the two of us. Together.

I licked his fingers languidly, and he stared at me so intently that the trembling in my body continued.

As the water in the shower cooled, and our bodies along with it, the adrenaline rush of our first mutual orgasm gave way to a startling new reality.

One that I could never, ever walk back from.

CHAPTER 19

RONIN

t wasn't an exaggeration to say that kissing Faise was the best thing that had happened to me in my adult life. And I'd experienced a lot of highs over the past twenty years.

Waking up wrapped in his arms this morning, and after everything that had happened last night, I realized I was going to take that leap. Step out on stage. Put myself out there. Risk our friendship for something more.

When I rolled over, I did what I'd been wanting to do for a while now. I kissed him. I'd shocked him for sure. And myself. But it felt natural, another step in our relationship. Did I know what I was doing? Fuck no. Did it feel good? Did I want more? Yes, and yes.

So, I dragged him into the shower, my heart beating out of control, my legs about to give out under me. Everything was about to change.

And when we kissed—a fulsome one this time—my world rocked louder than any show I'd ever performed.

Like discovering sex for the very first time, I was addicted to Faise's taste. The urgent way he brought us to orgasm was something else. It unleashed a hunger, an intensity that I'd never felt with anyone else.

I came so hard, so fast, I should've been embarrassed. But I wasn't. I was still reeling from the fact that it had happened at all. And my vivid fantasies had nothing on the real deal.

But as soon the orgasm was done, my brain kicked online, and I remembered why he was here in the first place. And who was waiting downstairs.

I kissed Faise gently, cupping his face in my palms. Unlike me, he had hardly any facial hair. On his face or his body. He was miles of smooth, golden skin, long and lithe, and sexy as fuck. My dick hardened again, wanting more, but play time would have to wait.

I noticed the large bruise on his face, and relived the moment when Dallas hit him. I rubbed my thumb gently over his tender cheekbone, wishing I could erase the mark. Erase any pain Faise ever had.

"Sorry to ruin the moment," I whispered. "But we gotta head downstairs. Ciara."

Faise nodded, "I know. That's why I said we had no time."

"I'm scared for her, Faise. What if he comes after her again?"

Faise stepped away from me, turned the water off, and opened the door to grab towels. I shivered. From the cold or from my worries, I didn't know.

"She's staying with us for now. We've got security, and she'll be fine."

"Yeah, but her job and stuff."

Faise quickly dried himself off and then took a second towel, wiping my body, head to toe, taking care not to disrupt my bandage. And I, needy bastard that I was (who knew?), let him. It was nice to be taken care of. When he kneeled and dried off my feet, I looked down at him. Imagining him taking care of me in other, filthier, ways. My cock was raring to go again but he'd have to wait.

When Faise finished drying me off, he stood up and took

my hand. Funny how a simple touch from my best friend could set my blood racing.

"No doubt it's going to be a shit time for a while," he replied. "But she's strong. Just like you. She'll be okay."

I nodded, still unsure but not wanting to voice the doubts in my head.

All of them.

As I looked at Faise, I wondered, worried, if I was gonna fuck this up. I didn't know anything about being a boyfriend? Was that what we were now? Lovers? Partners? None of those words seemed big enough to fit how I felt about Faise. It was that, but more, deeper than anything else. He was my world. I don't know why I didn't see it sooner. Or maybe I just took for granted he'd always be there.

We stepped out of the bathroom and I gave in to temptation and pulled him back into my arms, taking his lips in a deep kiss as we stumbled into the bedroom.

Between languid kisses, we managed to get dressed. Faise borrowed a pair of my sweats and a t-shirt. The clothes were enormous on him, but he looked cute as fuck. Of course, he ruffled when I told him so.

"Cute? Don't even," he scoffed.

"You are. Adorable," I teased, kissing his head as we headed down the stairs.

"That's worse!" he grumbled but the smile on his face told me he didn't mind at all.

I playfully slapped his ass—as I had a habit of doing with my boo—and he turned to glare at me.

"Baby, don't start that now."

Baby? Fuck. Had he really called me that? I was light-headed again, tripping on the stairs, nearly falling down.

"Careful, love," Faise whispered. "We don't want a return visit to the hospital."

Love? Baby? The words filled me with a high, a warmth

that spread throughout my entire body. If anyone else called me that, I'd gag. To me, endearments weren't sexy at all.

Until they were. But only with him.

I was distracted, but in the best way.

Until we finally made it downstairs and I spotted my sister, Regan, Lennie, and Ailey waiting for us in the living room. Along with our PR rep, Zoe, and our lawyer, Elias Kain. Ever since we split with Bandit, me and the guys hired our own lawyer, on retainer, to ensure that we had objective advice. No more label lawyers.

Walking over to my sister, I sat down beside her and gave her a gentle hug. "How're you doing this morning?"

"Okay. The sedative helped me sleep but I'm still exhausted. And scared."

Her face was pale but the red marks on her neck were turning purple. Just like that, I was so angry I was ready to scream. Faise sat down beside me and squeezed my thigh, his reassuring touch the only thing keeping me from spiraling.

"We'll keep this as short as possible. Dallas has been charged with assault, but his lawyer has arrived and is pushing for bail. In addition to that charge, I'd strongly suggest you file a restraining order. That way, if he tries to approach you again, he'll be arrested. Also, you need to be prepared for his accusation," Ailey paused and leaned forward. "He's claiming that the three of you attacked *him* in that alleyway. Given your injuries and the eyewitnesses from your security team, I doubt his claim will go anywhere. But the video footage shows the street, not the alley. There's no audio either, and the actual assault was not caught on tape. Given what Ciara has told us about his abusive behavior, I'm not surprised he's denying everything and pointing the finger at anyone but himself."

Elias interrupted, "Given the evidence I've seen so far, I doubt anything will come of his claim or that charges will be laid against you. Our best chance of hitting him back will be civil court. I'm also ready for him to counter-sue if he continues with these claims that you attacked him. He's going to use your rockstar reputation against you, claim you were high or just entitled and lashed out at him."

"The news of the assault has already hit the major outlets and social media," Zoe interjected. "An anonymous account claims to have video from the incident. Maybe someone at the party? Or a bystander walking by?"

"I'm going to follow up on that with you," Ailey added.

"And that's not all," Zoe sighed. "There are rumors that Faise relapsed and attacked Ciara and Dallas."

"What?" I launched off the couch. "This is bullshit! This asshole abuses my sister, drags her into that alley, cuts me, hits Faise, and he's the one who's the victim? Fuck this! He's not getting away with it!"

My head was about to explode.

"I've already issued an official statement denying Dallas' claims and confirming our side of the story," Zoe replied.

"It's not our side, Zoe. It's the truth," I snapped. "It's the fucking truth!"

"Ro."

Faise called out to me and I stopped talking. He motioned to my sister. When I looked down, she was shaking. Hard.

I sat back down and took her hand. "Sorry, Ci. I'm sorry."

Shit, my temper was probably triggering her. I was acting like such an idiot. I didn't know what to say to her or how to deal with this.

"Hardwick's team is working to track the stories. We're on top of it," Zoe continued.

"Stories? These are lies," I countered. "Don't give me the public relations speak. What's really being said about us? Do I even want to know?"

"Most of your fans are rallying behind you."

"Most?"

Ailey stood up. "Sorry, but I need to get back to the

precinct. Between the footage, eyewitnesses, and the photographic evidence of your injuries, I doubt Dallas's claim will go anywhere. But, for now, keep a low profile and file that TRO. And if you have any other questions, reach out to me. I'll keep Elias posted on any updates as we move forward."

I nodded, unsure of what else I could say. I was still too angry.

Lennie escorted her out of the room, and I looked to Zoe.

"How bad is it? And don't bullshit."

Zoe shook her head. "Like I said, your fans are behind you, but—"

"Maybe I should head back home," Faise announced suddenly.

"What? No!"

"You heard what Zoe said, Ro. The media think I relapsed and attacked you guys."

"No, I said there was a rumor circulating—" Zoe started.

"Whatever," Faise bit out. "We know how this works. Wouldn't it be better if I hide out for a while until the news dies down? Keep my distance from them?"

I didn't want that at all. I didn't want any distance between us. Ever.

Zoe shook her head. "What's best for you and Ronin and Ciara is a united front. If anything, I'd prefer you stay here for a while. That way, if the paps do get a shot of you, they'll see that nothing has changed between you and Ronin. Still supportive. Still besties."

More than that. I hoped.

I looked at Faise, but he refused to make eye contact. My stomach flipped over and not in a good way. Then I wondered if what had happened upstairs was the start of something incredible or the end of it.

My phone buzzed. It was a group text from Brodie and Holls.

> Brodie: Are you guys okay? We're coming over.

> Holloway: Daws and I are on our way. How about we jam? A bit of distraction might be welcome.

I tapped out a quick reply.

> Ronin: Sounds like a plan. The police just left. Talk when you get here.

Then I glanced over at Zoe. "Holls and Brodie are heading over."

Faise's phone rang, and he walked out of the room to answer it. I heard him say "Av" and it made that insecure part of me flare to life again. Would Faise change his mind? What if everything that had happened this morning was all we had?

Stop. This is Faise. He wouldn't do that.

"What about my sister?" I asked Zoe, then turned to Ciara. "Ci? Do you have any active accounts Zoe should know about?"

It was the first time Ciara smiled since she arrived. "I work in social media, Ro, of course I have accounts. I've shut down my personal one. I texted my boss this morning and requested an emergency leave. Given what happened and all the negative publicity, I'm confident they're going to fire me."

"I'm sorry."

"It's okay. I'd need to quit anyway. You were right. After what happened, I can't go back to New York. To be honest, I wanted the big city dream, but the reality wasn't good. Maybe if I hadn't been so damn lonely when I arrived, I wouldn't have let Dallas treat me this way. I don't know. And now your name's being dragged through the press. It's all my fault. All of this."

"Hey, no," I reassured her. "None of this is your fault. He's the asshole."

"I need a job, though. Or something. I just can't sit around for the foreseeable future doing nothing."

"As it happens, I'm looking for someone to work behind the scenes," Zoe offered. "Copywriting. For other bands in our roster. What do you think?"

Ciara bit her lip. "Remote?"

Zoe nodded. "Freelance."

"Thanks. Can I think about it?"

"Of course."

Faise ambled back into the living room, finally meeting my gaze.

"Everything okay?" I asked him.

"Yeah. Averell just wanted to check in and see how we were doing."

Yeah, right. He wanted to check in on Faise. I wanted to say something snarky but I held back.

"I also reached out to my therapist," Faise continued. "She has time to see us this week. Ciara first, then you and me, individually."

"I think that's a great idea." I reached for my sister with one hand, and Faise with the other. "The sooner, the better."

CHAPTER 20
FAISE

always knew my addiction would come back to bite me on the ass.

Not the good kind.

Just the thought of those rumors that I'd gone off the rails and hurt my best friend and his sister made my stomach heave. Bad enough they'd been assaulted, but now this? Jesus Christ.

Celebrity life had its upsides, but this part, having your worst moments splashed across entertainment news, this was a shitload to deal with. People could say anything they wanted about you, throw accusations, and insults out like it was nothing.

As much as I avoided socials, I was just like everyone else. I wanted to know what was happening in the world. And I wanted to be a part of it.

But now? Now I wanted to hide, and I wasn't sure when, or if, I ever wanted to be back out there again.

Of course, Averell had to call. I wasn't in the mood to talk to anyone, him least of all.

I just wanted to forget last night ever happened, so I told Averell I was fine and that was that. My tone was abrupt, and he didn't push. Which I appreciated. Hooking up with him would've been a mistake anyway. A last-ditch attempt to get over Ronin. Which was ridiculous. I was never getting over him.

And now I didn't need to. Ro wouldn't change his mind about us after that kiss, would he? Okay, it was more than one kiss.

Just thinking about the two of us in his shower had my blood running so hot I swore I had a fever. I wasn't ill, but I was feeling out of sorts.

My entire world had shifted, and I didn't know where to find my footing.

I wasn't all hearts and flowers and my life is suddenly perfect this morning. The doubts that swirled in my mind were never far from the surface, always teasing me that I wasn't good enough. Not even for my best friend. And of course, when the doubts surfaced, so too did my desire to get high.

Addiction cravings came in waves and starts, and the wave was cresting high today.

Reaching out to my therapist was necessary. For Ciara, for Ronin, and for me. I had a sore face from last night, but I hardly felt the pain at all. It was the shock of seeing my best friend and his sister being attacked that still reverberating through my body.

If I'd lost Ronin…

I couldn't imagine that. Or, if I did, it wasn't good. And it made me question how I would cope. My therapist had suggested to me that being so close to Ronin, for so long, could be a path to co-dependency. But I never saw me and him that way. What was wrong about sharing so much? I'd never questioned if our bond was healthy or not. For the most part, we were thriving. Always me and Ro.

But what if this change wasn't? What if being lovers brought us down?

I loved Ronin, no question, no doubt. Just like the air I breathed every single day, he was necessary to me.

But what kind of love did he need? He'd always been happy being friends, nothing more. Was he really all in with being my lover now or was he just reacting to the shock of last night? He said he was jealous, but maybe that was just a reaction to me pulling away lately. To the idea of having to share his best friend with anyone else.

So many questions floated around in my mind, buzzing around like white noise.

I was tempted to reach for my emergency anxiety meds, but I didn't want to start down that road. A road that led nowhere good. I only had a few pills, but still. Numbing myself wouldn't help matters. I knew myself. I'd just want more. To not worry, to not feel at all.

I couldn't have that now. I needed to feel everything.

I so wanted to stay here with Ro but part of me was tempted to head home and isolate. To sit at my kit and drum my frustration and insecurities away. The one thing I always understood was music. And when I played, I never had to ask myself the tough questions.

I just… was.

Doing something, anything, to keep busy was always helpful to my state of mind.

Once Zoe and Elias left, I headed for the kitchen and started making breakfast. I wasn't a great cook by any means, but my mom made sure I learned the basics.

"After we eat, Len can take you home to grab more of your stuff," Ronin stated as he sat at one of the bar stools around the island, watching me.

I'd cooked in his kitchen so many times, and yet today, I was nervous like I never was. I felt Ronin's stare on me and not in the usual way.

Opening the cabinets, I reached for a frypan, but it nearly slipped out of my hand.

Then I knocked over my cup of coffee. And I burnt the toast.

"Fuck!" I exclaimed as I tried to focus, but couldn't.

"If you want to stay here, I mean—"

"You heard what Zoe said."

"Yeah, but I only want you to stay if you want to. You can take one of the guest rooms if that's what you prefer."

I nodded, avoiding Ro's eyes. I was raw, needy, and vulnerable. I wanted to believe that he could be mine, in all the ways I wanted, but he hadn't touched me since we'd left his bedroom and now he was suggesting I stay in another room? I was confused. He was always in my personal space and now he was giving me more of it? What the hell?

But I didn't have time to reply to his comment because Brodie and Holls had arrived.

They joined us in the kitchen and gave us each hugs. After we'd assured our friends that we were okay, the guys sat down around the island, while I continued to work on breakfast. Such as it was. Burnt toast and scrambled eggs. Ronin had a shit ton of prepared meals in the freezer, but I hated microwaving anything, eggs most of all.

I stood at the stove, stirring and stirring, my mind whirling, until I realized that the toast wasn't the only thing burning.

"Shit!"

"You okay there, Faise?" Brodie asked.

"Fine, I'm fine."

I dumped the eggs into the garbage and started over.

"I can't believe that asshole is claiming you guys attacked him. What the actual hell?" Holls commented. "You better sue that motherfucker."

"Elias is already working on it."

"Can we talk about something else?" I asked. "Please. Anything."

"How about we work on some new songs today. Rock out the stress. Ro?"

"Yeah, I'm all for that," he replied as he sipped on his coffee. "Let's check out our new studio. Jesse told me the setup is state of the art."

"Sure, or we can jam at my place," Brodie offered. "Wherever you feel most comfortable."

"I'd like to see the studio," I added. "Plug and play and forget about the last twenty-four hours."

Ronin's cup fell out of his hand, and it crashed onto the counter, coffee spilling everywhere.

"I mean, I want to forget about last night," I corrected as I handed him paper towels to clean up. I finally met his gaze, while my heart pounded out of control. "Not this morning."

"What happened this morning?" Brodie asked, glancing between the two of us with sharp eyes.

"Nothing," Ro and I answered at the same time.

I turned back to my cooking with shaky hands. I grabbed more eggs, cracked them into the bowl, and whisked, adding cheese, grated onion, salt, and cumin. Then I poured the whole thing in the heated pan and carefully, this time, stirred until it was set.

I plated up the food and we all dug in.

"Are you sure about that?" Brodie suggested as he stuffed in a mouthful of eggs. "You two are acting weird."

"What?" Ronin's voice cracked and I bit back a laugh. "No, we're not."

"We've been here ten minutes already, and you've yet to touch Faise," Holls added. "Something is off."

"Everything's fine. Normal. Like it always is," Ronin assured them.

It was anything but.

Instead of sitting beside the guys, I stood facing them and scarfed down my breakfast. A quiet tension filled the room, as everyone ate. Well, Ro and I ate. Brodie and Holls shoved in bites of food in between staring at us. Then Brodie took his fork and gently poked Ronin in the arm.

"Dee, what the fuck!"

"Just checking to make sure it's really you and not some cyborg version of my friend."

"Well don't!"

I glanced at Ronin and sighed. "Tell them."

Ronin's mouth fell open, but no words came out. I was shaking so hard, I dropped my fork and it tumbled unto the floor.

"God, I need more coffee for this conversation." I turned around and bent over to pick up the utensil.

"Holy shit!"

I whirled around at the sound of Brodie's voice.

"What?"

Ronin's face was flushed, but he was staring at his plate.

"Ronin was eyeing up your ass like *it* was breakfast. Does this mean you two finally—" Brodie paused and mimed jerking off.

Holls sat there with his fork halfway to his mouth, eyes wide, waiting for our answer.

Instead of replying, I walked around the island. My legs were wobbly, my hands cold, but my heart? It was so fucking full when I looked at Ronin. He turned without pause, opening his arms to me.

Fuck everything else going in my head. The worries, the angst, the doubt. Nothing was right without Ronin.

I slid into Ronin's arms and kissed him.

"Does that answer your question?" Ronin whispered when we came up for air.

Mine? Yes.

Our band brothers? Hell no.

CHAPTER 21

RONIN

knew the way Faise was pacing in my kitchen that he was all up in his head. I knew my boo. He was worried that I was going to change my mind. That everything that had happened this morning was a mistake, but it was far from that.

Our timing on stage was always spot on, but here, now, we were out of sync like we never were. Nervous, restless, struggling to find our groove in this brand new world we'd woken up to. A world where he and I were lovers, not just best friends.

And now I just wanted one damn moment alone with him.

When we finally stopped kissing, I turned to look at Holls and Brodie. My band brothers were staring at us like they'd never seen us before. Even though they joked about me and Faise being a couple all the time, ever since we started playing together, I don't think they ever thought that it would happen. It was going to take all of us time to get used to this reality.

Still, I didn't want to go back. I couldn't.

Why had it taken me so long to realize what all the

touches, hugs, and cuddles, meant? It was like I'd been wearing foggy glasses for years. When they finally cleared, all I could see was this beautiful man standing right in front of me.

"I can't believe it," Brodie kept repeating.

"You bugged us about it often enough, why can't you believe it?" I asked.

"You finally managed to grow some balls and go for it."

I rolled my eyes. "Speaking of which, why don't you guys head off to the studio and me and Faise will meet you there? Later. Much, much later."

"I think I'd rather head to the studio first. We need our normal routine right now more than ever," Faise added, slipping out of my arms.

I didn't like that one bit. His leaving or his answer.

"Ooh, burn," Holls quipped.

I gave Holloway my best finger, then stared at Faise. What the hell?

"It's been a lot in twenty-four hours, yeah?" Faise nodded and took my hand in his, giving me a reassuring squeeze. "Let's go have some normal. Jam, blow off steam, then we can come back here just the two of us."

Was he having second thoughts? I didn't like feeling this uncertainty between us. I always knew what he was thinking and vice versa. Didn't he want to be alone with me in the same desperate way that I wanted to be alone with him?

"If we're going to do this, Ronin, we're going to take our time," Faise continued. "I'm not going to fuck this up. You mean too much to let that happen."

He was right. I'd been dealing with these feelings for a long time, I just hadn't been ready yet to face them. With other guys I could just fuck and forget. Walk away. But Faise? That wasn't happening. That meant I had to stop thinking with just my cock. Faise needed to know that I was all in with him.

"Awe, did you hear that Holls? They're in love," Brodie teased.

"Like I said," I bit out, turning to Brodie. "We'll meet you over there."

Brodie and Holls smiled and stood up, reaching over to give us a hug.

"If you guys change your mind, we understand."

"We'll meet you at the studio in half an hour."

Music had always brought us together, and we needed that now more than ever.

We said our goodbyes and then I went in search of my sister. Before I went anywhere or did anything, I needed to make sure that she was okay.

I knocked on her bedroom door and when I didn't get a response, I opened it slowly. Ciara was fast asleep. It reminded me of when we were kids and I would babysit, checking up on her. Funny how that never goes away. No matter what, she'd always be my baby sister.

Satisfied that she was resting, I was finally ready to contact my mother to tell her exactly what had happened last night. She'd left me a voicemail this morning, when we were talking to Zoe and the police, and I'd texted her back, saying everyone was all right and that I would call soon. But I couldn't hold off on talking to her any longer.

I headed back out to find Faise still in the kitchen. "I'm going to get changed and call my mom. You know where everything is. Take anything you need. And feel free to wear my clothes."

"Sounds good," Faise replied. "I'll meet you by the front door in twenty."

After giving me another kiss, Faise headed upstairs. I picked up my cell phone and tapped my mom's number. She answered on the first ring.

"Ronin, what's going on? Are you and Ciara okay?"

"Like I said in my text, I'm fine, Ciara is fine too. Well, as fine as she can be right now. She's been keeping a secret from us. Her boyfriend Dallas has been verbally and physically abusive for months. They came to our launch party last night, and I knew something was off. He got pissed and lured her outside. Thankfully, I went after them, Faise too, but things just exploded after that. Ci's shaken up. And she doesn't want to return home to New York. Dallas is a police officer so you can imagine what's going through her mind."

"Oh my God, I knew something was wrong when she refused to call me back. The news said you were injured, what happened?"

"Dallas caught me with a broken beer bottle, and I had some stitches but I'm fine. He also punched Faise. Thankfully, Dallas was arrested and Ciara's filing a restraining order. All this to say, she's going to be staying with me for a while. She's right to be worried about going home. This guy is off the rails."

"I can't believe this," Mom paused, her voice muffled. "Thank God she came to you, Ronin. I'm getting on the next flight down to Nashville."

"I think that's a great idea. You can stay here with me and Ciara and Faise."

There was a significant pause on the other end of the line.

"Faise is staying at your place, too? That's good. He and Ciara get on well and she needs the support."

"She does. Text me the flight details and I'll have a driver pick you up."

"I don't think I need—"

"Yes," I insisted. "This Dallas guy might be out on bail tomorrow. He's volatile as fuck and we don't want to take any chances. I'll send a driver and one of my bodyguards."

"Okay. Can you tell Ciara to call me back? I need to speak to her."

My mom's voice finally broke, and I could hear her sobs.

"I will."

"I'll see you soon, honey."

"Bye, Mom."

I hung up, my hands shaking. I could use a drink, but it was too early in the day. Even for a rockstar like me.

Instead, I made myself another cup of coffee, decaf this time, and drank it slowly while texting Len about my mom's plan to head down here.

"Hey."

I turned to find Ciara standing behind me, tears on her face, her phone in her hand.

"I talked to Mom," I explained. "And told her everything that happened. She's flying out here as soon as possible."

"I know. She just texted me. She's been trying to call me all morning, but I just didn't have the heart to talk to her. I feel so ashamed. Like I let her down. Hell, I let you down."

"You haven't let anyone down. But maybe let her in, yeah? I know it's easier to keep these things bottled up inside but trust me, doing that will only do more harm than good. I saw that with Faise when he went through the worst of his drug addiction. If you don't talk about what's bothering you, it just festers. I'm always here. Faise is here, and Mom's going to be here too. Just tell us what you need, and we'll do whatever we have to. We're gonna get through this as a family."

Ciara nodded and wiped her face.

"Me and Faise are heading to the studio to jam for a bit. Do you want to come along, or do you prefer to stay here? Do you feel safe with one of my bodyguards?"

She nodded. "I'd rather stay here, thanks. I'm still shaky and I hardly slept last night. I just want to rest and then watch some TV, try to take my mind off things."

"Are you sure? I don't want you to be alone with no one to talk to."

"Brodie's assistant Bibi reached out to me. She's going to stop by in an hour and keep me company for a while."

I was enormously relieved at that. "Bibi's great. But don't

tell her any stories about me from growing up, yeah? Otherwise, she'll never let me hear the end of it."

"Don't worry, Ro, your childhood secrets are safe with me," she whispered. "I know I haven't said it often enough, but you are an amazing big brother. I don't know that I would have been able to get through Mom and Dad's divorce, or school, or any of it, without your support. I just want you to know how much I love you."

I reached for her, for a hug that we both needed.

"Have fun at the studio," she whispered. "Make a lot of noise. And don't worry. I'll be fine."

I nodded, and she headed for the living room.

Getting out of the house for a bit would be good. I headed upstairs to my bedroom, but when I got there, I paused. Faise was sitting on my bed, still dressed in my clothes, staring at his hands like he was waiting for an answer to a prayer. I didn't move a muscle. I just stared and took in the sight of him.

He looked so right in my bedroom, on my bed.

I'd never imagined that being in a relationship was something that I'd ever want. But looking at Faise now, it was like he was always meant to be here. And when he looked up at me, I had serious doubts that he and I were going to make it to the recording studio at all.

In his gaze there was heat and passion, but also trepidation, worry.

I knew that with my best friend I couldn't just say the words. The only way to reassure him that I was in this for good was by showing him, not just telling him. If I had paid attention, I would've realized sooner that my need to always be in his personal space meant more than friends. I always had a need to touch him. But it also worked the other way. I needed his touch as much as he needed mine.

"Move in with me," I blurted out.

Faise's mouth opened and closed.

He shook his head. "What?"

"You heard me. Move in with me. After we finish up with the rehearsal studio, we're going to go by your place, grab as much of your stuff as we can, and bring it back here. This is where you belong. With me."

"What about taking things slow?"

"Sex, yeah. If you want. But everything else, no. You can stay in another bedroom if you're more comfortable with that, but I want you here, in my home. I want to hear your laugh, I want to talk to you all day, every day. I want to wake up and see your beautiful face. You need to know that this is so far beyond fucking. I'm ready. And I'm not looking back."

Faise nodded, standing up. I walked over and pulled him into my arms. He smiled, wide, and when his dimples appeared, I was a goner.

"I want that too," Faise replied and kissed me languidly. "It already feels like this is where I'm meant to be. It already feels like home."

It certainly did.

CHAPTER 22

FAISE

After Ronin told me all about the call with his mom, and Bibi coming over to stay with Ciara, we headed out to the recording studio with Lennie.

Our phones blew up with messages from other friends, musicians and the like that had heard about what had happened, offering their support. It meant a lot.

It was overwhelming, but in a good way.

Just like when Ronin took hold of my hand as we left the house. And he hadn't let go of it since. Not when our bodyguards stared at us, and not during the entire car ride to the studio. I don't know if we were followed by the paps. I'm sure we were, but I didn't care to know. I was so overloaded at this point that pounding out a whole bunch of songs on my drum kit was just what I needed. No matter what, I could always count on sessions to help me figure shit out.

Jesse was already at the studio and greeted us at the front door. When he saw my hand in Ro's, he paused and gave us a quick grin. But his eyes told a different story. And for a moment, I felt guilty. I couldn't imagine how devastated I'd be if I'd told Ronin how I felt and he didn't feel the same. I totally got why Jesse's band had broken up. If I had to work day in and day out with the man I was in love with, but could never have, I wasn't sure I could make it either.

Jesse motioned for us to come inside. And wow, the new recording studio was even bigger and brighter than our old one. All our instruments were already in place, ready to go. Everything was organized in such a manner that it hardly needed fine tuning at all. And given that Jesse was a musician too, it made sense.

"I'm gonna do some work and sit with Ace. Let me know if you guys need anything."

We thanked him and headed into the recording booth.

Brodie and Holls were already seated, strumming their guitars to a new tune. When they spotted us, they smiled and waved us over. Ronin still hadn't let go of my hand and it made me giddy.

"Well, well, if it isn't the Wayward Lane love birds," Brodie quipped.

"Shut up and play," I grumbled, suddenly self-conscious.

Until Ronin brought my hand up to his lips and kissed it, then led me over to my drum kit. Only then, when I was seated, did he let go of me. Even still, when he wandered over to pick up his bass, the look he gave me told me that as soon as we were done here, we were heading home.

To his bedroom. Wait, ours now.

And that bed? We were gonna wreck it. Hard. So much for going slow…

"Given that you and Ronin are fucking now, I figured you'd be in a much better mood. Bored already?" Holloway teased.

I rolled my eyes. "Not all of us need to kiss and tell."

"Oh, but you do need to tell," Brodie chuckled. "We gave you all the deets when we got sexy with our men. Now it's your turn."

"There's nothing to tell. Yet," Ronin declared. "Except hot as fuck handjobs in the shower."

"Ro!" I bit out, feeling hot all over.

I was barely able to comprehend coming all over my best friend, never mind telling other people about it.

"Since when are you shy when it comes to bragging about sex?" Holls snickered and pointed at me. "This from the guy who fucked twins while we watched."

"Okay, all right," I conceded. "But that was different. That was hook ups. This is—"

I looked at Ronin for help. What we had together was more than fucking. And I didn't want to share that with anyone. Not even Brodie and Holls.

"Say no more," Brodie relented, and his expression turned serious. "I'm happy for you guys. Don't fuck this up."

"We won't."

I hoped. I was worried I would fuck up for sure. Ever since rehab, I felt the weight of other people's expectations, or rather, my interpretation of them. I didn't want to screw up my life again. My relationship with Ronin least of all.

"It's all well in hand," Ronin replied with a sinful smile.

I squirmed on my stool, willing myself not to get aroused right now in front of the guys.

"Sounds like," Holls replied with a cheeky grin and then shook his head. "Okay, no more joking around. Now that I've finally finished working on 'Running Start', let's see how it sounds."

I glanced at the sheet music and read it through to the end. We pulled on our headphones and started to play.

Holls did the intro with a guitar solo, Ronin and Brodie joining in, then finally, me. Unlike our rock anthems, which were heavy on drums, this one was slower, softer.

I let myself get carried away by the music, listening to Brodie and Holls sing about running away from their feelings. Holls had written the song about his boyfriend, Dawson, but I felt myself and Ronin in every note. This song was going to be a hit with our fans. I could picture the crowd singing along with us.

As someone who once believed that I'd never fall in love, if I could relate to it, chances are the fans would too. I wasn't big on rock ballads in general. I preferred our high intensity, hard rock songs. But something about this one, at this time, got to me.

Finally admitting to Ronan how I felt about him, there was no way I could put my emotions back in that bottle again.

Then I remembered Ronin's poetry. Had he written about me? I was feeling pretty inspired myself, even though I'd never tried my hand at songwriting. I was an intuitive musician, not a writer. And, to my mind, I was the least talented musician among us. But days like today, when we got in our groove, when our harmony hit just right, even I could admit that I had a talent that I hadn't fully appreciated or accepted.

Drummers always sit at the back of the stage, in our own world. There's a synergy that singers and guitar players have with their fans that drummers don't. We can't touch the audience like the rest of the band. That's not to say that we're not appreciated or important. It's just a different thing.

On tour, between sets, I'd bang out a drum solo for the crowd. Those were the times when my nerves hit. Because it was just me. No voices, no guitars, nothing but my sticks and my dreams. Fans loved it, and it gave me a chance to make that connection with the crowd. One that was important. Without a human touch, music is just waves of atoms. It has no meaning and no energy.

Just like my life without Ronin. No energy, no color, no life.

We got to the end of the song, but I was so caught up in staring at Ronin singing—to me, with me—that I forgot there were other people watching us.

Until Jesse knocked on the glass partition. He held up his

hand, stopping us. Then he opened the door, and we slipped off our headphones.

"Sounds great, but Faise, your voice is too soft. You need to focus on your diaphragm. We want to bring up the vibration level."

I nodded. Singing was not my strong suit either. Some drummers were good at both, a few were great, but me, not so much. And being distracted by Ronin wasn't helping matters.

"Okay, let's try it again," I said.

This time, I closed my eyes, shutting off everything outside of my own voice, the words rolling out of me. In that moment, there was no frustration, no uncertainty. Just the heady feelings that were tumbling around inside me like a tornado picking up speed.

Jesse was right. When we hit the chorus this time, shit, the four of us were magic. I got the same feeling that I did when I was on stage, chills running through my body, the incredible rightness of the moment giving me a high that nothing, no drug could ever give me. It was difficult to explain, but when you felt it, you knew.

When we reached the end of the song, I opened my eyes to find the guys staring at me with shocked expressions.

"What?" I asked, removing my headphones. "Not good?"

"Not good? Shit, Faise, you've been holding back on us," Brodie stated.

I waved him off, but he shook his head.

"I'm serious! Holy fuck. Holls? Ro?"

"I heard it too." Holls nodded and smiled at me.

Ronin got up, bass still in hand, and walked around my kit. He leaned down and kissed me, teasing me with his tongue.

"Why have you been hiding all this time?" he whispered to me.

"What?" I looked up at him, smiling against his lips. "I've always been right here in front of you."

"No. Not like this. You're so fucking incredible when you let go. When you believe in yourself. I can't even—"

Ronin stopped talking and took my lips again, the kiss deeper, longer. I was drunk on him.

"Uh, guys," Holloway interrupted.

Ronin leaned back and turned to him. "Now we're ready to play."

I wasn't. I had a boner that wouldn't calm and a heart that was close to bursting wide open at any moment. This was going to be our fastest recording session in history because Ronin and I needed to be alone.

"Jesus, it's fucking hot in here." Brodie pulled at his t-shirt and gave us his usual smirk. "All right, let's do two more songs. Then, I need to go home to my husband."

"Fucking right," Holls agreed and fanned himself.

Amen to that.

CHAPTER 23
FAISE

We recorded three songs that afternoon. They weren't finished yet, but we had a good start.

Six hours later, we were tired but wired, happy with our studio time. I still worried that me and Ronin being lovers would change our dynamic. That somehow our songs, our sound, would be different and not in a good way. Relationships among band members were always a volatile kind of thing. Even when you weren't lovers.

But when sex came into play, well, things changed. Some bands broke up over it, some wrote hit songs. There was a lot of pressure for me and Ronin. As happy as Holls and Brodie were for us, there was fear there too. And I wasn't ignorant to it.

We'd stopped off at my place on our way back to Ronin's to grab my clothes, my laptop, and other personal items. My hands were still shaking as we loaded up the SUV.

Settling in the back seat, Ronin took my hand in his and brought it up to his mouth, kissing my knuckles.

"Stop thinking so hard," he interrupted my musings.

"I can't help it."

"Then I'll just have to find a way to distract you," Ronin whispered as he pushed me down on the back seat.

"Ro," I warned him, my face heating.

It was hilarious, considering all the sex I'd had in front of other people.

"Your sudden shyness is too fucking adorable."

I let out a frustrated groan. "I told you how I feel about that word."

Then he kissed me, and I forgot all about words. Except 'more' and 'please' and 'yes'.

The weight of his body, the way his lips took possession of mine, it was all very sexy, insistent, demanding. Like being caught in a massive wave, I was pulled under, deeper, drowning in his ocean blues. I licked into his mouth, and swirled my tongue around his, sucking hard. His answering groan had me shifting, our hips colliding. Fuck, I needed more of his kisses. I could live off them alone.

Suddenly, a throat cleared. I'd forgotten that Lennie was in the car with us.

"We're back. And your mom has arrived."

Lennie's statement was like a cold shower, and I startled, then pushed against Ronin's shoulder.

"Give us a minute," Ronin muttered as he sat up and pulled me with him.

Lennie got out of the car and closed the door. Ronin was about to kiss me again when his phone buzzed.

Kissing—and everything else—would have to wait. Again.

"Stay on the other side of the car," I cautioned Ronin.

His wicked chuckle told me I was in so much trouble.

A few deep breaths, and a few minutes later, we exited the car. Lennie shook his head at us, leading us inside.

Ronin's mom, who was just shy of my height, greeted us on the other side of the door, pulling Ronin in tight and hugging him hard. And he was a big man to move.

"Ciara's resting. I'm cooking dinner. Why don't you boys go and get washed up."

"It feels like high school all over again," I said as I greeted her with a hug.

"I hope not. I couldn't take the smell of Ronin's gym bag ever again."

"Mom!"

"What? It's the truth. I used more bleach during your teenage years than I did throughout my entire life."

"Okay, we get it," Ronin sighed and shook his head, his hair falling out of his messy bun.

I bit back a laugh as we entered the foyer.

I was home.

When the four of us settled down to dinner a short time later, memories of my childhood came flooding back.

For years, Callie worked two jobs to support Ronin and Ciara. And after Ronin's dad cut off contact, she was the only parent they had. It was clear the way she'd always put their needs ahead of her own, that she loved Ro and Ci, and would do anything for them.

Ronin loved staying at my parents' place on the weekends, but once a week, we'd have dinner with Ciara and Callie at their apartment. Only now did it hit me how lucky I was. To have not just one home, and one family, but three.

After dinner, the four of us sat down to watch movies.

Normally, I sat on one end of the couch and Ronin on the other, but not anymore. He beckoned me closer with a crook of his finger and I had no hesitation moving into his arms. Then I realized that we hadn't said anything to his sister or mom about us.

I snuggled into Ronin's lap, leaned back against his chest, his arms around my waist. Fuck, that was better than good. I never wanted to leave.

His mom glanced over at us and smiled but said nothing. Her eyes told me that she'd always known. Ciara offered us a blanket and then moved to sit beside her mom, holding her close.

I sighed.

"Good?" Ronin whispered, his hot breath teasing my ear.

I shivered and ran my hands along his forearms, linking my hands with his. "So good. Not sure you're gonna be able to move me from this spot."

"That's the plan."

The movie started, but I wasn't paying attention to the screen. All I could focus on was the feel of Ronin's body against mine. The heat, the rapid drumbeat of his pulse, the brush of his hard cock that sat snug against my ass. He squeezed my arms and kissed my neck with gentle nips and playful licks. He was keeping it PG in front of his mom and sister, but underneath that blanket was a whole different story.

Halfway through the movie, I was so turned on I started squirming in his arms. Then he massaged my neck and shoulders, easing all the tension out of my body, one languid touch at a time. He rubbed my scalp, my temples, then worked his way back between my shoulder blades, and down to the upper swells of·my ass.

When his arms wrapped around my waist again, I was pretty sure I was going to melt into a puddle right there on the couch.

Next thing I knew, the movie was over, and Callie and Ciara were saying goodnight. Then it was just me and Ronin, alone.

"You ready for bed?" Ronan asked.

My tongue was so tied I couldn't answer him, so I nodded instead. I gently eased off his lap, and he slid out from under me, standing up, the blanket falling to the floor.

"Come here."

I kneeled on the couch facing him, and when I saw the bulge in his crotch, my mouth watered.

Then we moved like we always did, towards each other, in sync. He bent down and I slid my arms around his neck, and my legs around his waist as he carried me through the house and up the stairs to his bedroom. My heart knocked hard against my ribs with every step. I knew, I just knew, that what was going to happen next was going to change us forever. And the way Ronin was looking at me, the way he held on to me like I was the most precious thing in the world? Fuck, it sent shivers up and down my entire body.

Sex with other men had always been hot and dirty and fast. There were never any deep emotions attached to it. It was just fun, casual fucking. But this, what was happening right here? I couldn't even believe it, never mind feel it. My whole world narrowed down to Ronin. We shared everything in life—music, laughter, highs, lows, and now, our bodies. Our love.

But he hadn't made to kiss me yet. I just knew that if we did, we'd never make it up those stairs. And with a house full of his family, it wasn't the time for an exhibitionist kink.

He carried me into the bedroom and playfully tossed me onto his bed.

I laughed, wasting no time stripping off my clothes, my skin on fire, my dick so hard it slapped against my stomach, red and throbbing, leaking pre-cum. Ronin groaned and leaned forward, licking the head of my dick.

"Oh, fuck," I moaned as I grabbed his hair, tugging on the long strands, needing more.

"Fuck is right," he whispered and gave my cock one more teasing lick before moving up my body, until we were face to face. I was naked and he was still dressed, and the contrast, the roughness of his clothes against my skin, it was electric. I let out a loud moan that probably echoed through the walls of his bedroom.

His lips hovered over mine. "I need you in my ass and I sure as hell want yours."

"I'm down with this plan."

"Good. Because I want you to wake up tomorrow and know that you're mine, I'm yours, and nothing and no one comes between us. Not ever."

"Yes," I moaned in response.

I wanted him in every way I could get him. And there was nothing I wanted more than to give myself to him.

"No condoms," I offered.

"Nothing between us."

I nodded. "Kiss me already."

"So demanding."

"Just wait," I teased him.

I was a quiet guy in general but bossy as fuck in bed. Most of the time. Then again, I'd never been in bed with my best friend, so who knew what would happen? I didn't like to submit to strangers. Most of the time I topped. But just the thought of Ronin coming in my ass was so hot that it burned away any hesitation.

Ronin's lips took mine in a possessive kiss, and I was only too happy to return the favor. His tongue sucked on mine, each deep, devouring touch better than the last. And each kiss had me wanting more. I slid my hands to his neck, pulling him in tighter, angling my head for a deeper connection. Our kisses went from playful to languid to downright filthy, as he aggressively fucked my mouth, taking ownership of my lips. His beard teased my skin, the burn so fucking heady I wanted more. Every nerve ending in my body was so alive.

When we finally broke for air, I pushed on his shoulders, and he fell to his back, taking me with him. I straddled his waist, and reached for his jeans, unzipping them with trembling hands, eager to see all of him. Eager to taste every inch of his gorgeous skin.

"Get this shirt off," I demanded as I slid my hand inside his jeans and my skin met his. "Commando? You dirty fucking boy."

Ronin waggled his eyebrows at me, and I shook my head, unable to stop the smile that spread over my face. I took hold of his heavy, rock-hard dick, giving it a long, slow stroke. Ronin's groan was loud, and so fucking satisfying.

Playtime was over. It was time to rock 'n' roll.

Ronin threw his shirt off, and I attacked his mouth. I tugged on his cock, stroking him off. He was leaking so much pre-cum that it made for a smooth glide.

"Stop," Ronin warned.

"What?" I nearly shouted, my hand stilling.

"Keep that up and I'll come too soon. And as sexy as a handjob is, I need more this time."

"I want to fuck you," I moaned, letting go of his cock and slipping down the bed. "I need to be inside you."

"Yes," Ronin grunted.

I yanked on his jeans, and pulled them all the way off, tossing them aside.

Seeing him fully naked and hard, for me, had my balls drawing up tight. I wanted to rub myself all over his body and come on those sexy abs of his. When he drew his hand up over his hairy chest and pinched his nipples, I jerked hard, like he'd just touched me.

I grabbed the base of my dick, willing myself to calm down. Holy fuck, he wasn't the only one about to come too soon.

"Get over here and fuck me already," Ronin whispered as he rolled over and got up on his hands and knees. He clutched the duvet in his hands, his knuckles white with strain, his forearms shaking.

And shit, I didn't know which view was sexier.

His round ass was right there, so fucking biteable and all mine. I kneeled on the bed and ran my hands up his hairy thighs, and under, cupping his heavy balls and then his dick, so hard, so hot, and all for me. Christ.

I leaned in and kissed the dimples on the swells of his ass, willing myself to go slow. I licked one cheek, then gave him a not-so-gentle bite, sucking on the skin, marking him. I was going to leave so many love bites on Ronin's body, there would be no question who he belonged to.

"Faise."

His voice was low and gravelly, full of desperation and need. He pushed his ass back and spread his legs.

I didn't need any further invitation.

CHAPTER 24

RONIN

Faise's hot breath on my ass was enough to send me coming all over my bed. God, just looking at him, looking at me, eyeing me up like I was a prize that he'd won, had my body on fire and my heart racing out of control. No one had ever looked at me with such want before.

When I rolled over and got on my hands and knees, I glanced over my shoulder to find him running his eyes all over my body. We'd always been possessive with each as friends, but this? This was on a whole other level I had yet to experience.

I didn't just want him. I fucking needed him. All of him.

My best friend. The man who made me feel like I was standing on top of the world.

Even when I fell, faltered, he was there. And I was the same for him. I don't know why the hell it took me so long to admit what was building between us, but now that I did, I didn't see anything else.

He licked his way down my crease and over my hole, and Jesus, my cock grew painfully hard. The filthy sound of him spitting on my hole was followed by his wicked tongue teasing me so good, sliding over my taint and down to my balls. Shit, I hadn't been rimmed in so long. And I was not prepared for the reality of my best friend eating my ass.

Faise did not hold back. Tormenting me with playful flicks, he slid his tongue over the rim, again and again, until finally, he pushed inside me. I grabbed hold of the base of my throbbing dick, willing myself not to come yet.

"Oh fuck, baby, that's so good," I groaned loudly. "Don't stop."

I'd never sounded so needy in my life. But I couldn't help it.

Faise grunted, teasing me with his skillful tongue until I was a writhing mess and my arms gave out.

"This is the sexiest ass I've ever had the pleasure to look at. Or taste. Or fuck."

The raw gravel of Faise's voice had another dirty moan slipping out of me.

Spreading my cheeks with his callused fingers, he pushed his face in my ass, licking, sucking, eating me out until I was whimpering. All I could do was kneel on shaky legs, head on the mattress, and take the awesome pleasure he was giving me. My climax kept building, my cock jerking hard, begging for touch. I was about ready to scream Faise's name when he gave me one last, tormenting flick and eased back.

"No!" I protested, but he swatted my ass cheek. "Fuck!"

"Exactly," Faise growled and leaned over my body.

He kissed each knob of my spine, until he reached my neck, where he bit down and sucked on the tender skin, marking me, making me shiver. His hard cock brushed the skin of my ass and Jesus, I was so ready for him.

"You better have a shitload of lube in your nightstand Ronin, or so help me—"

Faise's gruff, impatient tone made me want to laugh. Something I rarely did with previous lovers.

"Yes, it's there," I replied, turning my head to stare at him. His golden skin was flushed and drops of sweat slid down his face and neck, his black hair falling into his eyes. It wasn't enough. I needed to see him.

While he reached over to the nightstand, I flipped over to my back, taking my cock in hand and pumping it slow and steady.

"Hurry the fuck up and get your dick inside me," I demanded.

Faise yanked on the drawer and pulled out the biggest tube of lube I owned. Throwing it beside me, he walked around and kneeled on the edge of the bed. I held my knees to my chest, opening myself up to him.

I looked down my body, slick with sweat, my cock hard, red, and leaking. I was a needy fucking mess.

Faise paused and glanced up at me, pushing one hand through his hair. I could finally see his eyes clearly. There was no mistaking the desire there, the longing, the heat.

But it was the tenderness that rocked me to my core. A look of pure adoration, of love, that hit me hard, like nothing else. The trembles in my body turned to shaking, and I closed my eyes. He was so much more than I could ever imagine.

"Baby, are you okay?"

Fuck, I didn't know how to answer that.

"Need you," I bit out.

Everything else was too much for me to say. A lump formed in my throat, and I felt dangerously close to crying. Me. I blinked away the rush of tears and took in the beauty of the man I'd loved nearly all my life.

Faise reached for the lube and slicked up his cock. Then he leaned forward and teased my ass with one finger, sliding it over my hole and gently pushing it in. With the lube and the rimming, there was more pleasure than pain. Still, I wasn't used to bottoming. It had been years. But suddenly, it was the only thing I wanted. I needed Faise inside of me. A part of me. He'd always been that, in my heart, but now we were joining in every single way.

"It's good, I'm good. More," I whispered.

Faise added a second finger, and took my cock in his other hand, jerking me off.

"I need to know Ronin. How bad do you want my cock?"

"More than anything," I panted, overwhelmed by pleasure. "Fuck me. Please."

"I'm gonna do so much more than that," Faise bit out, stopping to add more lube, and this time, a third finger. I was so full as he began to push in and out, fucking me with those talented fingers of his. Then he crooked them and nailed my prostate.

"Faise!" I shouted as intense pleasure rippled through my body. "Don't stop!"

He teased me again, and every time his fingers grazed over my prostate, I nearly came off the bed.

"You ready?" Faise asked.

"I've been ready for a while."

Not just for this, for sex, but for us. Faise leaned down, so close, but then paused.

"Kiss me," I demanded.

"But I just had my mouth—"

"Faise," I growled, releasing one hand from my knee to reach up and grab his neck.

Our mouths crashed together, and fuck, tasting myself on him was so freaking hot. With one last kiss, he leaned back, spread his knees, and notched his dick to my ass. His bare dick. Pushing slow but steady, I glanced down, watching as he slid inside me, filling me up, giving me a pleasure that was so powerful, so primal, all I could do was growl his name.

I'd always thought of him and I as two halves of one whole.

And now, right here in my bedroom, I finally understood what that meant.

Faise

If I only had tonight, I'd be better than good.

Years of frustration, yearning, full-on pining for my best friend, and finally, incredibly, we were here. In his bed.

And not as roommates or best friends or bandmates, but as lovers.

I always thought Ronin was a beautiful man, but now that he was *my* man? Beautiful was too bland a word. For him, and for what was happening between the two of us.

Inch by inch, I slowly slid inside his body, feeling the tight ring of muscle give way. He tilted his hips, taking more of me, taking me all the way in and fuck, bareback was a heady pleasure. Something I'd never experienced with any lover. Only with him.

"Fuck, Ronin… you… I… holy shit."

"That's an understatement," he urged as he slid his legs around my waist. "Fuck me."

I gritted my teeth, willing myself to go slow. I wanted it to last, to savor our first time together. But my impatient BFF was having none of it.

"We have all night," I whispered, panting, trying to hold on to my control. "I want to make it good for you."

He slid his massive hands over my ass and pulled me in tighter, squeezing my cheeks hard.

"Ronin," I warned.

Like that stopped him. The cheeky bugger slid one finger down my crease and teased my hole. I punched my hips forward, filling him up, all the way.

"Yes," he moaned. "That's what I want, baby. Need you so bad. Don't hold back."

Jesus Christ, when he called me 'baby', goosebumps popped up all over my heated skin. There would be no holding back. Not this time. Not anymore.

I rocked into him with tight strokes, watching every expression on his face. His big blue eyes stared up at me, and I shuddered at what I saw there. He'd always been mine. And now he was, in every way.

"I'm yours," he moaned.

Grabbing onto his thighs, I pushed his knees against his chest and pounded his ass, taking what was mine.

So much for going slow.

"That's it," Ronan groaned. "More. harder."

I took his cock in hand and stroked him off in time with my thrusts. The bed was shaking and creaking underneath us as I set the pace, fucking into him harder, faster, my control all but obliterated as Ronin panted, staring up at me with wide eyes.

"Faise."

My name had never sounded better. And knowing that I was about to spill my load in Ronin's ass, I was shaking hard, wanting more but at the same time, wanting it to last. I never wanted this feeling to end.

I'd fucked around with a lot of men, but I'd never cared about anyone's pleasure more than my own.

My climax built, along with all the emotions I'd been fighting. All the years of wanting my best friend. My heart was beating faster than any drum I'd ever played. Ronin gripped my ass cheeks tighter, pulling me in so close that there was nothing separating us. Not a breath, not a whisper, not an inch of skin.

I revelled in Ronin's moans, watching as his body grew as desperate as mine to reach that perfect point of pleasure. And I knew, after watching him have sex so many times, that he was close to coming. His cock jerked hard in my hand, and the telltale rumble that erupted from his chest told me he was almost there.

I stroked his dick harder, faster, never letting up.

"Right there, baby, that's it!" Ronin groaned as I fucked into him with a savage intensity. "Oh fuck!"

His body jolted, hot cum lashing my hand, his abs, his gorgeous cock.

Licking his lips, he panted and stared up at me, and my climax was just within reach. So close. The intensity was overwhelming, and I just knew I was going to be wrecked in the best way.

"That's it, love," he whispered, his face flushed with heat and sweat. "Come for me. Come in my ass. Mark me."

Ronin's words pushed me right over the fucking edge. The orgasm slammed into me, blistering hot, my vision blurring, my body quaking as I unleashed in his ass. Hot cum surrounded my cock as I continued to fuck into him.

Pretty sure I screamed loud enough to wake up Ronin's entire household, not to mention the goddamn neighborhood.

I was sweating hard, my body trembling, my lungs gasping for air, just like at the end of one of our shows. Except, I was naked and inside Ronin and this was better—fuck I couldn't even believe it—so much better than performing.

Collapsing onto his chest, his big arms slid around me, holding me tight to him. I couldn't breathe and I didn't care to.

Then, the tears came. The wave of emotions that I couldn't control. Fuck. I blinked away the wetness, trying to get a hold of myself before he noticed.

"Look at me," Ronin urged.

I shook my head, too overwhelmed. I was so fucking raw right now.

"Baby."

My head shot up. Couldn't help it. Hearing him call me that was just the sweetest sound in the world.

"Yeah?" I blinked. One tear managed to slip out and down my cheek.

"Don't be shy. Not with me," he whispered and tapped his lips. "Kiss me."

And yeah, I kissed him. Long and hard.

Was there any other way?

CHAPTER 25
RONIN

With Faise on top of me, his half hard dick still in my ass, I was too blissed out to move an inch.

And feeling his cum inside me? Don't ask me to describe it, I'd be here all night.

Speaking of all night, once I caught my breath (would I ever?) it was my turn to return the favor. Maybe I'd start off with a blowjob first. And yeah, picturing Faise fucking my mouth was just as hot as everything else between us.

Not just that.

It was intense. Primal in a way that had me wanting to pound my chest and run through the streets, yelling 'this man is mine'. For guys like us, who'd all but run screaming from that kind of ownership, it was telling. I saw the vulnerability in his eyes, the tears he couldn't hide and fuck, it made me fall that much harder for my boo.

He was moving in here, with me, and that was that.

Forever. The end.

Well, not the end. To me, it was just the beginning.

I shifted, kissing the top of his head, and he let out a sigh that was pure contentment. It made me smile and squeeze him tighter. My cock was already chubbing up, ready for round two.

I'd never been fucked so thoroughly before. No. Fucked was not the right word. If anyone asked me what it was like sleeping with my best friend, I wouldn't know what to say. Or rather, there was too much.

Do you have eternity?

There was no weird tension like there was sometimes with a stranger. No pretenses, no show. No pretending to be something I wasn't. Most people I'd fucked around with loved the idea of screwing me because I was a famous musician. That was fine, it was what it was. I soaked up their adoration too, so it worked both ways. But they didn't get the real me. They got my rockstar persona.

Some musicians lived that way twenty-four seven—at shows, backstage, and in their day-to-day. But I had to keep something for myself. For me, and my friends and family. Otherwise, when the time comes to leave that spotlight forever, what are you going to do? Too many musicians couldn't handle it when their fame waned. I didn't want that. I was not going to be a shadow haunting the stage.

"I'm going to give you back some of your advice," Faise muttered as he finally lifted his head up and looked at me. He gently pulled his cock out of my ass, and I felt more cum slip out of my hole. I'd never fucked bareback and it was the hottest thing ever. "Stop thinking so hard."

I laughed and rolled him over, blanketing him with my heavier body.

"I was just thinking about how incredible this feels," I confessed, cupping his face in my hands. "I never have to be anything but myself with you. And even if we didn't have music, we'd still have each other."

He turned his head and kissed my palm, his soft lips teasing my skin, sending a shockwave through my body. Just like that, I needed him again.

I bent down, taking his lips in a heated kiss.

We made out for ages, with sultry kisses and languid sighs, one taste more decadent than the next. His hands moved down over my back, to the swells of my ass, pulling me in closer. Our dicks were ready to go again, straining hard against each other, and I tilted my hips, needing more friction, needing to feel every inch of his skin against mine.

I kissed my way down his jaw, along his tender neck, and across his smooth pecs. I slid my tongue over one nipple, over his piercing, and sucked hard. Faise grabbed my hair in his hands and tugged me closer, urging me on, writhing beneath me.

"Love that," he moaned. "More."

I kissed my way over to his other nipple, licking it and giving it the same attention. When I slid my tongue around his piercing, Faise let out a filthy groan worthy of any porn star.

"Jesus Christ, I could come again. Just like this."

"That's a sexy idea, but first, I want to fuck you," I whispered, moving my mouth down his body, kissing every inch of his chest, his abs. I slid one hand down to his ass. "I want you to walk around with my cum in your ass."

Faise gripped my hair harder and hissed. "Holy shit, Ro, stop talking and just do it."

I laughed out loud at his impatience, and the feeling was so fucking good. Only with Faise.

"Get on your knees," I commanded. "And hold on to the headboard."

"Still too much talking and not enough fucking."

I grinned, and sat up, rolling him over with ease.

He grunted and humped the mattress. "Yes, please. You need to do that more."

"You like it when I manhandle you?"

"Without question," he moaned and pushed up onto his knees, his taut ass on full display. He glanced over his shoulder and gave me a saucy wink. "Well, big boy? I'm waiting."

"I'm lubing," I quipped as I fumbled around for the tube of lube.

It took me three tries to open the damn thing, and every time, Faise laughed harder, so hard, the bed was shaking underneath us.

"You need help, baby?" he chuckled.

I flipped him off and then, finally, flipped the cap open.

His throaty laughter echoed in the room. It made my dick hard and my pulse race. Needing inside him now, I slicked up my cock. My erection was so hard, I was lightheaded. I pushed one thick finger inside him, watching his tight pink hole take me in.

"Fucking shit, that's sexy," I groaned.

"Ngh. Yes," Faise whispered and pushed his ass back.

I slid another finger in, stretching him, fucking him until he was begging.

"I'm ready," he panted.

"Not yet," I replied, and added a third finger.

I had a big dick (not to brag, but yeah) and there was no way I was going to rush this part of the process. I wanted to make it as good for him as he'd made it for me. And knowing that Faise didn't bottom often, I wanted to be sure he was prepped enough. He came first.

Once I'd added more lube, and the glide was easier, we were good. I used one hand to push his head and shoulders down to the mattress, holding him there. At this angle, his ass was all mine, his tight hole a temptation that I was not going to resist.

"This good?" I asked, wanting to be sure that he was okay with being held down.

"Hottest fuck of my life and you haven't even gotten inside of me yet," he replied, his answer muffled by the duvet.

I slid my other hand over his ass, memorizing the feel of his skin under my heated palm. Fuck, Faise was smooth all over. I notched the head of my dick to his pretty hole, and I watched as his ass swallowed me up. And without the barrier of the condom, the heat around my cock was unreal.

"Oh God," Faise whimpered. "More, Ronin. Give it all to me."

"I wish you could see how beautiful you are."

Faise moaned, shifting, spreading his legs wider.

"And your ass around my bare cock is just incredible."

Gripping his hips tightly, I punched my hips forward, rocking into him. Every time I thrust, the headboard rattled against the wall, making a loud racket. Shit. The last thing I needed was my bodyguard breaking down the door.

Just the thought of anyone else seeing Faise's body like this, hearing his moans of pleasure, had my possessive streak running hotter.

I rutted in and out, setting a punishing pace, fucking into him. It was too good and I knew I wasn't going to last long. Sweat trickled down my face and my neck, my chest. I was panting like I was running a goddamn marathon. Or like I did at the end of our performances when I would run across the stage.

But this high was one that could never, ever, be duplicated.

I slid one hand down around Faise's hip and gripped his leaking cock in in my hand. I tried to time my thrusts while stroking him off, but I was too far gone. I pulled Faise back against me as I fucked into him in a frantic rhythm. He cried out my name, and begged me to go harder, faster. Begging me for more.

His body shuddered, and his dick jerked in my hand, hot cum lashing my skin. Pleasure knocked the breath right out of me as I gyrated against his ass, coming deep inside him.

And when I looked down and saw my cum dripping out of his ass, around my dick?

I'd never seen anything sexier.

Pulling out of him gently, I scooted back down the bed and leaned down to lick his hole. Faise jolted, let out another needy groan, and then collapsed on the bed. I kissed my way up his body. He glanced over his shoulder, and I didn't hesitate to take his lips in a mauling kiss. Tasting him and my cum. So dirty. So delicious.

"What the hell was that?" he asked me when we finally came up for air.

"That was years of edging. Give me a minute, and we'll try for round three."

I blanketed his body with mine, unable to move an inch.

"Too heavy?" I whispered.

"Don't you dare fucking move."

CHAPTER 26
RONIN

woke up the next morning with sore muscles and a stiff cock. But best of all, a full heart. The last one I felt most of all.

Waking up next to Faise was the same as it always was, but oh so different. There was no mistaking the fierce ache inside of me, a longing for more.

I finally had a moment to take it all in. This incredible man beside me.

Faise's lips were swollen and red, beard burn covered his face, neck, and chest, and there were love bites all over his body. And we hadn't even gotten to round three. We both knocked out cold after I collapsed on him, two rounds of epic sex enough for one night.

For last night, at least. Today was another story.

Who says fucking your best friend will ruin everything? If anything, it was just the opposite. I wanted more kisses, more time with him, more waking up like this.

Why the hell hadn't we done this sooner?

"Stop staring and kiss me," Faise muttered, his eyes shut tight.

"Look at me and I'll do just that."

He blinked and opened his eyes. Staring into those warm pools of amber, the ache that had settled in my heart intensified. Instead of doing what he asked, though, I got up out of bed, scooped him up in my arms (sheet and all) and carried him bridal style to the bathroom.

"Ronin, what the hell are you doing?" he squeaked.

"Taking care of my boo," I laughed. "First, we shower, then we come again, then we go back to bed."

"We're going to need food at some point if we're going to keep fucking like rabbits. Otherwise, we'll both collapse and Lenny will have to take us to the hospital, stuck together, glued to each other with our cum."

"There are worse things that could happen," I teased.

I let him down gently and pulled away the sheet. Mmm, his naked body was a sight for these eyes. He was fucking gorgeous. Long and lean, and best of all, mine.

Ignoring my stare—and my hard on—Faise opened the shower door, turned on the water, stepped inside, and motioned for me to follow him. I walked over to the cabinet first, pulled out two disposable toothbrushes and paste, and then joined him. Once we were both minty fresh, the morning makeout session was on.

That is, until someone knocked on the door. No, not the bathroom one, my bedroom door.

Grunting my annoyance, I grabbed a towel and slid it around my waist then padded out of the bathroom to see who was at my door at this hour of the morning.

It was Len standing on the other side. "Sorry to disturb you guys, but Zoe is here and so is Elias. They have an update about your sister's case."

"We'll be down in a few minutes."

I closed the door and walked back to the bathroom. Faise had his head tilted back as he washed his hair. I wanted to stand there and admire him, but unfortunately, there was no time. Once I made sure that my sister was feeling better and settled, I'd plan a vacation with Faise. No phones, no paps, no interruptions.

"They've got an update on Ciara's case," I told him. "I'm going to get dressed and head downstairs."

"I'm coming with," Faise replied as he quickly rinsed off. "But first, we need to change your bandage. I hope to hell you didn't tear any stitches last night."

"Don't worry, the only part of me that isn't sore this morning is my chest."

"Did I hurt you?" Faise asked.

"Of course not. Did I hurt you?"

He shook his head, his smile so wide it made my breath catch.

"I'm a bit sore but it's the good kind," I explained to him. "Besides, isn't having more sex the cure all?"

Faise rolled his eyes at my bad joke, turned off the water, and reached for a bath towel. Once he was dried off, he checked my wound and changed my bandage.

With that done, I headed back out to my closet to grab sweatpants and t-shirts. It was only then that I remembered Faise's suitcases. He'd packed up his favorite clothes and his bathroom toiletries yesterday. I loved the fact that his stuff would soon mix in with mine. It made what was happening real.

We quickly got changed and headed downstairs to find my mom and Ciara sitting down with Elias and Zoe, chatting away. All four sets of eyes turned to us, and the conversation in the room ceased.

"What's going on?" I asked.

Zoe cleared her throat. "We heard from Ailey. The good news is that all the evidence and witnesses support your claims that Dallas assaulted you and that you and your security team acted in self defense. There won't be any charges laid against you, or Faisel. The bad news is that Dallas was released on bail and he and his lawyer are talking to the press. He's denying he did anything wrong, and according to my source at Entertainment News One, he's accusing you and the band of abusing your celebrity status. Of course, it's bullshit, but at this point, there's nothing that we can do to stop him. Unless he slanders you. To counter this, we need to have our own strategy. I'd like to set up interviews with major news sites so that you can get your side of the story out there."

I shook my head in disbelief. "Not only is Ciara abused by this asshat, and we're assaulted, but now we have to defend ourselves? Can't we just let the lawyers take care of this? Why do we need to say anything?"

"We don't have the luxury of sitting on this," Zoe continued. "You know how quickly public opinion can shift. It's best to get ahead of this type of thing rather than let someone else control it."

"I agree with Zoe," Elias added. "She's monitoring all the social channels and entertainment sites to see if Dallas steps over the line. If he does, you can guarantee we'll sue him. In the meantime, get your faces out there and show that you're the injured party in this whole thing. You might also want to consider having your sister take part in some of these interviews."

"I don't think she's ready for that," I replied, my gut tightening. "Ci?"

"I'm not," she replied and my mom put an arm around Ciara's shoulders. "It took me a while to face what was happening. And if not for coming down here, I don't know that I would've admitted what was really going on until much later. I just can't talk to the media about this right now. If you want me to give a statement, I can do that. But no interviews. I'm just not ready. I'm sorry."

"Of course, you're not ready. And I don't expect you to do this." I glanced at Elias and Zoe and then my mother. "I'm the one the press want to talk to and I'm the one whose face is splashed all over the news. And I've dealt with difficult interviews before. This is nothing that I can't handle. Leave my sister out of it."

"All right," Zoe replied with a nod. "That's fine. I had a talk with Averell this morning and he's fully supportive of my plan to get ahead of this story. I'll set up the interviews and make sure that Elias and I are with you. That way if there's any questions that you're unsure about answering, we're there to assist. We're not going to let you go through this by yourself."

"Can't the reverse be true?" Faisel asked. "I mean, Dallas has been charged, not found guilty yet. Are we allowed to comment on what happened or will *we* be accused of slander?"

"The arrest is public knowledge," Elias assured us. "Like I said, I'll be there with you to help answer any questions and to monitor what's being asked and how you should respond."

"We've still got rehearsals and recording to do," I added. "And then we're heading out on tour again. So, we're going to have to schedule these interviews as soon as possible."

"I'm on it," Zoe replied, and picked up her phone, typing away.

"And I want to be with Ronin. For every interview," Faise stated, and took hold of my hand. "That's not a suggestion, but a demand."

"Understood." Elias's phone buzzed. "Excuse me, I have to take this."

"If you need privacy, you can use the music room. Last door on the right."

Elias nodded and headed down the hallway. Faise and I finally took a seat on the sectional. My mom and my sister smiled at us, and I was wondering why. Until I remembered that Faise was holding my hand. My face heated but I made no move to let go of him.

"And we'll also have to have a plan for this," Zoe pointed to our interlocked hands. "Or am I jumping ahead?"

I glanced at Faise and the smile on his face had me reaching over to taste it.

"Nope, you're right on time."

CHAPTER 27

FAISE

While Ronin took his sister to her first therapy appointment, I stayed behind at his place and unpacked.

Wait. I guess it was *our* place now.

Things were moving at lightning speed and yet, this wasn't much different than our day-to-day life or living with him on the road. He was always in my personal space anyway.

Except, now we exchanged hot morning kisses. And cum. And we held hands.

I loved that. All of it.

God, listen to yourself. I sounded like Brodie and Holls.

Not that that was a bad thing. Just unexpected.

I mean, I've loved Ronin all my life. First as my best friend, then, as the man I wanted more than anyone else. I didn't think I could feel any more for him.

But I was so wrong.

Because after last night, I was ready to do something I've never, ever done. Yup, I was ready to write that fucking rock ballad. Me. I probably had gigantic heart eyes that everyone could see.

Fuck it. I was too happy to care what anyone else thought.

Just as I was opening my second suitcase, I heard a phone buzz. Shit, it was mine. I'd all but forgotten about it for the past day or so. I searched the room and finally located it in the jeans I had on yesterday. When I glanced at the screen, I saw my brother's name.

"Hey bro, what's up?" I answered.

"What's up? Are you kidding me? Are you okay?"

"Of course, why?"

"Dude, your face and Ronin's is all over the news, not to mention that guy who attacked you. I've been texting like crazy and worried out of my mind."

Shit, I'd been so caught up with Ronin and his sister, I forgot to warn my own family. I probably had dozens of frantic voicemails and texts.

"Fuck, I'm so sorry. I better call Mom and Dad, too," I paused and ran a hand over my face. "I'm fine. Ronin is too. Well, he was cut and had stitches, and I have a bruise on my face, but we're okay. It's Ciara we're worried about. That asshole who attacked us was her boyfriend. He's been abusing her."

"Oh no. Where is she now?"

"Ronin just took her to a therapy appointment. She's going to stay with us for a while. The guy's a cop, so she's frightened as hell and doesn't want to go back to New York."

"No doubt. I'm glad she's staying with you guys. Are you living with Ronin now?"

"Um—"

Oops.

"Yeah. Well, I think. I mean, temporarily. I'm here for now. Or longer? I don't know."

"Faise?"

"Yeah?"

"You sound drunk? Are you sure you're all right?"

Drunk? Maybe on love. And dick. But definitely not from alcohol. But maybe I needed a drink for this conversation.

"Not drunk, but Ronin and I…we—" Holy fuck, I was shaking now, barely able to hold my phone. "We slept together. I mean, it's more than that. You know how I feel about him."

There was a pause on the other end of the line.

"I do know. You've loved him since you were ten. And now, it's more? I'm so happy for you guys! Finally."

"Really? I thought you'd tell me this was nuts."

"Are you kidding? The way he looks at you like you're the only thing in the world? Not to mention all the touching and calling you 'boo'? I mean, I know friends can be affectionate, but still. Anyone with eyes knows what's going on with you two. Mom and Dad called it years ago."

"What?"

"Sure. Nana and Dada too."

"Okay, then," I laughed, relieved. "Now enough about me, how're you doing?"

"I'm good. I'm sleeping better and working out again. And of course, I'm talking to my sponsor every day."

I needed to check in with mine. My urges hadn't spiked dangerously, despite the stress of the past few days. But I wouldn't take chances. Just when I think my addiction is behind me, that's the moment the sneaky bastard comes for me again.

"The paps still follow me occasionally, but not like before," Rae added. "And I've got a few job interviews coming up in July. I thought, before then, I might take a trip down to see you. If that's okay? If I'm not interrupting."

"Of course. We'd love that! Next week? We're heading out on tour beginning of June to start our US leg, but you're welcome to join us. Pretty sure Ciara will head out with us, too."

"You're sure?"

"You're family, of course, I'm sure. I'll ask Bibi if she can arrange your travel."

"That would be awesome. I'll see you soon, then. And call Mom and Dad so they don't worry."

"Doing that now. Love you, Rae."

"Love you too, Faise."

I tapped *end* and then tapped on my parents' number. One ring later, and my mom answered.

"Faisel Douglas Reed, it's about time you called us back! We've been worried sick since we saw you on the news!"

Mom pulling out my full name (Douglas? Total cringe) was a sign that I was in deep shit. I felt like a naughty teenager again.

Then I glanced over at the messy state of Ronin's bed. Naughty was the least of it.

"Sorry, but between the police and the hospital, and talking with our PR team and lawyers, it's been crazy."

"What happened? Is everyone okay? Who is this Dallas Bledsoe?"

"Ciara's boyfriend. Now ex. He was threatening her, Ronin intervened, and things escalated. Thank fuck I went after him. Who knows what would have happened if—"

An enormous lump filled my throat, making it impossible to swallow. I couldn't think about 'what if's'.

"But we're good," I continued. "Ciara's still in shock, though. Dallas has been abusing her for months. She was acting strange, and when we finally met up with them, Ronin and I knew something was wrong. Don't think he ever expected this, though."

"Is she still with Ronin?"

"Yeah, we're all at his house. It's not a good idea for her to be alone just yet. Their mom flew down yesterday."

"Well, that's good. I'm glad Callie is there. And you are too. You sound different, honey? Are you sure you're fine?"

"I am," I cleared my throat. "Me and Ronin, we're together."

"Of course, you are. It's always been that way."

"No, I mean, together, together. As in, a couple."

A sharp inhale on the other end of the line was followed by silence.

"Mom?"

"I knew it! I didn't know when, but I knew it would happen! Are you happy, honey?"

Was I happy?

I walked over to the bed and flopped down on it like a starfish. Everything felt unreal.

"I don't think I have enough words, Mom."

"You finally told him."

"It's been eating at me for so long. I never imagined—" I was getting choked up and I placed a hand over my eyes. "I almost can't believe it."

"I always knew you loved him. But I worried that he didn't feel the same way. Or, that he didn't want anything more than friendship. You were both so set on being single forever. That's what you said. I never believed you, but given Ronin's family history—"

"I know."

Would Ronin change his mind? He wouldn't. Right?

A sudden tightness in my chest had me sitting up. But I wouldn't let that fear ruin what was turning out to be the best thing that had ever happened to me.

"I'm going to take it day by day. I can't worry about what might happen in the distant future. That kind of anxiety is what triggers my addiction."

"You're both older now, and hopefully, wiser. Just remember, there's going be a period of adjustment. Be patient with him. And yourself."

"I've been patient for years, that's not the problem. I worry, he'll change his mind."

"It's scary, all the unknowns, but you know what feels right. Trust in that. And in him. I know he loves you, but if he's never been in a relationship before, there's going to be growing pains. I suspect that ever since his father left, he's afraid to put his whole heart out there. I can't imagine how he felt, losing his dad like that. Ronin puts on a good show, but he's just like you. Sensitive. And you're going to need to be mindful of that. Don't be surprised if at some point, he pushes away."

"No matter what, he's it for me," I confessed. "I'm not going anywhere."

"Spoken just like your father," Mom chuckled. "I was the same, you know. I fell hard and fast for your dad, but I was scared. I was always torn between doing what my parents wanted, what was expected, and what I wanted as an individual. Your dad wasn't the man my parents wanted me to marry. Even though I was born in New York, my parents held firm to their cultural traditions, and your dad and I were very different. And I worried about that. How would it affect our daily life? If we had children? There were so many questions and worries in my head that I almost changed my mind."

"What? I didn't know all this."

"It's not something I wanted anyone, outside of your dad, to know. It wasn't my love that was in question, it was everything else that came along with it. Falling is one thing. Living a life together, well, that's a far more complex reality."

It was. And being in the public eye didn't help either.

I could picture the headlines now. As soon as the press latched on to our relationship, they'd be plotting our demise. After all, that's what kept the tabloids going. There would always be stories, and rumors about someone we were spotted with. I did my best to ignore that shit now, but no doubt, some of that stuff got to me. And there was pressure too. If we hit a bump, how would that affect our music? The future of the band?

"It's a lot. And given our celebrity, there's going to be scrutiny on the two of us. I mean, given that we're rockstars, there's always trolls we have to deal with. Hateful bullshit because we're gay. And then, sometimes, I don't know if I'm the best thing for him. My addiction is never going away. What if I relapse? Is it fair to put him through that?"

"That's a question you need to ask him," my mom sighed. "Those conversations are tough, honey, but you have to do it. If you love him and you want to be with him, you can't keep those thoughts to yourself. You tend to keep things bottled up, but you can't. Not with Ronin. Not if you love him."

She was right. I'd done that for so long, and it didn't do me any good.

Like any first time—on stage, coming out, admitting my failings, falling in love—my nerves were riding high. But on the other side there was honesty, being true to myself. And what didn't kill me, made me stronger.

I needed to be that. For me and for Ronin.

CHAPTER 28
RONIN

A WEEK LATER

Me and the guys spent a week in the studio, recording more songs, and getting ready to head out on the road again.

We had a concert in Nashville tonight, and then we were headed down to Florida, Georgia, and the Carolinas for the next few weeks. Then it was a flight to LA on June 30th for our concert there on July 1st, and San Francisco on the 4th. Up the west coast and across the country until we landed back in Nashville at the end of July. We had August off. It wasn't the whole summer like we'd wanted, but hey, that's rockstar life. And when you sign with a new label, you gotta put in the work.

You also have to play while you're in demand. Time passes and new bands hit the stage. Fame is fleeting and so is the opportunity to make the most of it.

While Brodie and Holls were busy testing out their guitars, seeing to last-minute details for our performance tonight, I went in search of my boyfriend.

Fucking hell, even after a week of calling Faise that, it still rocked me to my core.

In the very best way.

He'd moved in a week ago and he was never moving out.

Faise's brother was headed down here for tonight's concert and would be joining us on tour for a month, along with my sister. Bibi had arranged to close my sister's lease in New York and got all her items shipped down here to Nashville. With Elias on site and security in tow, Dallas hadn't dared question anything.

Faise and I had done a few interviews as per Zoe's plan, but we kept our comments on the incident with Dallas to a minimum. Except to say that he was the aggressor, we were filing charges, and our lawyers were taking it from here.

We didn't comment on our relationship yet. Part of me didn't think we had to. The press knew how close we were, along with everyone else. But I knew that for Faise, it was important to make that public declaration. There were still times when I saw the worry in his eyes, the fear that I was somehow going to disappear tomorrow or change my mind.

I reassured him every day, with every touch, that I was here to stay. But he needed more than sex to understand. He needed the words. So did I. But like everything in my life, I always found it easier to show rather than tell people how I felt.

And Faise was holding back too. Like he was afraid if he said the words, it would break the spell, the magic that had been the past week.

I walked downstairs to our dressing room, and found him sitting in one of the chairs, twirling his sticks in one hand and reading his phone with the other.

"Baby," I whispered and stood behind him.

He met my smile in the mirror, placed his phone and sticks aside, and stood up. Walking around the chair, he slid into my arms, holding onto my waist. I leaned down and kissed him and fuck, I'd never get used to doing that. My heart pounded out a heavy beat, fast and strong.

"Showtime in an hour," I murmured and kissed him again. "You ready?"

"Like you need to ask."

"Where's Rae?" I nodded, looking around for his brother.

"He's in the VIP room with Ciara, Dawson, and Van."

"He looks so much better. I think he's finding his way back."

Faise nodded. "It hasn't been easy, but he's worked his ass off. I just hope, you know, being on the road with us is okay. I mean, none of us are into drugs anymore, but still. We can't escape it in our business. Half the people we know get high all the time."

"We'll do whatever we can to support him. And the same holds true even if he were at home. You know that. Getting drugs is as easy as ordering food from an app."

"You're right," Faise nodded and bit his lower lip. "And hey, just like me, you can't hide forever. At some point, you have to face temptation head on."

I was so proud of him, and I wanted him to know how much. I cupped his face, leaned down and kissed him again, savoring the fact that I could do this without pause. That he kissed me back with the same intensity. It was a passion I'd only ever felt with him. Maybe it was finally time to tell him exactly how I was feeling. How much I wanted us.

"Baby, I—"

My comment was interrupted by a knock on the door.

"Hey guys, sorry to interrupt," Bibi announced in her booming southern accent. "But you're needed on stage ASAP."

With a frustrated sigh, I took Faise's hand, and guided him out of the room and back upstairs.

Brodie and Holls were pacing back and forth, while Jesse and Elias were deep in conversation beside them. The fact that our lawyer was here was not a good sign. And then I noticed that every member of our security team, including our lead, Regan, was here. Something big was going down.

"What's going on?" I asked, letting go of Faise's hand.

"Our show's been cancelled," Brodie hissed.

"What? Why?"

"A threat was called in," Holloway added. "They had to shut us down."

"Someone called the box office ten minutes ago," Jesse explained. "Claimed they were going to shoot up the venue to 'get rid of all the nasty queers'. Each band member was mentioned by name in a very explicit threat."

"Fucking hell!" Faise blurted out.

I shook my head. "That's never happened to us before. Jesus."

I glanced over at Faise, and he looked like as horrified as I felt. Brodie and Holls too.

Elias nodded. "Chances are it's just some asshole being a psychotic prick and shooting his mouth off. But we can't take that risk. The police have been contacted and Regan and her team are on high alert when it comes to your security. I'm sorry."

"We've played at this venue dozens of times and without any problems. Why here? Why now?" Faise asked.

"I don't know," Jesse replied as he ran an agitated hand through his hair. "But we're doing everything to find out."

"What about the rest of our concerts down south? We're supposed to leave tomorrow to head to Florida."

"So far, it's still a go. Unless something else happens in the meantime," Regan offered. "Rest assured, security protocols are in place. Three-step process for ticket holders prior to entering the venue and we've updated our screening technology to catch any potential weapons. And we're increasing the size of your protective detail."

Dawson, Van, Ciara, and Rae stepped out of the wings to

join us. The worried look on every one of their faces told me they were also having a hard time digesting this news.

Dawson walked up to Holls and pulled him in tight. Holls in turn, buried his face in Dawson's chest as his boyfriend leaned down to whisper in his ear. Van did the same with Brodie, kissing his husband and rubbing a soothing hand down our frontman's back.

Rae and Ciara headed for me and Faise. Our family did not need this. No one did.

"Everything's going to be fine. The show's cancelled but it's just one event," I reasoned and reached for Faise's hand again. Both of us were trembling, but we interlocked our fingers tightly. "It's a one off. Some weirdo playing a rotten fucking prank. It means nothing."

"Do you think this is Dallas?" Ciara asked Elias. "Do you think this is him trying to get back at me through Ronin? Some twisted type of revenge?"

My sister looked at me, her face pale and her eyes filled with a guilt that didn't belong there.

Regan nodded. "Given what you've told us about him, and the fact that he's a narcissist who still denies hurting you, it wouldn't surprise me in the least. He's suspect number one at this point. The police are trying to pinpoint the origin of the phone call. We'll know more in the next few days."

"If they can trace it," Dawson interjected. "If whoever called in the threat used a prepaid cell, they probably got rid of it already. It's nearly impossible to trace. And don't forget, the guy's a cop, he's not stupid."

"Or he might be desperate enough to slip up, like Holloway's stalker," Elias added.

"What about Bandit?" Brodie snapped. "I wouldn't put it past Greg to pull something like this as payback for not renewing our contract. They've had several bands drop from their label since we left. I hear it's a shitshow over there."

Elias shook his head. "Personally, I think that scenario is

highly unlikely. If this person is found out, they're going to face serious charges. I don't think Haddley would risk even more fallout for his business."

"I agree with Elias. Let's wait and see what the police can gather. Remember that these concert dates and venues are common knowledge, so that means a large pool of suspects," Jesse offered. "Meantime, it's back home for everyone. No going out, no visitors. Rest up. We meet at the tour bus pickup location at noon tomorrow."

"I'm so sorry, Ro," Ciara looked at me. "If I hadn't—"

"Hey." I reached for my sister with my free hand. "We don't know that it's him. And if it is, they're going to get him. I don't want you to think about that bastard anymore. He's not going to fucking take you, or our music, or anything away from us."

"Ronin's right," Faise added. "And it's not like we haven't had haters before. Especially since all of us are out. We haven't had to cancel a show before, but we've had threats aimed at us. That's not new. And none of it has to do with anyone but the assholes who spew hate."

"This has happened before?" Rae asked. "How come you never said?"

"Why would I do that? And worry you, Mom, and Dad? No. It happens everywhere we go. Queer people are always harassed, and yeah, it's shitty, but unfortunately, that's our life. But we've never let that stop us. And we won't."

"Faise is right." Brodie nodded. "We're not going to stop doing what we love because of a few haters. Never."

"Can we have a moment, just me and the guys? It'll only take a minute," I asked everyone.

My sister and Rae headed off stage with Van, Dawson, Elias, and Jesse. Regan and Lennie stayed on the stage but walked a few feet away to give us privacy.

"Do you think there's any chance Hardwick will cancel our contract?" I asked. "I mean, first the launch party and now this? We're only a few weeks in and fucking hell, this is crazy."

"That's a question for Elias but as I understand it, no. And bands have gone through similar shit before with stalkers, threats, band members getting arrested, you name it," Brodie insisted. "For now, we keep calm, we listen to our security team, and we go about our business. I meant what I said. I'm not letting some sicko stop us. This is our life."

"Agreed," I stated.

"All in." Holls nodded.

"Always," Faise added.

All four of us grabbed onto each other, holding tight. We'd been through a lot together, and there would always be bumps in the road.

But one thing we never questioned was our loyalty. To our music, to our fans, and most important of all, to each other.

CHAPTER 29

FAISE

THE FOLLOWING DAY

After a sleepless night, Ronin and I, along with our siblings, headed with our detail to the tour bus pickup.

We had two buses for this trip—one for me and the guys and our security, then the other for Rae, Ciara, Regan and the rest of our team. Ronin and I had suggested to Ciara and Rae that it might be safer to stay at home. They refused, insisting that what we needed right now was family around us. I couldn't argue with that.

Holls and Brodie were already on board, and Van along with them. Dawson wasn't traveling with us on the southern leg of the tour because he needed to stay at home with his son, Jaxon. Come July though, Dawson was going to fly out to the west coast to join us.

Regan and Jesse had no further updates to share from last night. Which was both a relief and a concern. On the positive side, no further concerts were cancelled. On the negative, they still had no idea who'd called in that threat. No knowledge of who, or why, or if it might happen again.

Everyone was now strung tighter than my drums. All we could do was trust in our team and keep moving forward.

I stalked to the end of the bus, shoved one bag in the overhead bin, then placed the backpack with my toiletries and electronics on my upper bunk.

Ronin did the same, but instead of piling his stuff on his bunk, he threw his old backpack on mine, then his favorite bass guitar.

What the hell?

"Keep putting your shit on there and I'll have no place to sleep," I muttered, grumpy from tossing and turning all night.

Okay, maybe not tossing. Ronin had wrapped me up in his arms and hadn't let go. His naked hugs were my new addiction. But still, I was on edge from lack of sleep and worry.

"That's the whole point," he snorted. "You're sleeping in mine from here on out."

"It's pretty cramped for the two of us in there."

"Baby, tight spaces are my favorite," he teased and leaned down to kiss me.

When his mouth touched mine, I forgot all about sleepless nights and cancelled shows.

"Oh God, am I gonna have to listen to this every day and night for the next month?" Holls grumbled as he walked past us, throwing his bag on the bunk across the aisle from Ronin's.

"You've got headphones, Iain," Ronin countered. "And considering that me and Faise had to listen to you and Dawson get freaky in the shower last time, I think turnabout is fair play."

"Freaky? That was nothing. And you call yourself a rockstar?" Holls quipped and gave us a choice finger.

Ronin rolled his eyes, pushed the bunk curtain aside and then pushed me down on the mattress.

I, of course, went willingly.

"At least that funky smell is gone," I chuckled.

"Not for long. You're gonna come all over me and these sheets in short order. Then I'll do the same. I want them so fucking dirty with our cum that I can smell us for days."

"Jesus, stop talking!" Holls shouted.

I couldn't contain my laughter. Fuck, that felt good. Laughter was something we desperately needed now.

And Ronin didn't let Holloway's complaint stop him. My boyfriend slid down over me, pulling the curtain closed.

"The audio's about to start, so this is your only warning," Ronin called out.

"Holls just headed down to the kitchen, but I'm happy to stick around and listen."

Brodie's sudden comment had me stifling another laugh. Then I heard Van's voice, a gruff, "leave them be."

There were footsteps, and silence after that. Well, not total quiet. I could hear the chatter from the front of the bus. Not that it stopped us.

Once Ronin and I started kissing, the world could have literally crumbled down around us, and I wouldn't have noticed. Or cared.

Ronin tugged on my jeans, and I sat up. Or I tried to.

I yanked off my t-shirt, but my elbow smacked the wall. "Ow, shit!"

Then Ronin leaned up to do the same and hit his head on the upper bunk.

"We need bigger bunks," I chuckled as he unzipped my jeans and pulled them off. "Or our own bus."

He paused when he noticed that I'd gone commando. My cock was already hard and aching. He reached for his own jeans, shoving them down his hips, his dick slapping against his stomach.

"Mmm," Ronin growled. "Seeing you naked in my bunk is my rockstar fantasy come true."

My man said the most ridiculous things sometimes, but he still charmed me. I shook my head as I reached for him, for the lips that wrecked my control. Every fucking time.

"You don't need to sweet talk me, baby. I'm a sure thing."

"I'm serious," Ronin bit out.

And then, he bit me.

Or rather, my neck, sucking on the skin and marking me. An uncontrollable shiver wracked my body. Why was each time with him better than the last?

"Oh, God."

"No, just me," he quipped.

Then his wicked tongue wasted no time, licking a sinful path down my pecs and over to my nipples. I'd never been more grateful to have piercings in my life. He teased one nipple, then the other, until I was a writhing, horny mess.

"Where's the lube?" I moaned out.

"Under the mattress. But we don't need it just yet. Lie back and let me suck you off."

I was down with this plan as he continued to torture my nipples, tugging on my piercings. The fierce pleasure made me cry out so loudly that there was no doubt in my mind that everyone on board heard me. I felt the bus moving, gently rocking us back and forth. It pushed us together and then pulled us apart. Inevitably, like magnets, we held tight to each other.

Ronin slid down the bunk and pushed my knees to my chest. When he swiped at my hole with his hot tongue, I let out another dirty moan.

"Oh fuck, baby. More, please."

"That's what I like to hear," Ronin whispered as he shoved his face in my ass. I loved the beard he was rocking and the way the scruff scraped against my sensitive rim. My mouth opened but no words came out. The pleasure was that intense.

"Fuck my face," Ronin urged. "Don't hold back."

I shoved my ass up, wanting more. Wanting it all.

He licked my taint, then sucked on one of my balls, swirling his tongue around the sensitive sac until my eyes rolled back in my head. He gave the other one the same attention, as he gripped the base of my dick in his big hand.

When his tongue licked the head of my cock, my hips reared off the bed, my body wound tighter than his bass strings. And then he sucked me all the way down, deep throating my cock in his warm, talented mouth. So tight, so wet, so fucking good.

My hands were shaking, and I couldn't hold onto my knees anymore. I let them go and rested my legs over his shoulders, as he continued to tease and torment my cock with long drags of his tongue and a suction that had my climax racing to the finish line.

I gripped his hair, guiding his movements as I pumped my hips, desperate for more. Ronin choked on my dick, gagging, saliva running down around his mouth. But he didn't stop, he kept licking and sucking, his groans around my dick getting louder. The vibration on my cockhead was amazing. He took me deep into his throat again, devouring me, and my hips pistoned frantically.

"You ready for my cum?" I panted. "It's all for you. Only for you."

Ronin moaned and sucked hard. Then he tugged on my balls, and I was gone. Flying.

Everything locked up tight, the pleasure sparking through my body like a shockwave as I came long and hard, a raw moan ripping out of my chest. I shuddered as I released in his mouth, watching my cum slip out around his reddened lips. I was sweating and gasping for air, my heart pounding so fast and wild that it was almost frightening.

I'd had plenty of orgasms and enjoyed lots of head.

But watching Ronin pleasure me was something else. He wasn't the only who just had his rockstar fantasy come true.

My spent cock slipped from his lips, cum dripping down his chin. He wiped his face and then reached down to his cock with the same hand, tugging hard, jerking off. And watching him using my cum to pleasure himself was so fucking sexy.

"That's it," I encouraged. "I want your cum all over me."

He pumped his hand, once, twice, and then his body jolted.

"Faise!"

His loud groan unleashed, along with his cum. All over my cock, my abs, and my chest.

We were both panting for air in this tiny bunk that was now hot as hell. Ronin wiped my skin with his t-shirt, tossed it who knows where, and dropped down beside me, pulling me in tight.

I swore I heard what sounded like someone clapping, but I was too tired to open the curtain and find out.

———

I woke up a few hours later, stuck to Ronin, sweaty and hot. No complaints.

And yeah, the bunk smelled like our sex.

When I reached over and pushed aside the curtain, the bus was dark. Everyone was probably asleep. Finally. No one had slept last night.

I glanced at my watch. We'd slept for six hours. Hell, we were more than halfway to Florida by now.

"Come here," Ronin whispered, pulling me back down over him.

Despite the darkness, I found his lips and gave him a languid kiss. Kisses that were life to me. I don't know if I'd ever get used to the way his mouth felt on mine.

One of his hands slid up to cup my neck, the other, my

ass, bringing me closer. No space between us. There was no escaping and that was fine by me.

Until Ronin's stomach rumbled, interrupting our sexy moment.

"Time for dinner, big guy," I teased.

He pinched my ass, and hauled me in tighter, mauling my lips, refusing to let go.

Another loud growl echoed in the bunk, and I couldn't help the rumble of laughter that bubbled up out of me. Ronin slapped my ass in retaliation.

"Okay, it's your responsibility as my boyfriend to feed me."

"But I already did," I quipped, running one finger around his swollen lips, remembering every sight and sound as I came in his mouth.

He playfully licked my finger, then bit down gently.

What were we talking about? Oh yeah, me feeding Ronin. The memory was so hot, my dick hardened painfully.

"You sure as fuck did," Ronin whispered. "But now your man needs real food. Cook for me."

"Are you going to be this demanding every day of our tour?" I asked him.

"Fuck yeah," he squeezed my ass. "Fucking, food, show, shower, sleep. Repeat."

"I thought you wanted me to walk around smelling like your cum?"

"Don't worry, after we eat, I'll get you good and dirty again."

"I heard that!" Holloway yelled out from across the hallway.

Ronin and I tumbled out of our bunk.

But only a good while later.

CHAPTER 30

RONIN

After Faise and I managed to unglue ourselves from each other, we showered, and joined Holls, Brodie, Van, and Jesse at the front of the bus for a late dinner. Faise cooked pasta, extra spicy as requested, and we stuffed our faces until we were too full to move.

Lennie was typing away on his laptop while talking to Regan on his phone. There was a palpable tension in the air, but me and the guys tried to ignore it and sat around shooting the shit like we normally did.

I was convinced that Dallas was behind the threat in Nashville. After all, it would be easy for him to make a phone call and fuck everything up for us. If he couldn't get to Ciara directly, he could get to me. I just hoped that that was the end of it and our Florida concerts would go ahead without question. But it got me thinking more about our security, and stuff that I'd always taken for granted.

Faise was right. We'd received threatening emails before. Homophobic bullshit that was thrown at us as we left a club, or walked down the street, or rants posted on our socials. But no one had ever shut down one of our concerts before. It made me worry. About the safety of my boyfriend, my band brothers, our family, fans, and our security team.

Was the person who'd called in that threat doing it for attention, just to fuck with us, or was there a serious intent behind the message? It made me think about incidents that had happened to other bands over the years. Shootings and assaults in crowded nightclubs and outdoor concerts. We'd heard about those things, but it never happened to us directly.

I nudged Jesse's shoulder and he turned to me.

"What's the latest?" I asked. "Please tell me there's some kind of news about whoever the hell did this to us last night."

He shook his head. "They're working on it. So far, we've kept the story out of the news. We issued a refund to all the ticketholders yesterday, but we didn't elaborate on the reason why. We don't want to incite panic."

"I can't believe I'm admitting this," Faise started. "But for the first time in my career, I'm kinda scared to go on stage. What if this wasn't a one-off threat?"

"Security has always been tight for your concerts," Lennie interjected. "And rest assured we're doing everything we can to keep it that way. The worst only happens when you're caught off guard. And we're not in that situation. Everyone is on high alert. Speaking from experience, if someone really wanted to hurt you, they wouldn't warn you in advance. They'd just do it."

That made sense.

"Unless it's someone unhinged like that guy who attacked Holloway two months ago?"

"Stalkers are different. They're obsessive, which makes them prone to impulse decisions and irrational behavior. I honestly think that whoever called in that threat was just doing it to rattle you. To make you fearful. And it's working. You just admitted you're concerned about being on stage. They're fucking with you."

"The bad kind," Holls muttered.

"So, you think we're safe for our upcoming concerts?" I asked.

"Yes," Len replied. "That's my professional opinion. And my personal one, too. Is that a guarantee? No. We always have to err on the side of caution."

Faise looked at me and I could tell that Lennie's opinion gave him some measure of relief. Would we still be nervous heading out on stage tomorrow night? Yes. But I was confident that our team would do everything they could to ensure everyone's safety.

"What about the interviews you have lined up for us, Jesse?" Brodie asked. "What do we say if someone asks why the concert was cancelled?"

"Our public relations line is that one of the band was taken ill and and that was the reason you couldn't go on. If the press tries to push any further, do not engage. Leave it to me for follow up."

"What if they suggest that the assault by Dallas is somehow linked to the cancellation?"

"No comment. Not until we know who we're dealing with."

"If we ever know," Brodie added. "Normally I'm not shy with shooting my mouth off, but suddenly, like Faise said, I'm nervous. Which is totally fucked up because I've never let anyone do that to me. It's not in my nature to be cautious or unsure. And we'd never have become this successful if we weren't fearless. I don't want this asshole to win."

"They won't," Lennie assured us. "We monitor threats every single day. Most turn out to be nothing. Yes, you should be cautious, but no, you can't let that stop you from living."

"Okay, enough heavy shit," Holloway sighed and pulled out a pack of cards from his pocket. "Let's play. Loser buys all the drinks after our first show in Tampa."

"You're on," I replied.

We finally started to relax, playing cards, joking around, doing our usual thing.

We arrived in Tampa near midnight. Since neither Faise nor I had slept last night, and only few hours on the bus, we were tired and went back to our bunk.

Unlike some tours where we'd stay at hotels along the way, we were sleeping on the bus for the next few weeks. It wasn't ideal but at least security knew where we were at all times, and we could leave at a moment's notice if need be.

The only difference compared to when we used to travel was that Faise and I were now sharing a bunk. We still hadn't talked about what would happen when we got back home, but given that Faise was already living with me, I assumed the next step would be for him to sell his house and move in permanently. That idea was the only thing keeping me from ruminating about the cancelled show.

We did several interviews that morning, and then got dressed and headed over to the venue for soundcheck. Despite Lennie's reassuring words, every errant noise made us jump. We were all on edge. Who wouldn't be?

Once I had my bass guitar in my hand, my nerves began to quiet. Strumming out a few random chords, I warmed my fingers up and let the music distract me. Everything else was the same, but I noticed that Ace, our sound engineer, and Tommy, one of our road crew, were quiet too. Brodie was resting his voice as usual. Faise sat behind his kit, his knee jumping up and down.

"Nine Gone Wrong?" I asked, looking around at my bandmates.

And my boyfriend.

We started the song, and I got lost in the rhythm, tapping out the tune with my left foot and then turning around to face Faise. Watching him get in the zone turned me on. And when he caught my stare and smiled back, all the hair on my body stood on end. It was hot as fuck in the venue, but I had chills and goosebumps all over.

How long had he been looking at me like that and how had I missed it? Or had I seen it and been afraid to face what it meant?

Whatever the answer, I couldn't look away anymore.

I continued to strum the riff and walked over to Holls. We played off each other, and I spun around again and watched Brodie do the same on his guitar.

By the time we reached the end of the song, I was ready to play all night. The energy that pulsed between us was an awesome thing. The way it always was when the four of us got on stage and let loose. Music had always been my escape. It made me forget about the fights between my parents, it made me forget that we were so poor sometimes we barely had anything to eat. And it gave me hope, a dream, and as it turned out, a better life for myself and for my family. It fed something inside of me, as vital as any bit of food or water I'd needed to survive. It was difficult to explain, but if you asked any other musician, they would tell you the same thing.

Whether you were playing to a crowd of 1 or 100,000, performing made you feel alive. It really was as simple as that.

I didn't take for granted that I got to do this every day, playing music with my friends, but especially with Faise. It was like one of those concerts that you just never wanted to end. One that you remembered for the rest of your life. I wasn't foolish enough to think that it would always be this way, but I sure as hell was going to enjoy living in the now.

We finished up the song with Holloway's heavy riff and our crew clapped loudly.

"Shit, that's good," Faise called out. "We needed that."

"Fucking right we did." Holls nodded and passed his guitar to Tommy. I slid mine off and did the same.

Soundcheck was done and now it was time for us to get

ready for the VIPs. We had a group at every show, usually sponsors and people in the biz. Personally, I preferred the meet and greet with the fans after the concert, but kissing corporate ass was part of the job.

First, we had to change and get our hair done.

Payton, our stylist, was already waiting in the dressing room, chatting with Lennie. Or rather, Payton was flirting, and Lennie looked like he wasn't sure quite how to handle the attention. And the last thing we needed right now was a flustered bodyguard.

"Payton, stop toying with Lennie and pay attention to me," I teased.

"No way, honey," Payton shook his head, his blond curls bouncing. "I could never steal you from Faise. I'm not that kind of man."

"Thank you," Faise muttered and then gave me the stink eye.

What? He knew I was only joking. Right? I would never.

I sat down on one of the chairs and Faise took the seat next to me. He slid his arm around the back of my chair, the gesture proprietary as hell. When I looked at his eyes, the fire in them sparked a deep arousal in my balls. Oh, I was in trouble. I leaned over and kissed his temple, then placed my hand on his neck, staring right back at him.

"Jesus, is it hot in here or is it me?" Payton asked.

"It's Florida, of course it's hot," Lennie added.

Payton's chuckle broke me out of my trance.

"I didn't mean quite so literally, darling." I turned to find Payton patting Lennie's arm. "You're too cute for words."

Lennie's face turned bright red as he stepped back, knocking over Payton's hairdryer and several bottles of styling products from the table.

"Shit!"

"It's all right," Payton reassured him. "I've got it."

Lennie shook his head and bent down to pick the items up off the floor.

"Let me, it's my fault. Sorry about that," Lennie muttered.

The bodyguard placed the bottles back on the table, then nodded to the door. "Anyways. Yeah. I just…um…I'm gonna just wait at the door. I mean, outside the door. In the hallway."

Payton's eyes latched on to Lennie's ass as he strode past us. Lennie quickly shut the door behind him, and Payton let out a sigh and fanned his face.

"God, that man is so damn gorgeous. Too bad my flirting has gone nowhere."

"I think he likes you," I offered. "Never seen him so nervous before."

"Really?"

"Are you kidding?" Faise added. "Lennie's always unflappable. Except with you."

"Do you know if he's dating anyone?" Payton asked.

Faisel shook his head. "No idea. He keeps his private life very private. Never heard him talk about dating or even hooking up with anyone."

"Hmm, a man who doesn't kiss and tell. Interesting," Payton mused with a glint in his eye. Then he smiled at us. "And how are you boys doing tonight?"

I let out a filthy grin that required no explanation.

CHAPTER 31

FAISE

SHOWTIME

After our hair and makeup was done, which seemed to take forever, I hustled Ronin out of the dressing room and into the private bathroom at the end of the hall.

I knew that Ronin was just teasing Payton, but still. I didn't like the flirting. A possessive instinct I didn't know I was capable of was suddenly all I was capable of feeling.

"Why're we coming in here—" Ronin started.

"The question isn't why, but when," I replied.

I reached up, taking his lips in a fierce kiss, showing him exactly what I meant. There would be coming all right. I was going to suck Ronin's cock down my throat until he came long and hard.

He backed me up against the door, and it was on.

I ran my hand frantically over his denim covered crotch, cupping his dick, feeling him harden under my touch. I unzipped him, delving my hand inside. His cock grew heavy, hot, and hard in my hand. He moaned my name so loud, and it was the best thing I'd heard all day.

Dropping to my knees, I pulled out his dick and gave the fat cockhead a teasing lick, swirling my tongue around the head and then sucking him down my throat. I gagged, and swallowed again, determined to take him all the way.

"Baby," he whispered when I finally managed to do just that. "So many times, I watched you doing this. Wanted you to suck me off. But I never imagined. And now, here... I... fuck... can't believe—"

My dick jerked hard in response to Ronin's admission, begging for attention.

I gripped the base of his cock in my hand and slowly pulled off.

"Same," I whispered, my voice hoarse. "And now this dick belongs to me. Not Payton, not anyone else. Me."

He nodded, and I teased him with more licks and then swallowed him down again, saliva running down my chin, my lips sore, my throat aching.

Ronin delved his hands into my hair, tugging, pulling, his moans and pleas getting louder, more desperate with each swallow. I sucked hard, feeling his cock swell in my mouth.

"Pull off if you don't want to swallow," he warned.

Was he kidding me?

There was nothing I wanted more than his cum. I kept bobbing my head, until Ronin's body locked up tight.

"Yes!" he screamed as he shot in my mouth.

I was so turned on that I came, without touching myself, in my pants.

Ronin's body jerked again, and he flooded my mouth with so much cum that I couldn't swallow fast enough. It spilled out of my mouth and down my face. No doubt, I was a filthy mess. My hair was ruined, my makeup too, and my clothes would need to be changed.

I'd have to run around like a mad man before the show started. But fucking hell, it was worth it.

Ronin's softened cock slipped out of my mouth, and he

leaned back against the sink, holding onto it like it was the only thing keeping him upright. He was panting hard, running his other hand through his long, dark hair.

"That's a new part of our pre-show warmup," he quipped, as his stood there, staring down at me. His face was flushed and his eyes were bright, the blue so electric, I couldn't look anywhere else.

"Thank fuck I don't have to hit any high notes," I whispered, my voice hoarse.

Finally, I stood up on shaky legs.

He reached for me, pulling me into his arms, resting his face in my hair. What started out as fast and frantic was suddenly slow and sweet. And fuck, why did that make my stomach drop out from under me? Like I was free falling.

A sudden knock on the door had me burying my face in his chest, not wanting to move an inch.

"You guys done in there or what? And I hope you didn't break anything. Our insurance doesn't cover sex related damages."

Of course, it was Brodie.

"We'll be out in five," Ronin replied.

Then he tucked his dick back inside his jeans, and I washed up quickly. But my lips were unmistakably swollen. Both of us looked fucked out.

Ronin opened the door, and I was not in the least surprised to see Brodie standing on the other side of it, giving us a shit eating grin.

"Payton won't be happy he'll have to redo your hair," Brodie teased.

I shrugged, too blissed out to care. Besides, that would put an end to any future flirting with Ronin. Maybe. Not that Ronin was looking anywhere else but at me. But we'd been in our own private world. What would happen when we were out at parties again, and clubs? He always drew attention, and he was never short of interested partners. Would I be enough for him?

I hated these doubts in my head. I never questioned his love for me as my best friend. But as a partner? I wanted to say I was confident that he wanted me and only me. He said it, I felt it. But exclusivity was not for everyone. And monogamy was not something he'd ever said he wanted.

"Boo?"

"What?"

I glanced at Brodie and Ronin, who were staring at me with concern.

"You okay?" Brodie asked.

"Yeah, just… ah." A rare flush crept up my cheeks. "I need to get changed."

"No shit." Brodie shook his head. "Meet you guys upstairs in ten."

He walked off and left me and Ronin standing in the hallway.

"What's wrong?" Ronin asked.

"Nothing. What makes you think anything's wrong?"

Ronan raised one eyebrow. "Everything was fine until Brodie mentioned Payton. You don't seriously think I was really flirting with him, do you? I was just trying to help poor Len. I don't want anyone else but you."

"I know that. It's just that you and me as a couple, it's all new. Amazing, incredible, but yeah, new. And, you know, you've always made it clear that monogamy isn't for you."

"It wasn't. I didn't want that with anyone else," he confessed and pulled me in tight. "But I need it with you. I'm sorry it took me so long to finally get my head out of my ass, but—"

I laughed at that. "We both took a while. But we made it."

He kissed me, and then gave me one of his unforgettable hugs. I didn't want to ever let go.

"Come on," he reached down and squeezed my ass. "You

need to change, and we both need to hydrate. Then, we're gonna rock the fucking house down."

He guided me back to the dressing room, where I selected another outfit and quickly changed. Payton was busy chatting up Holls, so I got him to fix my hair.

After a round of razzing by Holls, I was ready to head upstairs. When Ronin popped his head in and winked at me, Payton patted my shoulder and told me he was happy for me. And Ronin.

"I need to snag me a big, beautiful man like yours," Payton sighed as he added texture spray to my hair to give it that bedhead look.

I didn't see the difference in my hairstyle from when I walked in here, after Ronin's hands had messed it all up. Tousled was tousled. Still, I had my creative art, and hair and makeup had theirs. It was not to be questioned.

"Well, you're on tour with us for the next few weeks and so is Lennie so—" I started.

"I don't know. I mean, I don't know if he's interested in me."

Payton sounded so unlike his usual confident self. He wasn't shy or uncertain.

"Only one way to find out."

"But isn't he always on the job?"

"There'll be times when he's off shift."

"It wouldn't work anyway. Between you, me, and my flat iron, I think I'm done with hook ups. I need a man who's going to stick around for more than one night. But with my work schedule, all the traveling, forget it."

Lennie entered the room and stopped short when he saw Payton. "You ready?"

Was he asking me or Payton?

"I'm good to go."

Payton stared back at Lennie, but no words were exchanged. I got up out of my chair and headed for the door.

Payton was right. It was hot in here.

———

I sat behind my drum kit, doing my warmup, waiting for the curtain to rise. Ronin and I did our usual pre-show clench, but this time, with a kiss. And lots of tongue.

Brodie and Holls made gagging noises, while Ro and I gave them our best fingers.

When Ronin took his spot on the stage, my nerves began to churn full force. I glanced over at the wings and spotted Lennie, Regan, and other team members watching. I also knew there was a shit ton of security in the audience. Not to mention the screening process for people coming into the venue. Still, the reminder that someone threatened to harm us at our Nashville show still lingered.

I don't think that fear was going away anytime soon.

Brodie turned around to face us just before the curtain dropped. The determined look in his eyes and the nod of his head told me that despite our fear, we were gonna be okay. I'd always admired his ability to say what he wanted, and the fact that he didn't take shit from anyone. He stood up for what he believed in. And that was always us.

The stakes had never been higher. I felt it, fuck, the whole stage was thrumming with nervous energy, and we hadn't hit a single note yet.

I nodded at Brodie, reading his expression.

No one's going to fuck with our family, our music, or our fans.

Our stage cue crackled in my earpiece and thank fuck my melodic brain clicked into gear.

When the stage lit up, and the curtain dropped, the roar of the crowd hit us like a sonic boom.

We started out with *Never Look Back* and the song had never felt more appropriate.

My arms and legs moved without thought. Kick on the downbeats. Snare on the backbeats.

It was my job to set the tempo, the mood, for all our songs. Ronin drove the rhythm with his bass, and Holls gave us melody lines and memorable solos. Brodie was the final missing piece, putting our harmony into words, driving the energy of the crowd higher and higher.

I joined in on the harmony when we hit the first chorus, but my voice was huskier than usual. Grittier. Even I could admit that it sounded pretty fucking sexy. And so was the reason why my voice was so low. Images of me and Ronin—in his bed, on the bus, in the bathroom—flashed through my mind, as bright as the lights that flashed around us.

And as soon as we were done on stage, I knew that being back in Ro's arms was the only place I wanted to be. Today, tomorrow, and every day after.

Forever was a long time.

But suddenly, to me, it seemed like no time at all.

CHAPTER 32

RONIN

Halfway through the show, on our break, we were downing electrolyte drinks and changing into another set of clothes, when Regan stepped up.

"I got an update from the Nashville PD. Unfortunately, they've had no success in tracing the call so far. On the positive side, it appears that this was a one-time thing. There have been no new threats or any hints of anything similar, but we're keeping a close eye on all comms. Either it's Dallas or someone saw the news about the assault and figured they'd cause trouble. This doesn't mean, however, that we're letting our guard down. Our security status is still on high alert. Unless it's a scheduled meet and greet with the fans, we're instituting a ban on outings like clubs where we have less control over the domain and who's coming near you. If everything is status quo over the next few weeks, then we'll reconsider our plan."

"I think we all agree that, for now, we'd rather be safe than sorry," Holls replied.

"Definitely." Brodie nodded, while he leaned against his husband.

"Fine with me," Faise replied.

"Me too," I added.

I didn't need to go clubbing anyway. There was only one man I wanted to party with, and he was standing right beside me. We'd have our own private dance as soon as the show was over.

Regan's earpiece crackled and she tapped on it. "What's up?... No, I don't recognize the name...if he's not on the list, he can't get in... hold on." She paused. "There's someone named Remy Harnett at the venue entrance. Said he's here to speak to Brodie about opening the next show? Is this for real?"

"Yup," Brodie replied. "Let him in."

"Advance warning next time, Brodie."

"Yes, ma'am," he replied to Regan, and she raised one eyebrow. "I'm not being sarcastic. I swear. Not with you. It just totally slipped my mind after the cancelled concert."

Regan nodded and walked off stage.

"Dee?" Holls turned to him.

"He's a country singer. Someone Van and I spotted at a local club back home. He's got a shitload of talent, but he hasn't been signed to any label yet. He mentioned he was gigging in Florida for the next month so I thought he might want to open one of our concerts."

"Country?" Faise asked.

"It's cool to have different opening acts in the upcoming shows. A crossover of sorts. Van and I have been toying with a few songs that would appeal to both our rock base and country fans. A mashup. We don't have it all worked out yet, it's just an idea."

"Could be interesting," I offered. "This guy Remy's good?"

"His voice is powerful," Brodie replied. "Guy could sing without a mic or a guitar no problem."

"Not to mention, he's got the look," Van added. "I mean, stage presence."

Brodie turned to his husband, and shit, there was practically smoke coming out of our lead singer's ears.

"What?" Van replied innocently. "It's true. You saw it too, *mon coeur*."

"Oh, so he's not just a great singer, but he's hot to boot?" I teased. "Tell us more, Van."

Van's face flushed but he shook his head. "Don't try to get me in trouble, Ro. You know what I mean. And it's not just me. You'll see for yourself."

"Hey, Jesse!" Holls called out. "Let me use your phone."

Jesse ambled over, passing us his cell. "What's going on?"

"Brodie invited a country music singer to open for us at the next show. The guy's here for the intros."

Jesse gave Brodie the same annoyed look that Regan did.

"What? Van and I were going to tell you," Brodie snapped. "Eventually. With all the security stuff going on, I just forgot."

Jesse rolled his eyes and glanced at Van. "I expected more from you."

Van shrugged. "Sorry, but like my husband said, we've been preoccupied. I promise you that it won't happen again. As soon as we know, you'll know."

Jesse nodded. I got it. He was in charge now and of course, he wanted to be in the loop. We were used to doing our own thing or doing it with Van. It was going to take some time for us to get used to working with a new manager.

Holloway googled the singer's name and me and Faise crowded around him. Several pictures popped up.

"Oh yeah, he's smoking hot," Faise announced.

I turned to my boo, not at all happy about that declaration. "You think so?"

"That long hair. The blue eyes. That smile."

Maybe this was a bad idea. "I don't like him."

Faise pinched my arm in retaliation.

"Ow."

"Be nice," Faise warned me. "The guy's probably nervous as hell."

"I sure am."

We turned to find the man in question, standing behind us, a guitar case in hand. He was exactly like his picture, tall and broad, with long, chestnut curls and a nervous grin. He was dressed in well-worn jeans, cowboy boots, and a blue plaid shirt that was half buttoned.

Van walked over to greet him first and Remy's smile turned from shy to big and bold. The guy would look great on album covers, no question. Brodie wasn't far behind his husband, taking hold of Van's hand and offering his other to Remy.

"Meet the rest of the guys, Ronin, Holls, and Faise. And our manager, Jesse."

"Remy Harnett, it's an honor to meet y'all." He nodded and shook our hands in turn.

His callused grip told me he was not holding that guitar for show.

"So, you're gonna open for us while we're in Florida?" Holloway asked.

"It'll be my pleasure. I just finished a gig in Tallahassee last night and drove straight down. Can't say no to an invite from Wayward Lane."

Jesse stepped forward and offered his hand. "Jesse Aimes, nice to meet you. First, we'll get your badge set up with our security crew and then you and I need to talk about the schedule."

"Course," Remy nodded. "Lead the way."

"Meet up with us in the VIP room after the show?" Brodie offered. "We can have a drink and talk shop."

"I'd love that. See y'all later."

Jesse motioned to the wings, and Remy followed.

"Guys! Five minutes!" Ace yelled out.

I finished the rest of my water and turned to Faise, who was smiling at me. "What?"

"You weren't really jealous, were you?"

I pulled him in tight and kissed his lips, tasting salt and sweat. "And what if I was?"

He punched his hips forward as his hands reached for my ass. "You're so ridiculous. You know you're the only man I see."

"I don't know, you looked pretty hard at that picture."

"I got hard, right here." He rubbed his body against mine. "And it's all for you."

I was about to lean forward and kiss him again when a towel was thrown at me.

"This is time to cool down, not heat up," Ace snickered.

I ignored our engineer and his joke.

"My bunk," I whispered. "As soon as the show's over."

"But what about Remy?"

"He can wait."

Faise squeezed my ass and let go. I was revved up and ready to perform.

For the concert, too.

———

After we closed the show, an hour later, we took our final bows.

Bibi then had us sign merch orders for the meet and greet. I finished mine in record time and decided to head to the tour bus first.

Lennie walked me over and stayed outside while I hopped on the bus, showered, and changed. I was hoping for a quickie with Faise before we headed to meet up with Remy and the guys.

Walking through the living area, I spotted my journal on the table and picked it up.

I often wrote when we were on the road, journaling about our trips. And sometimes, I wrote my secret poetry. Not that I had any outstanding talent, but it was my creative outlet. One that I didn't want to share with anyone. Well, only Faise knew about it. It bonded us, like so many other things we shared, just us two.

I sat down on the couch and flipped the notebook open. But as soon as I saw the handwriting, I knew that it wasn't mine.

It was Faise's. The words were laid out before me and, before I knew it, I was reading.

…It's getting worse. I can't watch him with every hot guy that comes along. The coke helps me forget, for a while, but it's never enough. Part of me wants to tell him. But I know that Ro will freak out. And I can't lose my best friend…

…I can't remember what happened last night. Or how I got home. I wiped my face and traces of white powder and blood were streaked on my fingers. When I rolled over, there was a stranger in my bed. Fuck, I hate when they stay over. I must have passed out before I could tell him to get lost. How many guys have I fucked lately? Too many to count. But I needed it. I need to fuck Ro out of my system, even though no matter who or how many times, it never seems to work. And snorting him away isn't working either. The hangovers are killing me. Thankfully, I still have a supply. Another hit and I won't have to worry at all…

… I didn't think coke would feel this good. And bad. Before, it was fun. But now, I need it more than anything. If I run out, I panic, and then everything, including my music, goes to shit. My life is shit anyway. Lately I feel like a robot. Travel, perform, take a bow, party, repeat. One city after another, the bright lights and eager fans all clamoring for a piece of us. It was awesome at first, all the beautiful people, the parties, the drugs, the attention. It was fun and heady. Until it wasn't. Because I hate that I have to share him with other people. Now he's all I think about. I can't stop. I'm messed up. Keeping my feelings buried is something I thought I was

good at. But it turns out, even introverts like me can't keep holding on to shit forever. I've been pulling away from him. I need to. Otherwise, I know for sure, I'll lose my mind. It's already happening. The white devil has a death grip on me and he's not letting go. Maybe that's okay. It can take me. Then I won't have this pain anymore...

Jesus Christ. What the fuck? I needed to stop reading. Put it away. Forget I ever saw that.

What the hell were you thinking?

I wasn't. And I thought I knew Faise. That we had no secrets, not between us.

But apparently, I'd been wrong.

The door to the bus opened but I didn't look up. Didn't need to. I knew who it was.

Suddenly, Faise was standing in front of me, and the look in his eyes made me break out in a cold sweat. I was guilty as hell, but at the same time, so fucking angry about what I'd found out.

"Why are you reading that? It's my fucking journal!" he snapped and pulled it out of my hand.

"I thought it was mine. It looks the same. I saw it on the table, and grabbed it by mistake. I'm sorry. By the time I realized... I—" Then my guilt turned to anger. "What the fuck, Faise? Why didn't you tell me?"

"Tell you what?"

"Don't!" I snarled. "The coke! The reason why you kept needing more and more. What you were going through. Tell me the truth!"

He threw the journal across the table. "Are you fucking kidding me? You saw me, you know what I went through!"

"Apparently not the reason why!" I yelled. "I can't... I mean—" My lungs seized up. I was so out of breath I could barely form words. "The reason your addiction spiraled. It was me?"

CHAPTER 33

FAISE

"**D**on't be so fucking egotistical! My addiction is about me, not you!" I shouted.

I was so fucking furious that Ronin had read my journal without asking first. My most private, inner thoughts. The place where I spilled my guts because I could. Because it was safe. Because there was no judgement there.

"That's not what you wrote."

I ran a hand through my sweat-soaked hair and stared at Ronin.

"Look, the fact that my partying got out of control, and it happened around the same time that I started noticing you as more than my best friend, yeah, it was shit timing. But it's not the reason for my addiction. I was unhappy about a lot of things. But I didn't know how to deal with it. Express it. Read the rest of it!"

"What?"

"Go on," I urged and pointed to the journal. "You might as well read the rest. Or I can give you a recap. You see, I also talk about my family and the pressure I felt about making it big. How I always felt secondary to Rae because I wasn't book smart like him. And there was the fact that I was the only queer person in my family. And the pressure to be outgoing and being under the microscope of the press when we became famous… you know all this. You know me!"

Ronin was shaking his head, like he didn't believe a word I just said.

"I thought I did. But you said it, right there, in your own words. *I* was the reason you started using more and more." Ronin paced the hallway. "I… I can't deal with this. I need to go. I need to be alone for a while."

He walked down the hallway to the back of the bus. I stood there, unable to move an inch.

When he came back down, he had his duffle bag in hand, and headed for the door.

"Running away when things get heavy?" I snapped. "Is that it? We're done? You're back to fucking randos?"

"I didn't say that! I just need some space to think. That's all."

"Yeah," I scoffed. "Go. Leave. It's fine. It's always easier to leave than to be the one left behind, right?"

I knew I'd hit my mark when Ronin flinched. That was a low blow. But I was so angry, so hurt that he wouldn't stay and talk to me, that I lashed out.

Ever since his dad walked out on him, he kept everyone, except his family, at arm's length. And sometimes me too. He felt deeply, more than most, but he wasn't comfortable with that fact. Ironically, I felt the same way.

"This is not about you," I reiterated, pleading with him to understand.

"How can you say that? You couldn't tell me how you felt about me, and you were so frustrated that you snorted your pain away. Don't tell me it's not about me!"

"Not all of it! And it's about us!" I shouted and slapped my hand on the table.

The sound of the door opening made me jolt, and I turned to face an irate Lennie.

"What the fuck is going on here?" he asked.

Ronin shook his head, his dark hair falling into his face. "I'm staying on the other bus."

Lennie's face fell as he glanced between me and Ronin.

"What he said," I replied and stalked off to the bathroom, slamming the door shut. I slid to the floor, gripping my head in my hands, the tears flowing free and hot. I kicked the shower door and then got up, turned on the water as hot as it would go and stepped inside, clothes and all.

I was shivering, despite the warmth of the water. Struggling, I stripped my wet clothes off and left them on the tile floor. Then I scrubbed myself raw and cursed myself for leaving that stupid journal where anyone could see it.

By the time I'd dried off, I was exhausted, drained. Then I realized, I'd forgotten my cell. I padded back to the living area, now dark and quiet, and picked up my phone.

Brodie: We're in the VIP room with Remy. Where the fuck are you guys?

Ronin: Not feeling well, talk tomorrow

Faise: Yeah, sorry. I'm done. For the night.

Was Ronin done with me forever?

Holls: Lennie says you're staying in the other bus, what's going on Ro?

Ronin: Not now

Brodie: What the fuck is happening?

Ronin knew. I might as well tell everyone else.

Faise: Ronin learned part of the reason why I hit the coke so hard. And now we're done. Any more questions?

I shut my phone off. I wasn't supposed to do that. Regan would have my balls for breakfast. But fuck it. I just wanted silence.

But I couldn't make myself walk back to my bunk. Ronin's bunk. Not after everything we'd done in there.

Fuck, Ronin had the right idea. I wanted to get off this goddamn bus. Unfortunately, there was nowhere else for me to go. So, instead of sleeping on my bunk, I grabbed a blanket and stretched out on the sofa. Not that sleep would come anytime soon.

Guilt ate away at me. Should I have told him when I came out of rehab? My therapist had urged me to confront my feelings about Ronin, but even then, I couldn't do it. The idea of losing my best friend trumped my need to come clean about all the reasons why I was using in the first place.

Fuck, would Ronin ever trust me again? Or would things never be the same? And why was I so torn up? He was the one who'd violated my privacy.

I heard the door of the bus open again, but I didn't open my eyes and I didn't move. I didn't want to talk to anyone. It was only when a gentle hand touched my head, that I opened my eyes to find my brother standing there.

"What are you doing here?" I asked.

"I passed Lennie on the way to the bus. He told me you and Ronin had a fight. What happened?"

I covered my face, pushing the heels of my hands into my eyes.

"Ronin picked up my journal by accident. There were things in there that I wrote when I was going through the worst of my addiction. The stuff I was feeling about him but couldn't tell him. He was shocked, angry, and horrified that he could be... a part of the reason why I couldn't stop using."

"You never told him how you felt?"

I shook my head, sitting up.

"In time, it would have happened. But ever since he and I

became lovers, I just couldn't. How could I talk about that? I don't want to relive the past. Fuck, I almost lost everything, including my life. I don't want to go back there. It's done. I want to forget about it and move on."

Rae sat down beside me and sighed.

"But you can't. And you and I are so fucking alike in this way, bro. Instead of talking shit out, like me telling my wife I was unhappy or telling our parents that I was broke, it was easier to numb myself. Ronin's in shock. You guys are so close and share everything. If I were him, I'd be upset finding out shit like that, too. I know these conversations are hard, but like you once told me, you have to do it."

"What if he won't talk to me? What if he—"

I was trembling hard, and Rae put his arm around my shoulder.

"He will. It's Ronin. Just give him a few days to wrap his head around what he read. Then, talk it out. Don't make the same mistake that I did. Tell him you love him. And show him. I know it's scary as fuck, but he needs to hear the words."

I nodded, blinking away more tears.

"I know," I whispered as I wiped my eyes.

"You want to watch a movie with me?"

I nodded, thankful and grateful that Rae was here. And as always, his big brother wisdom was right.

Both me and Ronin needed time to sort through all this.

———

An hour later, and halfway through the movie, I glanced at my phone. It was just after 2 am. Rae was asleep on the sofa beside me. Van, Brodie, and Holls finally joined us on the bus.

"I'm fine," I replied before anyone could ask. "And don't worry. We'll work it out."

"You better," Brodie smiled at me. "'Cause we love both of you."

"Aw, Dee," Holls gushed, grabbed our frontman, and gave him a loud, smacking kiss on the cheek.

"Ew, gross. I said them, not you," Brodie snorted and pushed him away.

Holls smacked Brodie on the shoulder, while Van shook his head at our ridiculous antics.

"You sure you're okay?" Van asked as he glanced at me.

I nodded in response.

Van started down the hallway. "I'm going to get ready for bed."

"I'll be right behind you, honey," Brodie whispered, his eyes locked on Van's ass.

"Thank fuck I'm sleeping out here," I grumbled.

"I'll keep you company for a bit," Holls offered, and sat down across from me.

Rae was still snoring away, sound asleep.

"Thanks."

Brodie sat down, too, and leaned in, gripping my knee. "How come you never told him?"

"What do you mean?"

"Faise." Brodie shook his head. "We were there. We witnessed your drug use going out of control. And every time we'd be out, and you saw Ronin with a guy, you hit it hard. It wasn't difficult to figure out why you were struggling. I'm not saying your addiction was all him, but your feelings for him played into it."

"I'm not denying that. But it's not the whole story," I replied. "And he didn't see it. And I could never say. I mean, for what purpose? To ruin the best friendship I've ever had? And once we started, you know—"

"Fucking," Holls offered.

"Yes, fucking," I sighed. "I didn't want him to know. Now he pities me. 'Poor Faise, he wanted me all these years and never said, and screwed himself over'. Yeah, that's attractive."

"This is Ronin we're talking about. He looks at you like you're the fucking sun and the moon and the stars. All of it. I don't think there's anything you could do or say that would change how he feels about you," Holls replied in a serious tone. "And take it from me, you can fight all you want, but your feelings win out in the end. It didn't matter how much I wanted to run from Dawson, something called me back. And if you want Ro, if you love him, if you trust him, you gotta be open. About everything."

I stared at Holls like I'd never seen him before. Brodie gave me the same look.

"Who are you right now?"

Holls stuck out his tongue.

"Oh, thank fuck, you're still in there," I teased and then reached for his shoulder, squeezing it.

"And thanks. You're right."

"I never get tired of hearing that," Holls teased and leaned back. "But I'm tired. I'm gonna hit my bunk. You sure you're all right?"

"I'll be okay." I nodded.

Brodie got up too. "Don't worry. He'll be back."

Once my friends were gone, I closed my eyes, knowing in my gut that Brodie was right.

And finally, sleep came.

CHAPTER 34
RONIN

After I boarded the other bus, I searched the cabinets and found a dusty bottle of vodka and a clean glass.

I poured myself a double, no ice, and took a long swig, the alcohol burning away the lump of anxiety that was lodged in my throat. I still couldn't believe that my best friend had kept his feelings for me secret all those years.

Why hadn't he said anything? What did that say about our trust?

"Ro?"

I turned to find my sister standing at the end of the hallway, her phone in her hand.

"What are you doing here?" she asked me. "Is everything okay?"

"Everything is—" God, where did I start? "I had a fight with Faise, and I needed some time alone. Sorry if I woke you."

She shook her head, and walked closer, then pointed to the glass in my hand. "I was still awake. Are you going to share that bottle of vodka or do you plan to drink it all yourself?"

Instead of replying, I reached for another glass, poured her a double as well, then passed it over. She raised her glass, and I did the same, clinking them together and muttering the word 'cheers'.

Not that I felt like celebrating. Room temperature vodka was my consolation drink, not the kind meant for good times.

"You want to talk about it?" she asked, sipping on her drink.

"Not now."

She nodded and took a seat on the nearby sofa. It was the same layout as the other tour bus. Only quieter. Cleaner, too.

Hey, we're four rockstars on the road. What do you expect?

"So, you couldn't sleep?"

Duh, Ronin. Ask the obvious question.

"Nope. I was thinking about the past few months," she started. "Wondering why I put up with Dallas's behavior. And the answer finally dawned on me tonight of all nights. I don't know why I didn't see it before. I was so desperate to hold on to the idea of him. Sticking it out, for better or worse. Or, in my case, just the worse part. I wasn't going to be like Dad and up and leave someone I loved, even if he was bad for me. Nope, I'd hold on to my relationship. I could make it work. Pride. It was all about pride. And insecurity."

I was the opposite. I never wanted to be in a relationship to begin with. But Ciara was right. Losing our dad made me wary. And guilty. He hadn't been that involved in our life before he left, but my coming out pushed him over the edge.

Faise was right. If you leave, or you don't get involved in the first place, you don't get left behind.

She took another sip and sighed. "Dad's rejection did a number on all of us. Left us with a hurt that still hasn't quite healed. And then, the one time I let my guard down, and finally let someone in, look what happened."

"You've been afraid to let anyone get close. 'Cause when you do, you give your whole heart. Everything. And that's scary as fuck."

She stared at her glass, then back at me. "It is scary. But it shouldn't be, not with the right person. Or if it is, it should be worth the risk."

"You always see the best in people. You did the same thing with Dallas. Did he know about Dad?"

She nodded.

"I'm sure he found a way to use that against you, consciously or not. He had you convinced that you couldn't live without him."

"He did. For a while. Until the first time he hit me. Then I realized, in my heart, that the whole thing was so wrong. But, by that time, I was so far in, I didn't know how to get out."

"You came to me. You got out."

She nodded and ran a hand through her hair. "I guess I did. Took me a while, though."

"Not everything works itself out in a day."

"Thank you for always being there. I probably haven't said it often enough," Ciara gave me a small smile. "I'm going to be okay."

"Yes, you will."

"And I'm happy to see you happy. And you and Faise have each other. That man loves you like crazy."

He did. But shit, just thinking about our fight, I...

"I found out something tonight," I confessed. "And I feel like shit. I should've been there for him. I mean, I was, sort of, just not in the way he needed. And I don't know why he kept things from me."

Ciara leaned forward, taking my hand. "I'm sure you did the best you could at the time. You're not a mind reader."

"I guess."

"Aren't you better off talking this out with him?"

My sister looked at me in a way I hadn't seen in a long time, her blue eyes sharp and knowing. She had a way of cutting through the bullshit that I admired.

I nodded.

"Then you know what to do." She finished the rest of her drink, handed me the glass, and nodded. "I'm heading back to bed."

"Thanks, Ci."

"It's after 2 am, go get some sleep," she called out as she headed back down the hallway.

I swallowed the rest of my drink, placed both glasses in the sink, and spread out on the sofa. Well, spread out was pushing it. It was pretty cramped for a guy my size, but I made do. I'd slept in far worse places.

No matter what, though, Faise was by my side.

Fuck, the thought of spending one night apart from him gave me a weird, painful feeling in the pit of my stomach. I reasoned it was the vodka, but my heart beating double time told me I was a fool.

I'd never sleep here. Those angry words between me and Faise would keep me up all night. So, I got up and headed for the door. When I stepped outside, Valen and Petyr were standing guard as usual.

"I'm going back to my bus."

They nodded, and Petyr fell into line beside me, walking me over. It was a short trip, but I guess our security meant business when they said they were on high alert.

When I got to our bus, I opened the door as quietly as I could.

I climbed the stairs, and spotted Rae asleep on the couch, Faise beside him. I walked over to him, slow steps, until Faise opened his eyes.

"Ro?"

"Come on, baby, let's go to bed."

"Am I dreaming again?"

"No. I'm right here, real as can be."

He rubbed his eyes, and his hair was sticking up on end. My heart clenched hard. He was the sweetest fucking thing I'd ever seen.

"Are you still angry?"

I shook my head. "We'll talk about it in the morning. I'm sorry I ran out of here."

Then, there was no more time for discussion. I bent over, picked him up, and carried him down to our bunk. I laid him down, and slid in beside him, pulled over the duvet, then closed the curtains.

I was still sweaty from the concert, but too exhausted to care.

Faise was in my arms. Nothing else mattered.

Faise

I woke up, confused. And hot, sweaty, and hard.

I blinked, and realized I was lying on top of Ronin. Somehow, my t-shirt was gone, and so was his, one arm slung above his head.

He came back.

I leaned down, nuzzling my face in his pec, then kissed my way over to the slope of his armpit. I inhaled his scent, rubbing my face against him. Fuck, I wanted to lick him all over. Every fucking inch.

No. Stop it. I could not let my dick distract me. We needed to talk.

"Baby?" he whispered.

I stared up at him, at the blue eyes that were home to me.

"I'm sorry I read your journal," he whispered. "As soon as I recognized your handwriting, I should have put it away. That's a total violation of your privacy and I get it if you're still angry with me. But, since I did read it, I also wish you'd told me sooner. About how you felt."

I shook my head, then kissed his chest again. "I was so raw at the time, and I wasn't ready to face it. I told you the truth. My addiction wasn't just about keeping my feelings for you a secret. It was a lifetime of insecurities. Of feeling like I didn't measure up to other people's expectations, of not being enough, and using drugs to escape my anxiety."

Ronin bit his lower lip.

"And how would you have reacted back then if I'd told you I wanted you? I didn't want to fuck up, not us or the band, but us most of all."

"I can't say for sure how I would have reacted. The only thing I know, the only thing I've ever been certain of, is that I love you. Friends first, and always, and now—" his voice cracked, hoarse with emotion. "Now as the man that I can't live without. Do you understand? I love you. I'm in love with you. Not just as you were, but as you are. You're everything to me. My one and only."

I trembled in his arms. When he reached up to cup my face, I realized he was shaking too.

Our bodies swayed together as the bus rocked. My world rocked along with it.

"I've been in love with you for so long," I confessed. "I love you so, so much."

Fuck, finally saying the words I'd held onto for years was exhilarating.

"I can't even explain it. It overwhelms me. I'm flying, and falling, but it's amazing. And I know I've made a lot of mistakes, but I promise, nothing goes unsaid between us. Not anymore."

He nodded, pulling me up close, taking my lips in a kiss that echoed our words.

Did Ronin just say he loved me?

"Faise, baby, are you okay?"

He gently swiped my cheeks with his thumbs, and it was only then that I realized I was crying.

This time, happy tears.

I nodded, leaning in to whisper against his lips. "I hope the shock absorbers on this bus are brand fucking new because we are about to give them a test they've never seen."

Ronin's booming laughter woke up the entire bus.

CHAPTER 35
FAISE

wasn't joking.

Now that we'd finally spoken our truth, there was no stopping the intense need to show each other what we meant.

Ronin's eager hands delved into my pants while I sucked on his neck, marking him.

"Get these fucking jeans off, now," he demanded, shoving my jeans down, gripping my ass cheeks so tight I knew I was gonna have bruises there tomorrow. "Get naked and fuck me."

Fumbling in the dark, we were a frantic tangle of grunts and moans, hard bodies, and soft sheets. There was hardly any space in here for Ronin, never mind the two of us, but to me, it was the sexiest place to fuck. Ever. Everything was more intense because there was no separation between us. It was heady—the smell of our combined arousal, the echo of our sighs and moans, the air charged with electricity.

I reached frantically under the mattress to find the lube, then slicked up two fingers.

Ronin pulled his knees to his chest, opening to me.

When I slid one finger over his hole, teasing him, he

growled so loud that I swear the walls around us vibrated. I pushed inside him, slowly, and he canted his hips, taking more.

"Hurry up," he hissed.

I drilled deep inside his ass, then crooked my finger and tormented his prostate.

"Yes!"

Ronin's shout was booming.

I added more lube and a second finger, not wasting any time but making sure he was good and stretched for the hard fucking both of us needed. My hands were shaking with want. I used my other hand to tug on his dick, so heavy and hard.

"Don't need any more," he groaned. "I'm ready."

Pulling out of his body, I wiped the rest of the lube over my dick and slid into his tight hole.

Ronin pushed his ass towards me, taking me in, while I rocked my hips, slowly, pushing inside him inch by inch, until I was fully seated.

There was enough light filtering through the curtains, enough that I could see Ronin's features clearly. He bit his bottom lip, his cheeks flushed, his eyes glazed over. So beautiful, and all mine.

"Love this, love being inside you," I panted as the heat around my cock intensified. Nothing between us. "Need you. Love you."

"Love you more," he replied as his body shuddered underneath mine. "Always."

"Yes."

My hips snapped, and I pushed inside him, as deep as I could go. It wasn't enough.

His big hands slid down and cupped my ass, pulling me in tighter, nothing between us. I fucked into him with short, tight strokes, face to face, my control slipping fast. I stroked his cock with the same frantic rhythm, tugging quick and hard.

"Ronin," I moaned.

"Baby," he called out, a husky plea that filled up all my empty spaces. "Fuck me full of your cum."

His words drove me right over the edge. Both of us jerked hard, coming in a heated rush, skin slapping together. My hips jerked hard, and I came so fast, I could barely breathe. Ronin's ass tightened, strangling my dick as I filled him up with my cum.

He reached up, taking my lips in a mauling kiss, sucking on my tongue. I let myself be devoured by him, consumed by the aftershocks that rolled through my body. The wild pleasure had me unable to stop, thrusting inside him, unwilling to let go. This, right here, this was where I was meant to be.

"I love you," he whispered over and over, kissing my cheeks, my temple, and then my lips again. "Only you."

I breathed in his words, letting them sink inside me, the trembling taking hold of me again.

Slowly, I eased out of him, and looked down, watching my cum slip out of his ass. The sight was so sexy, so freaking hot, shivers ran up my spine.

"I love you, too," I replied, clutching tight to him, burying my face in his neck. "Ronin."

I gave his skin a teasing lick, then kissed my way down over his pec, sucking on one of his nipples. Needing more, I leaned over and licked the edge of his armpit, tasting musk and sweat and something that was all Ronin.

I wasn't kidding when I said I wanted to lick all of him. He clutched my hair tight in his hands, letting out a filthy moan.

Suddenly, he wrapped his legs around my waist and rolled, taking me under.

"We need to rip out the top bunk so I can sit up and ride you," he growled.

"I'm down with this plan," I grunted, sliding my hands over his ass, rubbing down his crease, rubbing my cum into his skin.

"How about you buy your own fucking bus so the rest of us can sleep?" Holls suddenly yelled out.

"Now where's the fun in that?" Ronin shouted back.

Shaking his head, Ronin gave me a wicked grin and leaned forward to kiss me. Our dirty moans couldn't be contained.

"I think I preferred the shouting!" Holls added.

"No problem," I replied. "Just wait."

―――――

A few hours later, after Ronin and I had fucked, mauled, and marked each other with as many love bites, and as much cum as was humanly possible, we ventured out of our bunk to grab a much-needed snack.

The bus wasn't moving anymore. We must've arrived in Miami already.

Holls, Van, and Brodie were already seated around the table at the front of the bus, a box of pizza between them, and cold beers to boot.

"I'm traumatized," Holls grumbled as he bit on a slice of pizza.

"What the fuck are you talking about?" Ronin scoffed and leaned over to grab two slices, passing one to me. I took a large bite, ravenous. The pizza was so salty and good that I let out a loud groan of pleasure. Ronin nearly dropped his slice on the floor.

"The two of you." Holls shivered dramatically. "I can't unhear it."

"You never had a problem listening or watching before," I countered, raising one eyebrow.

It was true. Rockstars aren't shy when it comes to the stage or the bedroom.

"That's different. You guys were with strangers."

"And?" Brodie smiled smugly and glanced over at us. "I have no problem with it. You guys are hot together."

Ronin put a protective arm around me.

Van sighed and gave his husband a possessive look. "Really, Dee?"

Brodie turned and winked at his husband. "No one will ever compare to you, honey. But you have to admit, that soundtrack was pretty inspiring."

Van cupped Brodie's face and swiped a thumb over his mouth. When Van brought his finger back to his lips and licked it, Brodie sighed.

"I'm done eating… pizza," Brodie whispered and stood up.

Our lead singer strutted down the hallway, with Van hot on his heels.

"More for us." Ronin nodded as he ate.

We sat down and finished off the pizza with Holls. And we tried to ignore the loud sex sounds that echoed from the back of the bus.

Okay, maybe Holls had a point.

"I think we're big enough now, we could each have our own bus. Or, three of them, since me and Ronin would share."

Holls grabbed a napkin and wiped his face. "I don't know. There's something special about the four of us being together. Like when we started out."

"So, you're not uncomfortable?" Ronin asked.

"Not at all, I'm just razzing you." Holls smiled at us. "Never seen either of you smile so fucking big, though. That'll take getting used to."

"That's what happens when you fall in love with your best friend," Ronin admitted, then kissed the top of my head.

Holls nodded. "Took you long enough to get your head out of your ass."

I snorted, then nearly choked on my bite of cheese and pepperoni.

"Hey!" Ronin grumbled.

"Who says I was talking just to *you*?" Holls replied, then aimed his smirk at me.

I took a long sip of my beer to clear my throat. "Hey, I'm a musician, give me a break. It's not like any of us ever expected to fall. Ever. Right?"

Holls and Ronin nodded in agreement.

All four of us had been single for so many years. The last thing any of us wanted when we started out at eighteen was a conventional life. We wanted our freedom, and we didn't want to be tied down. Because there was always another show, another city, another man we wanted to explore. How do you sustain a relationship when you've always got one foot out the door? And, given our celebrity, there were so many guys vying for our attention. It was heady at the time.

Why choose one person?

In the end, though, we didn't choose love, it chose us.

This was the year we all turned thirty. A new decade, a new beginning. But deep down, one thing remained the same. We still wanted to play our music, and travel, and meet the fans. But maybe being a working musician and having a relationship wasn't mutually exclusive. Sure, it would take a lot of work and sacrifices. There would still be times when we'd be separated from our partners. Me and Ronin less so than Holls and Brodie. But it would happen.

There might be occasions when Ronin wanted to play a solo gig or maybe work on his own music. Same thing for me. What did I want to do outside of drumming? There had to be something. Because one day, my knees would give out, my shoulders would too, and I wouldn't be able to play at the same intensity as I did now.

Plus, there were other things to consider. Like family.

Was that something Ronin wanted? I'd never put much thought into having a family of my own. But now that Ronin and I were together, the idea was floating around in my mind. Having kids together would be a major step, something I didn't think I'd ever want. But maybe, just maybe, I wanted that with him.

I was getting ahead of myself. Happily so, but still.

Then I noticed that the noises down the hallway had quieted.

Brodie swaggered back down the aisle, like he did on stage, in his unbuttoned jeans, his lips swollen and red, his trademark grin in place. He sat down beside Holls and grabbed one of the bottles, taking a long sip.

"Fuck, I needed that."

"The beer or the blowjob?" Ronin quipped.

Holls shook his head, chuckling, and held up his beer bottle. "It's been a crazy ass year, but the best one of my life. And there's no one I'd rather share it with than you guys."

"Cheers to that," Ronin nodded and held his bottle up.

I did the same, clinking their glasses.

"To family," I offered.

"To family," Brodie repeated.

The boys of Wayward Lane would always drink to that.

CHAPTER 36
RONIN

After a successful week in Florida, we continued our southern leg, on to Georgia and the Carolinas. Every concert was packed, sold out, and without incident. The storm had finally passed, and things were looking up.

Now we were excited about the heading to the West Coast. We flew out to LA first. Then San Francisco, then up to Washington and Oregon. It was home to some of our most ardent fans, and it was always a kick ass time.

And me and Faise?

To outsiders, maybe the change wasn't noticeable. But to us? There was a freedom in embracing our feelings. And getting to know Faise as my boyfriend, my lover, blew everything, including my mind, away.

The only hitch came when we arrived in LA. Averell was already in town, working along with Jesse to book us in at all the right parties and places to be seen. The guy knew his shit and was probably going to market the hell out of us and make us richer. But I didn't like the fact that he thought he had a chance with Faise.

Past tense.

I knew Faise didn't want anyone but me, but still. I'd always been possessive of my boo, but lately, well, it was a whole other level. All I could see was how much attention he got from interested guys. Of course he did. He was smoking hot. Sexiest man I'd ever met. Watching him behind his kit, it was like I was seeing him play for the first time.

But if any guy so much as looked his way or tried to flirt, the death glare came out and I was not fucking around.

I surprised even myself with my reaction. But thankfully, Faise was turned on by my caveman antics.

Here's how it went down: Faise got flirted with after our concerts, I growled at whoever the culprit was, my man pulled me aside, and we found a bathroom or any hidden nook to fuck each other's brains out. Once I came, in him or on him, and he smelled like me, I was good.

And just thinking about meeting up with Averell made me want to do the same thing.

Only, we were disembarking our flight and there was no time to join the mile high club.

Maybe on the way back home.

Rae and Ciara were here for the California shows, then Rae was heading back to Rhode Island and my sister, to Nashville. She decided she wanted to stay near me, and Hardwick had offered her a temporary job working social media write ups for another band. She still had big city dreams, but she was now thinking international. Maybe London or Paris. If I knew my sister, it was going to happen. She'd been keeping up with her virtual therapy sessions and I could see her coming back to life, each day better than the last.

Rae was doing well too. He and Faise had regular talks with their sponsors, staying aware of any stressors that might trigger their addictions. And Faise finally opening to me, and to his brother, it made their relationship, and ours, closer than ever.

"Averell's going to meet us at the hotel for dinner," Jesse announced as he glanced at his phone. "Then he's got a full schedule for the night. Press ops, private parties, you name it. The tour and your next album is all the entertainment news can talk about."

But I didn't think about that. I was worried about spending a whole night with a man who wants *my* man.

A hand on my back had me turning around.

"You ready for tonight?" Faise asked me.

This was a big one. Not just for our careers, but for us as a couple. We were going public with our relationship.

"Yes." I leaned down and kissed him. "So ready. You?"

He smiled against my lips. "I'm so fucking excited. I hope the press are positive."

"I'm sure Jesse's got it under control."

We walked out of the plane, and our security team got us inside the SUVs in record time.

When we traveled to LA, we always stayed at the same hotel. It was renowned for hosting musicians, actors, and other celebrities. Impromptu performances by some of the most legendary talents in show biz were not uncommon. And the staff at the hotel were discreet. A rarity in our world.

With just enough time for a nap, a shower, and a change of clothes, we found ourselves in the lobby of the hotel at just after nine, starving. The food here was also a high point, with great seafood and a wine list that was bigger than any book I'd ever read.

Lennie and Regan escorted us to a private room, where Averell was seated at a long table. He was busy typing away on his phone. He stood up when he spotted us. Dressed in another sharp suit, a practiced smile in place, he nodded and shook our hands in turn.

Until, suddenly, the smile on his face vanished. He was

probably surprised that my sister and Faise's brother were joining us. Then again, Wayward Lane was a family, and including our relatives in events was nothing new to us. And if Averell didn't like it, too bad.

Rae sat between Averell and Jesse and started asking all kinds of questions about Hardwick's marketing plans and what kind of stats we were driving. That was all white noise to me. If the fans loved us, the albums were selling, the concerts were sold out, I was happy. The business side, I left to the professionals.

Averell seemed surprised at Rae's level of interest and his knowledge of business, but none too pleased when Rae began to ask more detailed questions. But at least Averell's attention was not on Faise. In fact, he'd hardly made eye contact with my boyfriend since we'd arrived at the table.

Thank you, Rae.

A waiter offered us water and menus. We ordered champagne to start, and a non-alcoholic version for those that didn't drink. Then we ordered dinner, and with drinks in hand, Jesse tapped on his glass and stood up.

"A toast. To a great band, a successful tour, and many more years to come!"

"I second that," Averell stated.

Dinner was a three-course meal, and by the time we were done, it was time to hit the media circuit. Just before we got up to leave the restaurant, Jesse leaned forward.

"You guys ready to launch?"

"No question," I answered, lifting Faise's hand, kissing his knuckles.

"What he said," Faise replied, staring back at me.

It was only me and him.

A throat cleared and we turned to look at Averell.

"Are you sure? Because once the news is out, there's no going back. The press will be relentless. Forget any kind of privacy."

"We've been living in the rock n' roll fishbowl for a while now," I countered, keeping my tone polite. "Pretty sure we know what to expect. And I'm not hiding. I'm in love with Faise, and he's in love with me. If anyone has a problem with that, they can fuck right off."

Hey, I said my tone was polite. Not every word.

Faise leaned over and kissed me, and Brodie and Holls whistled so loud, I'm sure the entire restaurant heard it.

"It's a shame we can't go right back up to our hotel room," Faise whispered.

"Later. Promise." I kissed him back. "First, I want to show you off. I want everyone to know that you're mine."

He licked his lips and I wanted to say, fuck the party. Let's make our own.

"Okay, time to get going," Jesse interrupted.

Faise wrapped an arm around my waist as we made our way out of the restaurant, Lennie, Petyr, and our entourage flanking us. Several people in the lobby stopped us and asked for autographs, which me and the guys gladly gave. Then it was out into the warm LA night and into a big ass limo.

Shit like this never got old.

Our first stop was a private party hosted by Montage Entertainment, a film production company. Jesse and Averell had pitched the idea of a rockumentary about Wayward Lane's rise to stardom and having Montage's film crew follow us on our next tour. Me and the guys had talked it over, but it still wasn't a done deal. It was a lot to have someone filming you 24/7 for weeks on end. Still, the genre was popular, and it might give a boost to our sales.

There was a formal press line and I recognized familiar faces, musicians, actors and the like.

Faise's grip grew as damp as mine the closer we got to the entry point.

"One last check," Jesse murmured as he adjusted my jacket and fiddled with Faise's hair. "You guys look great.

Remember, any questions you're not sure about, leave it, smile, and keep walking down the line."

My heart was pounding so hard it was all I could hear.

Brodie, Van, and Holls were behind us, and gave us a reassuring pat on the back.

When the line finally moved, and just before it was our turn to step out, I glanced down at my boyfriend.

I was nervous for sure, but I wasn't changing my mind. And the determined look in his eyes told me he was the same. With our hands interlocked, I pulled him as close to me as he could get. We didn't need to utter a fucking word; our body language said it all.

"Let's do this."

Like Faise, I always found this part of our life overwhelming. When I didn't have my bass guitar in hand, I needed distraction, so I played it off with jokes. My go to for any situation where I felt uncomfortable. But my humor vanished in the face of all the cameras and bright lights. This wasn't any ordinary junket, and we weren't on stage.

Flashes popped, so many, so fast, that it became difficult to see anything but spots in my eyes.

"What's going on here?" one reporter yelled out.

"I'm holding my boyfriend's hand. But thanks for pointing out the obvious."

There was a smattering of laughter in response. Okay, maybe my sense of humor hadn't completely shut down.

Faise leaned into me, and I let go of his hand, wrapping my arm around his waist, pulling him in tight. Then I turned my head and kissed his temple. There was a frenzy of call outs and more flashes.

Jesse motioned for us to walk closer to the press line. I swallowed hard, readying myself for the onslaught of questions.

"Faisel! Ronin! Over here!"

A familiar reporter smiled at us. "Janine Taylor, eNews

Now. There have been rumors about your friendship being something more for years. Have you two been keeping it a secret all this time?"

Faise shook his head and leaned into the mic. "No, this is a recent development. But one that we're very happy about."

"What about the future of the band? Aren't you worried about the repercussions if your romantic relationship doesn't work out?"

"No, we're not," I replied with a smile. "We've been best friends for twenty years. This is just one more evolution of our relationship. Faise and I are a permanent deal. Forever."

"That's serious. Does this mean a proposal isn't far off in the future?"

Both of us let out a nervous laugh. We were expecting those kinds of questions, but the shock of hearing them wasn't lost.

"You're going to have to stay tuned to find out."

CHAPTER 37
FAISE

There was a proposal.

No, not me and Ronin. Not yet...

Dawson had flown to LA for the weekend to visit Holls. And, after our July 1st sold-out performance, Holls proposed to his boyfriend. Privately. The next day, the press release had our fans going wild.

The Wayward Lane family had another reason to celebrate.

And tonight, we were doing just that. Our security had allowed us to attend an exclusive club with invite only privileges. No paps, no unscreened guests, and no problems.

"So, you guys set a date or what?" Brodie asked as we sat at a table, downing shots of tequila. "Or are you gonna be like me and Van, and run off to Vegas?"

Dawson and Holls were too busy making out to pay Brodie's question any attention.

"Hey, fuckers!" Brodie yelled out over the music. "You're getting married! Plenty of time to suck face later."

Dawson gave Holls one last kiss and turned to give Brodie

a dirty look. Not that it had any effect on our frontman. Dawson might look scary as fuck with his fauxhawk and intense expression, but all of us knew the man was a gentle giant.

"There's no rush," Dawson replied as he held up his hand, admiring the gold ring. "So, no Vegas wedding."

"Well," Holls started. "I wouldn't say no to getting married sooner rather than later. But, no matter what, we gotta plan it out. No elopement. Jaxon needs to be a big part of our day."

Dawson's son. Holloway's soon to be stepson. Holy shit. To think of Holloway, who, only six months ago was your typical rock n' roll fuckboy, as a stepdad, was crazy. Crazy, funny, and surprisingly, perfect. Our friend had a big heart and when he loved, he did it all the way. With his mom long since passed, and his dad now out of his life, Holls had gone and created his own kind of family. First with us, and now with Dawson and Jaxon.

For musicians like us, having that kind of support is what keeps you grounded. Too often, the attention, the fame, the accolades, it all goes to your head. But fame doesn't last forever.

For the past twelve years, we'd busted our asses building our music careers, so our personal lives were all about fun. And we enjoyed our bachelorhood. We were on the move constantly and we didn't need anything but our dreams, our music, and plenty of sex. But love? Please. That was for songs and shit.

Or it was. Now it was our life.

"You don't have to have the wedding in Vegas but how about the bachelor parties?" I offered, raising a glass.

"I'm down with that." Holls nodded.

Everyone clinked glasses, then downed our shots.

"Fuck, what a difference a year makes," I muttered. "How the hell did we get so lucky?"

"It's all Van," Brodie insisted as he turned to his husband. "You started it."

"Me?" Van scoffed. "You mean, you."

Brodie kissed Van's confused expression away. "You walked into our lives five years ago and nothing's been the same."

"You guys would've made it to the top, with or without me," Van replied.

"That's not what I'm talking about, honey. All that shit's great, but without your love, it doesn't mean anything."

Van leaned in and kissed Brodie long and hard.

Until Holls gave Brodie back his own advice. "Suck face later."

No surprise, Brodie made a rude gesture with his fist.

"Dee's right, Van," I offered. "We met you and things changed. It wasn't just the record deal, it was your belief in us, your unwavering support. Through the good times and all the bad shit that came along. It gave us the courage to be better versions of ourselves, not just in our music, but in our life. And because of that, great things happened. Love happened."

I looked at Ronin and he leaned down to kiss me.

"Faise, that has to be the corniest fucking thing to ever come out your mouth," Brodie announced. "And yet, it's the goddamn truth!"

We all laughed and cheered to that.

Ronin

After another round of shots, we hit the dance floor and partied until the wee hours of the morning.

We stumbled out of the private event at 3 am, joking, bickering, you know, being our usual selves. It was a short walk from the exit to the SUV, and I noticed that the streets were lined with partygoers. LA was like Vegas. The shows, the parties, they go on all night.

Suddenly, I heard someone shouting.

Lennie and Petyr yelled "gun!" and shoved us to the ground so hard, my bones rattled, and the breath was knocked right out of my body.

What the fuck?

My ears were ringing as screams filled the air. People scattered like a stampede.

I blinked and suddenly, Dallas was there in front of me, tumbling to the ground. Regan was on top of him, knee to his back, yelling out orders as more security team members rushed around them.

Dallas was back in New York. How could he be here? Now? What the hell was going on?

Then I realized that Faise was underneath me, shaking badly. But I knew enough not to move. To stay where I was, shielding Faise. I'd protect him no matter what.

"Is everyone okay?" Len asked as he ran back to us, phone to his ear.

Regan and Petyr tied Dallas's hands behind his back. The guy was yelling his head off, swearing and struggling to get loose. Other team members were holding on to him. He wasn't going anywhere.

I rolled off Faise and checked him over. He launched himself at me, and I gripped him harder than I ever had. He was hyperventilating.

"It's okay, baby. Everything's all right," I reassured him.

Jesus Christ, was it? Faise's shaking calmed a bit as I rubbed soothing circles on his back.

"Dee? Holls?" I called out and finally looked around.

Van and Brodie, as well as Dawson and Holls, were lying on the ground nearby, same as me and Faise, shaken but okay.

"We're fine. I think," Brodie called out. "I don't know

what the hell just happened, but thank fuck for our security team."

Police sirens wailed in the distance. Here we go again.

"Please tell me that asshole's not going to get out on bail this time," I whispered to Faise.

Then, I fainted.

———

I woke up in the hospital. Again.

Faise was asleep in the chair at my bedside, his dark hair sticking up on end, a soft snore echoing in the room. Just the thought of that asshole hurting him... Shit, my eyes welled up.

Fuck, hold it together.

Then I spotted my sister standing by the window, Regan beside her, talking in whispered tones.

"Ci," I called out.

"Ro." She turned her head and blinked away tears. "Oh my God, I'm—"

"Don't even say it. This is *not* your fault. It's that fucking prick. He's going to jail and staying there this time."

"I'm sorry," she whispered as she walked over to me, Regan by her side.

"Is everyone all right?"

Regan nodded. "Everyone is fine. Shaken up, bruised, but good."

The relief was overwhelming.

"Dallas confessed to the call-in threat at the Nashville concert," Regan confirmed. "And then he followed us, here, across the country."

"But how did he find out where we were tonight?" I asked.

"He's a cop so he's not without resources. According to his phone, he'd been tailing us since we landed in LA. He's smart, and more resourceful than I anticipated. The how and why is still being worked out, but he's going to be charged with serious offenses and I highly doubt he'll be making bail this time. I'm just annoyed that I didn't spot him until it was almost too late. Thankfully, our team was on guard, and we got to him in time."

"*You* got to him in time," Faise announced.

"Baby," I whispered as he stood up and leaned over. This time, he was the one giving *me* the bear hug.

"Don't ever scare me like that again, Ro," he whispered in my ear.

"Same."

My head ached and my hands, shit, when I looked down, my hands were red, scrapes covering my palms. But nothing was bleeding or broken, thank fuck.

"Is our concert in San Fran still a go?" I asked.

All I wanted was a return to normal.

Regan cleared her throat. "With Dallas arrested, and given his confession, our major concerns are gone. It's still a go. But only if you guys are okay and if you want to perform. That's up to you, Jesse, and the label."

"Ro, what about your hands?" Faise asked.

"They're just scrapes. I've played with worse."

Holls and Brodie entered the room, along with Dawson and Van.

"I'm fine. I want to get out of here. What time is it anyway?"

"Almost noon," Regan replied. "The police will want to take your statement, then we can go."

Once a doctor gave me the final okay, the police arrived. And Elias. There were tons of questions asked and answered and by the time I was released, I had a massive headache.

We headed for our bus, and once all our security team was back on board, we left LA for San Francisco. No delay. And with good reason. The press had gotten hold of the story and none of us felt like talking just yet. Zoe could deal with any pressing issues until we had a few days to recover.

I worried about what this setback would do to my sister. If Dallas would try to come after her, or us, again. All the questions the police asked were rattling through my brain. My body wouldn't settle.

Faise and I headed for our bunk but neither one of us said a word. I just held onto him, knowing how dangerously close I'd come to losing him again.

But he was here, in my arms. Where he was meant to be. Where he would stay.

I had my share of doubts about how I was going to handle being in a relationship. Worries that were valid.

But loving Faise was not one of them.

CHAPTER 38
FAISE

JULY 4

There was no better way for us to welcome the 4th of July than with a concert.

Were we shaken up? No question.

Were we going to let the fans down and cancel the show? No fucking way.

With Dallas arrested, I didn't worry that we'd have a repeat of the other night. Or that we'd have any trouble from him again. According to Elias, Dallas was facing so many charges that he'd probably spend the next decade or so in jail. Not to mention the civil cases we'd file against him.

But Ronin was still worried. He was quiet, not like his usual self. I understood. We were all worried about Ciara and how she was handling things. Maybe it was being on the road, maybe it was being surrounded by our crew, and our security team, but as far as I could tell, Ciara seemed to be doing okay.

We'd spent most of the previous day talking about what happened. And we reassured her again that it wasn't the first, and probably not the last, scary incident we'd face.

Holls had been attacked by a stalker a few months ago and Quinn, one of our former bodyguards, had been shot in the process. Quinn was okay (he was working with Dawson as a private investigator), but the whole thing had given us a stark wakeup call. The bigger Wayward Lane got, the more attention we'd attracted—good and bad. It was something we'd have to deal with from here on out. And anyone involved with us was the same.

Ronin was the one I was worried about. He didn't want to let me or Ciara out of his sight.

To be fair, I was the same. With him, with everyone in our family.

I called my sponsor and talked for nearly a half hour. A record for me. But I didn't want any anxiety to fester.

Then I reached out to my therapist, and set up a time for me and Ronin, and Ciara to talk about everything that had happened.

After that was done, I wandered through the concert venue to find my boyfriend on stage, alone (besides our bodyguards), strumming away on his bass. He had bandages on his palms, but he insisted he was fine to play.

"Hey," I called out as I stepped onto the stage.

I thought Ronin had spotted me but the jolt of his body and the fact that he missed a note, was telling.

"Hey, baby," he asked me without looking up. "What's up?"

"I could ask you the same. You've been unusually quiet. Are you sure you're doing okay?"

He shook his head and continued to play.

"Ronin?"

"I don't want to talk right now. I just need my routine. I'm fine."

I wasn't going to push. Not yet. Like me, Ronin was stubborn. When he was ready, I would know. But if it didn't happen soon, I'd have no choice.

Our road crew started to fill the stage, getting our equipment in place. Ace and Tommy helped us with soundcheck, but it took forever. Shit was misplaced, the mics kept glitching, and tempers were short. Brodie especially. After belting out one chorus of *Sideline*, he suddenly stopped, swore, and walked off the stage.

Jesse told us to keep going and Van went after his husband.

Things went downhill after that.

The opening band, Killmine, were delayed due to their flight, so we'd be going on earlier than expected. We'd become fast friends with their lead singer, Nate Filier, and his band brothers when we performed in their hometown of NOLA in October. But even the prospect of hanging out with those guys again didn't improve the somber mood.

We got changed, as usual, and had our hair and makeup done. But that routine too was filled with a chilly silence. Then we hung around, just the four of us, before showtime. Van brought us a round of much-needed tequila shots, but instead of celebrating like we usually did, we just drank and said nothing.

It was the weirdest pre-show experience in my life.

What the fuck was going on here? Brodie was pacing the length of the dressing room, anxious in a way I'd never seen him before. Then he sat down on the couch and gnawed on his fingernails. And he wasn't the only one acting strange. Holls was busy typing on his phone, instead of telling us every detail about his night with Dawson. And Ronin? He was sitting beside Holls, staring into space like a zombie. He wasn't cracking jokes or shooting the shit.

I was the least vocal member of the group, but I was done remaining silent.

"Knock it off!" I yelled out suddenly.

Brodie stopped walking. Holls stopped typing. And Ronin finally looked up at me.

"I know we got the shit scared out of us the other day but we're all fine. The guy's been arrested, and we're safe. It's over. Are we upset? Yes. Are we going to let this setback screw with our music? No! We have fans out there expecting a kick-ass concert. Not just a good one, but a great one. One that they've saved for. One that they'll remember for the rest of their lives." I paused and ran an agitated hand through my hair. "This isn't just what we do, this is who we are. Now get the fuck up! We have a show to rock!"

I stood there, hands on my hips, out of breath. My heart was pounding so fast it was about to crash right through my rib cage.

Brodie was the first to move, stalking up to me with that wicked glint in his eye. I prepared myself for a verbal whiplash.

Instead, he gripped my shoulder tight and nodded.

"You're right," he whispered. "I'm sorry."

Say what? Brodie never apologized. It was as rare as me losing my shit just now and yelling.

"Faise is right," Brodie said as he turned to Holls and Ronin. "Look at us! It's like we're ready to run and hide. And that's fucked up. We've always performed no matter what— sick, stoned, and everything in between. Not to mention, we've done it despite the nasty trolls and the haters. We always, always, get out there and give it our all. No matter what. And tonight is no different. Fuck that asshole! He's gone and we're here. We can do this. I'm ready."

Holls stood up next, offering a smile that had the knot in my stomach finally easing.

"Me too," Holls nodded. "We're not going to stop doing what we love. Haters gonna hate, but fuck them."

Ronin was the last one to stand up.

The look on his face was absolute shock. I worried for a split second that he was going to do a runner.

Until he walked up to me, gripped my neck tight, and

pulled me in for a hard kiss that knocked the remaining breath right out of me.

"Do you have any idea how much I love you?" he whispered against my lips, oblivious to our band brothers standing beside us. "And how sexy you are when you call us out on our own shit?"

"You liked that?" I teased, nipping his lips.

He nodded.

"Someone had to do it," I added. "You guys were too quiet. Even for me."

"So," Holls interrupted. "Are we all in?"

Ronin kissed me again, not letting go. "Baby, I'm ready to rock this fourth of July because you've lit *all* my fireworks."

"Holy shit, could you be any cheesier?" Holls called out. "Your dirty talk is so lame."

"Faise, I think your dick's melted Ronin's brain," Brodie snarked.

I let out a laugh, relieved that things were back on track.

Someone tapped my shoulder, and I gave Ronin one last kiss before turning to our friends.

"What?"

"Suck face later," Brodie reminded me. "We have a show to do."

Yeah, we did.

Ronin

My boo was incredible.

And sure, maybe my line was cheesier than fuck, but it was the truth. Faise's passionate plea sparked a fire in me like nothing and no one else. And I needed that kick in the ass tonight.

We all did.

The fact that it was my boyfriend doing the kicking, though, was a surprise. He was the last person I expected to rally us. Normally, that was Brodie's domain. But watching Faise step into his power? The way he fought for us?

Sexiest thing ever. I didn't think I could fall harder. But I did.

A half hour later, we were on stage, facing the biggest crowd of our career. With over sixty thousand people inside the stadium, the roar of the crowd was incredible. It was hot as fuck already, because hello, California in July. And it only got steamier when the lights hit us full force, and we started playing. We kicked off this concert with *Nine Gone Wrong*.

I'll never forget that moment when the fans belted out the first chorus. The energy around us soared. Goosebumps popped up all over my skin as I looked around at my band-mates and recognized the awe in their expressions too. At everything we'd accomplished. At how far we'd come.

Then Holls joined Brodie at the mic, performing our latest song, *Running Start*. The song he'd written for Dawson. The crowd went nuts, cheering and clapping when Holls called his fiancé on stage.

By the time we'd reached two and a half hours in, every-thing except our pants—or in Brodie's case, his kilt—was thrown off and into the crowd. We were drenched in sweat, exhausted, but never so fucking happy.

By that time, Killmine had arrived, and Nate and his boys joined us to sing a duet of *Filthy Pain*.

After that, we left them on stage as we took a much-needed break. We hydrated in the wings and watched Killmine live up to their name, totally rocking their set. It was so cool to see how far they'd come since their first perfor-mance with us back in October.

When we hit the stage again, we were amped up. And thankfully, the sun was starting to set so the temperature finally dropped. Nate and the boys joined us for our last song, *Never Look Back*. We were all sweaty and shirtless by that point.

Well, everyone except Nate, who strutted back out in in his jeans and a black leather jacket. Grabbing the mic, Nate thanked our crew, and called out Tommy and Ace. We encouraged both guys to step out of the wings and take a bow with us. After all, we couldn't do a show like this this without them.

Faise was still sitting behind his kit, so I walked around and held my sweaty hand out to him, encouraging him to stand up. When he did, I slid my arm around his waist and pulled him out to center stage. Nate passed me the mic.

"Let's hear another round, please, for this incredibly talented man."

Faise shook his head but waved to the crowd.

"Faise is not just my best friend, and my bandmate, but he is, in fact, the love of my life."

There were cheers and whistles and more applause as I leaned down to kiss him.

Suddenly, fireworks exploded overhead.

And our celebration? It had just begun.

EPILOGUE

FAISE

A YEAR LATER

"Come on, boo!" Ronin called out. "We're gonna be late!"

I was already sweating through my shirt, despite the air conditioning, and my suit jacket was next. Damn restrictive clothing.

"This is the last time I ever wear a suit," I grumbled.

"Stop complaining," Ronin replied. "You look sexy as fuck."

I stared at my reflection in the bedroom mirror. The black suit fit me perfectly, but I hardly recognized myself. Anything except jeans, t-shirts and running shoes was totally out of character.

"This shirt collar is choking me. And not in a sexy, kinky way."

Ronin's laughter filtered through the suite. The sound made me smile.

"Either unbutton it or get used to it. You'll be wearing that shirt for hours."

"Why are these things so formal?" I asked. "We're rock-stars. We don't wear suits. Except our birthday ones."

Ronin stepped out of the bathroom in slim cut, navy dress pants and a white button down, his long hair loose in those messy waves I loved. My man was gorgeous no matter what. Still, as soon as we were done at this event, the clothes were coming off. And staying off.

"It's a wedding, so deal with it." He shook his head and smiled at me. "By the way, we have a stop to make before we pick up Brodie and Van."

"For what?"

Ronin didn't answer me.

"Baby?" I asked.

My boyfriend was busy getting his suit jacket on. "I'll explain on the way."

Something was up with him these last few days. But I'd let him work it out in his own time. When he was ready to tell me, whatever it was, he would. No matter what, we were partners, in all aspects of our life. There were no secrets, and nothing was left unsaid.

It was hard to believe that we were celebrating one year together as a couple. So much had changed and yet, it felt like no time at all. That's what happens when you fall in love with your best friend, and he falls right back.

I grabbed my cell and texted Brodie, letting him know we were on the way. Ronin's sister and mom had already left for the venue. They were helping Bibi organize the wedding.

Ciara had gone through a lot of therapy, and she was doing great. She'd decided to stay in Nashville and was now working full-time with Hardwick. Dallas's confession about the concert threat eventually led to him pleading guilty on the assault charges. He'd been in jail for the past year and would stay there for the foreseeable future. Thank fuck.

Ronin's mom moved down here as well, not far from us. Our home was always filled with family, music, and laughter.

But that wasn't all. My brother Rae had also moved here. He got a job as a marketing director for a beverage company, and he was loving it. The only ones who hadn't made the move were my parents. Guaranteed, as soon as Ronin and I had kids, they'd be selling up and joining the rest of us.

Not that we were in any rush to do that. I relished having Ronin all to myself.

Well, he'd always been mine. And now he was in every way, and I was his, too.

Ronin slipped up beside me and held out his hand. Palm to palm, fingers interlocking tightly. It was simple, really, but holding Ronin's hand made my heart take off running. Every fucking time.

"You ready?" Ronin asked me.

I nodded.

Lennie and Petyr were waiting outside our door and escorted us to the SUV.

"Looking good, gents," Lennie stated. "Any thoughts about today? Twenty bucks says Holls faints before he makes it up the aisle."

"Make it fifty," Ronin offered.

I nudged my boyfriend with my sharp elbow. My lethal weapon.

"Ow, that hurts."

I rolled my eyes, not believing Ronin's complaint for a second. Then I placed a gentle hand on his waist and started rubbing the same spot. He pulled me in close, leaning down to kiss me.

"Don't start that here," I warned.

"What? Why?"

"You know what happens when you start kissing me. We can't be late. Not today." I smiled at him. "And stop taking bets. I talked to Holls this morning. He's not freaking out at all. But he's worried that Dawson might be."

"No way," Petyr commented. "Dawson's been ready to marry Iain since last year. It's all he talks about."

"It's true, he's nuts about him. Ugh, all these couples in love," Lennie muttered as he opened the back door. "Crazy rockstars."

"Hey, we're so *not* that."

"Not anymore," Ronin chuckled. "Okay, maybe sometimes. But not like before."

"Yeah, we're settled now," I argued. "Grown up and shit."

Lennie scoffed. "Really? Is that why you paid that stripper at Dawson's bachelor party to pull me up on stage? While I was on duty?"

"You weren't on duty," I replied with a dirty chuckle and slid inside the car. "Admit it, you enjoyed yourself."

The group went wild that night when poor Len lost his shirt, and nearly his pants. The guy had a ripped body that everyone in the crowd appreciated.

"I'd rather face a drunken mob at a concert than that." Lennie's face flushed, and he shook his head. "I can't dance for shit. It was the most awkward five minutes of my life."

"Are you kidding?" Petyr chuckled. "The audience loved you. I'd never seen so much cash thrown on stage."

Ronin nodded and slid in beside me. "He's right, Len. Maybe you could work the pole on your off hours?"

Lennie gave Ronin a choice finger and then slammed the door.

Ronin and I shared a laugh. Despite all the growing we'd done, deep down, we were still the same bratty teenagers who liked to play loud music and joke around.

I was pretty sure that Holls and Dawson's wedding today would be the same—full of laughter and music, an all-night party that would be the talk of the town. The event was being held at their home, which was a short drive from our place.

Lennie pulled out of the driveway and headed west.

Wait. We were going in the wrong direction and my curiosity engaged.

"Where are we going?" I asked.

"I told you, just a quick stop before we pick up Dee and Van."

"For what?"

"You'll see," Ronin replied.

I swallowed down my remaining questions. I loved Ronin and I trusted him without pause. So, wherever he was leading me, I'd follow.

We drove by sprawling ranches and suburban dreams, every passing mile busier than the last, as we headed into the city. When we reached Brooklyn Street, I realized that this was the route we took to get to our recording studio. But why would we need to stop off there before the wedding?

We didn't. There was no reason.

Suddenly, my heart beat out a frantic rhythm, so fast and hard I could feel it pulse in every part of me. Ronin's hand was damp as he gripped mine tighter.

And when I turned and stared into his summer blues, I knew.

Ronin

Faise knew me so well, I swear, he often knew what I was going to do before I did it.

I'd been planning this for months. Working on it in secret. Which wasn't easy when we spent nearly every day together. And night.

Lennie pulled up to park on the busy city street, and Petyr opened the door for us.

My boyfriend didn't utter a word. Not a question, not a comment.

When I looked in Faise's amber eyes, it was like being

home. No matter what happened in life, he was that to me. Always had been. Always would be.

But I was still nervous as hell about today and when we stepped inside the building, my heart raced out of control.

Lennie and Petyr escorted us into the recording studio, did their rounds, and then slipped out the main door to wait outside.

I guided Faise into the booth, turning on the editing board, and the mics, and then motioned at the two chairs that sat in the middle of the room. There were no instruments today, just me and Faise. Every word that happened in this moment would be recorded. For me, for him, but most important of all, for us. For all time.

"Wondering why we're here?" I asked, tremors running up and down my arms. Hell, my whole body was vibrating like an amp. To my own ears, I sounded breathless, and no wonder.

It isn't every day that you propose to the love of your life.

"Kind of. But I'm in the best hands," Faise replied as he sat down across from me. "So, I'm leaving the explanation up to you. When you're ready, I'm ready."

I was.

In the dim lighting, and surrounded by soundproof walls, every word, scent, and sound magnified. He smiled slowly, and the beauty of it, like the sun rising on a lazy summer day, completely wrecked my heart.

Just like the first time we met, being near him was the only place I wanted to be.

I reluctantly let go of his hand and reached for the notebook in my jacket pocket. When I pulled it out, my hands were shaking so hard I nearly dropped it.

"I wrote something," I confessed, my voice cracking, hoarse with emotion. "A poem that belongs only to you."

The page in front of me blurred until I blinked, unshed tears wanting loose.

I reached out for his left hand and his tremble matched mine. Clearing my throat, I managed to find my words.

My heart is a rhythm known only to you
And I don't care what they say
Baby, I don't think like they do
Neither do you
Playing hard, moving fast, the fans, the fame
But it's not a game
Living with you, loving too
Is a road that bends, never ends
We chose this life, no regrets except
One year, two
Beyond the set, ten, twenty is too few
Together, forever
Our love is one rhythm
The song that's me and you

I slid off the chair and went down on one knee, pulling the ring box out of my pocket. Thankfully, without fumbling.

"Faise, baby, I love you more than anything. Will you marry me?"

Faise launched himself at me and we nearly toppled over.

"I take it that's a yes?" I chuckled as I squeezed him tight.

"I love you too, Ro, always, so it's a million times yes," Faise whispered as he turned his head and kissed me.

We didn't need words after that.

Faise

The wedding was simple but beautiful, and the outdoor setting was perfect. It was sunny and warm, just like our friend. Holls and Dawson were both wiping away tears as they said their vows, Holls promising that the only running he'd be doing from now on was to his new husband. I couldn't be happier for Iain and seeing him with Dawson, and their son, Jaxon, made me think about everything I wanted with Ronin.

Once the reception got started, me, Ro, and Brodie headed over to give our band brother hugs and congratulations. Of course, I kept my left hand in my pocket, not wanting anyone to notice the ring and make a fuss. After all, it was Holls and Dawson's day.

"So." Holls stared at me.

"So?" I asked.

"Show us the fucking ring, Faise!"

"You told them?" I turned to Ronin.

"Of course."

I pulled out my hand slowly and held it up, Holls, and Brodie crowding around me.

"Is that a bass clef?" Holls asked.

"Yup," Ronin replied. "In blue diamonds."

Brodie whistled. "You done good, Ro. And we couldn't be happier for you guys."

We had a group hug and when we pulled back, Brodie wiped his eyes. Our frontman was crying, holy shit.

"Someone take a picture to confirm this moment. Brodie is tearing up," Holls quipped.

"Well, speaking of good news—" Brodie paused. "Shit, maybe I should wait."

We all stared at Brodie. It wasn't like him to hesitate about saying, well, anything.

Holls shook his head. "No way. Spill. What's going on?"

"Van and I are…we're… holy shit, I'm so overwhelmed, I can barely speak." Brodie bit his lower lip. "Our surrogate is pregnant. We're having twins. A boy and a girl."

We stood there with our mouths open.

Holy. Fucking. Shit.

"When?" Holls asked.

"In six months."

"Oh my fucking God!" Ronin yelled and everyone at the reception turned to stare at us.

"A little louder, Ro. I don't think the rest of Nashville heard you."

Then we group hugged again, but this time, we were all in fucking tears. Van and Dawson walked over to join us.

"Be prepared, guys," Van warned with a grin as he held Brodie tight to his side. "In short order, two mini-Brodie James will be unleashed into the world."

"That's a lot of attitude and snark," Dawson chuckled.

Brodie gave the groom a choice finger.

"And you're gonna have to stop doing *that* in front of the kids," Dawson reminded him.

"Christ."

"You gonna trade in the sports car, Dee, and buy one of those big ass minivans?" Ronin teased.

"Fuck, no."

"You'll have to stop swearing too," Holls quipped.

"Shit," Brodie blurted out. "I have a bad feeling their first words are not going to be suitable for preschool."

"Yeah, but they'll be the coolest kids around," I assured him.

Holls grabbed Brodie's arm. "Holy fuck! I just had the best idea. Jaxon and the twins, along with Faise and Ro's kids, can start their own band!"

Ronin's eyes nearly bugged out. "We just got engaged, Holls. Slow it down."

I laughed at my fiancé's expression and took hold of his hand. "Don't worry, baby. We've got plenty of time."

"Nah, I agree with Holls." Brodie nodded. "Get moving on those kids, Ro. We have another band to form."

Van groaned and pointed to his hair. "This is all going to turn white in no time."

A waiter passed by and offered everyone a glass of champagne. And yeah, we needed it. There was a fuckton to celebrate.

"Let's have a toast," Brodie offered. "To Iain and Dawson, on their wedding day, to Ro and Faise on their engagement, and to the second generation of Wayward Lane."

"To the best of friends." Ronin winked at me.

"Rockstars forever," Holls quipped.

"To our family," I added. "To love."

Everyone held up their glass.

"To love!"

Thank you for reading 4-EVER!

Want more of the Wayward Lane MM rockstar universe? Read about Brodie and Van in Punk-In, and Holloway and Dawson in B-Mine.

Find all my books here.

ABOUT THE AUTHOR

Ava Olsen writes steamy and dreamy MM romance with heartwarming characters, sexy banter, and ALL the romantic feels.

Sign up for my newsletter for the latest updates, cover reveals, and bonus scenes: http://avaolsenauthor.com

FOLLOW ME

ALSO BY AVA OLSEN

Sutton U Crew: MM Sports Romance

Catch

Bar Down: MM College Hockey Romance

Rule Breaker

Play Maker

Heart Taker

Stand Alone (enemies to lovers)

Happily Never After

Wayward Lane MM Rockstar Romance

PUNK-IN

B-MINE

4-EVER

Wayward Lane Backstage

Don't Fall For A Rockstar

Don't Fall For A Bodyguard

Don't Fall For A Dreamer

Voyagers Series

Oh Buoy

Starboard

The Cockpit

Endeavor

Nauti or Nice

Stand Alone (Voyagers spin off)

Co-Star

NY Nights

Novel Affair

Troublemaker

Unforgettable You

NY Nights Bodyguard Edition

Hate to Love You

Love Like Yours

Never Knew Love

Stand Alone (novella)

Long Time Coming